Thomas Trofimuk
DOUBTING YOURSELF TO THE BONE

A novel

Cormorant Books

Canada Council   Conseil des Arts
for the Arts   du Canada

ONTARIO ARTS COUNCIL
CONSEIL DES ARTS DE L'ONTARIO

The publisher gratefully acknowledges the support of the
Canada Council for the Arts and the Ontario Arts Council
for its publishing program. We acknowledge the financial support
of the Government of Canada through the Book Publishing
Industry Development Program (BPIDP) for our publishing activities.

Printed and bound in Canada

NATIONAL LIBRARY OF CANADA CATALOGUING IN PUBLICATION

Trofimuk, Thomas 1958–
Doubting yourself to the bone / Thomas Trofimuk.

ISBN 1-896951-86-4
ISBN-13 978-1-896951-86-7

I. Title.

PS8589.R644D68 2005   C813'.54   C2004-906522-X

Editor: Marc Côté
Cover design: Angel Guerra/Archetype
Cover images: Woman by E. Dygas/Getty Images;
Spruce Forest by Duncan Murrell/Getty Images
Author photo: Randall Edwards
Interior design: Tannice Goddard
Printer: Friesens

CORMORANT BOOKS INC.
215 SPADINA AVENUE, STUDIO 230, TORONTO, ONTARIO, CANADA M5T 2C7
www.cormorantbooks.com

DOUBTING YOURSELF TO THE BONE

for my lovely girls — CL (my first reader)
and Mackenzie (my first daughter)
for Leah, closest friend, who pointed me
in the direction of the title

and

for WTT senior, my dad, who truly loves the game of hockey

one hundred fifty-eighth day:

the creek is clear and cold
laughing her wet face all along the stones
I stop and plunge my aching wrist
pray that the medicine therein bless the pain
wash me and mine

at first I thought it was because I would not let go
then know, no
it is after the weight lifts
that we feel her heaviness
the absence of weight can be disconcerting
all this is the letting go

— PAULETTE DUBÉ

PART ONE

I

LEAVES

Ronin james bruce looks at his wife, who ardently believes in the activity of raking leaves. A woman who loves to tell stories. A woman who is barely holding onto a secret.

"I'm not trying to be argumentative."

"Yes, you are," Moira says.

"Well, help me to understand this obsession you've acquired for leaves," Ronin says. "No one ever rakes up leaves in a forest, and all over the world they seem to survive."

"This isn't a forest. This is the city. People rake up their leaves in the fall. They pick them up. It's what's done. It's what we're going to do. And I'm not obsessed."

Ronin and Moira are standing on the front porch of their house, at 47 Larch Way, in Edmonton, looking out at their narrow yard covered with leaves. A heavy, wet snow had come at just the right time. The leaves fell straight down — no fluttering to the ground for this crop. There were few survivors. The street and yard are thick with the remains of summer, and these leaves are frozen into place. A cold front had dropped down from the Arctic following the snowfall, and anything that might have been wet snow was frozen solid.

"I really think it can wait until spring," Ronin says. "The world will not end if these leaves spend the winter. Besides, how are you going to rake with everything frozen?"

"It's supposed to warm up on the weekend. That's when we'll do it."

"Did you say *we*?"

Moira almost smiles and sits on the front step. Ronin sits beside her and can feel it coming — one of Moira's stories.

"Imagine this," she says. "What if there were these two people who loved each other a great deal and fall was their favourite time of year. Each fall they rejoiced in the cool weather that flowed into the city from the underbelly of the mountains. The clouds hung above the city like dusty grey blankets and the temperatures hovered around zero. They would revisit favourite sweaters and leather gloves, corduroy trousers and sturdy boots. For them, there was a melancholy inside this season that was not connected to any life experience. Perhaps melancholy isn't the right word. They didn't feel sad exactly, more like a crystallized understanding of the movements of life."

"I can see where you're going with this."

"No you can't," Moira says. "Wait. Listen. It was their favourite time of year. And leaves! How they loved to rake the leaves."

"I'm actually smelling leaves right now. Rotting leaves. Fertilizer and a big pile of ..."

"... wit is just educated insolence. Let me finish. They would take turns. While one raked, the other followed and read from collections of poetry. They would read their favourite poets and new ones as well. One year they memorized 'The Love Song of

J. Alfred Prufrock.' Can't you see them? He's raking and she's reading 'Prufrock' ..."

"Please don't recite the entire poem, I like this poem, I'd need to have a decent drink in my hand. And really, isn't this scene just a bit precious? Poetry while raking leaves?" Ronin looks at her. She's a gorgeous mountain woman. Big old woollen socks, bought by the dozen at the Army and Navy are bunched and fallen at her ankles. Pale-green long johns and an oversized fleecy. Her eyes are a ferocious hazel colour. She's pushed her glasses up into her hairline, something she does when she's arguing because she thinks it makes her look more serious.

"But isn't it a beautiful fall poem?" Moira pushes her hands deep into the pockets of her fleecy.

Ronin moves his leg against hers. It's a good yard. There are tall, arching elms on the boulevard. Two maples in the centre and lots of flower beds around those trees. It's an older neighbourhood in transition. Young families are moving in as the older folks move away. More and more kids show up on Halloween each year. The Halloween barometer, Ronin calls it. There's a new silver Volvo S80 out in front of the house. It reminds him of a dinky toy he had as a kid. He's not certain when Volvo made the switch, but in his mind the company used to have a very distinct, classic design. A box on wheels that would run until the floor rusted out; cars that seemed to go on forever. Now, Volvos look like any one of a dozen Japanese imports. They don't look like ugly shoeboxes anymore and seem less reliable. Moira can bring home cars whenever she wants. She sells them for a living; Volvos and Jaguars. She's very good at what she does. Moira has an education degree — a master's. She started off in philosophy and floundered into an education career in her second year. She could teach if she wanted, but for now she makes more money and works far less than any teacher Ronin knows. Although selling cars is probably a lot less rewarding than teaching, it seems to be working for her.

He drives a '76 Plymouth Fury, a rust experiment with a rebuilt engine, a new transmission and a very fine stereo. There are rips in the seats and it's been in two accidents in exactly the same intersection and with drivers who inexplicitly went through red lights. He now avoids that intersection. It's tried to kill him twice — no use tempting the fates. But the car is heavy and, with the proper tires, it does all right in snow.

Ronin stands up. "I'm going to bring out the flask."

"Why not the bottle and a couple of the good glasses?"

Moira means the set of four glasses he'd picked up at a discount store for ten bucks. They felt right in the hand; someone took care to design them with that in mind. Narrow and square on the bottom, they flared out at the top. You could really get your nose in there and take in the aromas of the whisky.

He pulls on a thick cotton camp coat before he comes back out. He places the bottle and the glasses on the top step. "I've been thinking about 'Prufrock.' Wouldn't you say it's closer to a winter poem? I mean the guy's contemplating growing old and dying."

"It's a perfect *late* fall poem! You're really starting to bug me. Anyway, these two people would drink wine from huge, fish-bowl glasses and play music as they raked. Mozart and Schubert. Once, they played Mozart's *Requiem* really loud and scared the crap out of the neighbours."

"They had lots of leaves?"

"They had lots of trees."

"I think your story needs some conflict, or tragedy, and soon, or you'll lose your listener."

"Oh, there's a tragedy all right. A chunk of ice falls off an airplane at 32,000 feet and it comes down onto their front step and kills the guy instantly." She giggles like a kid.

"Very funny. Do these people have names?"

"Of course they have names." She cups the drink in both hands and sniffs at the whisky. "Moses. Moses and Katya. He's a writer, and she's a lawyer."

"A Biblical hero — an Old Testament prophet — something charmingly Russian. And the hunk of ice from the airplane?"

"It kills their cat."

"Moses lives then?"

"Yes. The cat dies."

"That's sad, but not really tragic."

"It was old."

"What's old for a cat?"

"Twenty-five years. Let me finish. This one fall, they're in their bliss. Katya is raking leaves and Moses is reading some Hemingway short story ..."

"Which one?"

"'The Big Two-Hearted River.'"

"Part one or two?"

"Both parts. So, the sky is heavy and dull and the uncaring flatness of its steely grey colour stretches from horizon to horizon. It's threatening to snow. They're playing Mozart's *Requiem* and when Moses suggests a glass of red wine, Katya says no. Moses is surprised. Katya loves her wine and this is a particularly nice pinot. He asks if she's feeling all right. She says she's fine ... it's just that she's pregnant."

"ARE YOU TRYING to tell me ...?" Ronin looks at Moira and then at the glass cupped in her hands. She hasn't touched a drop.

She points at him. "Daddy," she says, then she places a hand on her chest. "Mommy."

"No."

"Yes."

"When?"

"Six-and-a-half months, roughly."

"Oh my God, we did it! We made life! New life! Why are you standing? Shouldn't you be sitting? Are you sure?"

"Yes, I'm sure. I'm pregnant, not sick."

"But shouldn't you —"

"Just come over here and kiss me."

"What about the leaves?"

"A clever ruse."

He is beyond himself with joy. This is unexpected and expected at the same time. He'd been tricking himself by thinking the chances of it happening were faint and it wasn't a big deal if it didn't happen. But it has happened and he's crazy with happiness.

Later, after making love very gently with Moira, he snuggles in behind her. She is asleep — her breathing is luxurious and long. A car door slams down the block. It's raining. It's very dark in the room. Ronin is not ready for sleep. He listens to the rain, watches the faint patterns of light and shadow on the ceiling. He begins to worry.

⟋

LAURA MARIE IS BORN inside a snowstorm just after midnight on April 15th. Moira insists on a natural birth. "I want to experience it to the fullest. You'll be with me and we'll do the breathing exercises. We'll be okay without freezing the bottom half of my body. I want to feel this — all of it."

Ronin loves her for this, loves her determination and zeal for life, but he asks the question anyway: "And if something unexpected happens?"

"That's why we'll be in a hospital."

A nurse makes the assumption that Moira is going for the epidural needle. She starts to explain how the needle works and how pleasant it will be to go through labour numb from the waist down. *No pain*, she says. *You won't feel a thing*. According to her, the vast majority of women in this particular hospital go for the epidural these days. It doesn't go well for the nurse. It's unlikely she will make that assumption again.

Ronin does not remember anything distinct about the snow, does not recall the passing of time. It had been like walking along a river, with big elms and poplars stretching peacefully while the snow scattered itself into the river and was swallowed up. The snow clung to the extended branches. Footprints were almost immediately covered over. A muffled silence. Then his daughter is crying. Moira is crying and shaking. And Ronin is there inside this dream, not thinking, only feeling. Happy and grateful and humbled. All of life contained in this single moment. Snow falls steadily past the window of the hospital room. It snows all night and well into the next day. He begins to consider this falling, frozen innocence as a substantial blessing. This daughter is a careful poem written in shadows on a white wall, early in the morning. Each breath is a stanza. He is in love. New feelings rise up, constantly surprising him. There is a growing sense of protectiveness toward creatures and things that are innocent. He walks around in a state of stunned awe. "How was it, how are you?" people ask, and he says stupid things like "great" or "I'm great" — when what he really means cannot be spoken. Only inside a deliberate silence could he come close to saying the awe-excitement-fear-exhilaration he feels.

~

THIS IS A DISTILLED JOY. Because there was a time before Ronin and Moira were married when she thought she might be pregnant. Their relationship was in the soupy, before-the-fridge Jell-O stage. Even then, through all the fear and apprehension, through the anxiety and shock, Ronin was thrilled. There was a little man, at the bottom of his being, who was jumping up and down, shouting *Yeah! Yeah! Yeah!* But he could barely hear him through all the fear. At the time, Ronin was not certain he had any fatherhood skills.

Why would he make a good father? He knew nothing about being a parent. Nothing! But who does know this stuff ahead of time?

"Are you sure?" he says from the other side of the initial shock wave. This is an utterly banal and ridiculous cliché. But sometimes clichés are brutally appropriate.

"Well, no, but I'm late."

"So this is a maybe."

"Take a breath. I'm just telling you there's a possibility and we should talk about it."

"Talk about it."

"Will you please start breathing? You can't talk if you don't breathe. I need you to talk with me about this."

"Yes, yes ... I'm breathing. But Jesus, Moira, are we through being kids? Are we ready to be parents? Am I?"

"Well, that's honest."

"I can't pretend that this doesn't scare the crap out of me."

"That's honest too."

He remembers calming down after a few days. It had started to seem less frightening and more interesting. Less disastrously life altering and more just life altering.

But Moira wasn't pregnant. One consequence of that earlier brush up against parenthood was a profound dialogue that hadn't been there before. Suddenly, there was freedom and vocabulary to talk about a bigger piece of life.

SARAH JANE ARRIVES, on October 1st, a year and half after Marie's birth. She's born three weeks early, on a warm fall day with only sporadic swatches of golden colour showing in the trees on the way to the hospital. There are trees in this city that, with the first hint of frost, seem to turn yellow overnight, and are on the ground a few days later. Others hang on for dear life. Ronin was thinking that, with one birth under his belt, the second would have less of an impact — that he'd not be as moved. It would somehow be diminished. But it didn't work like that. It was different and just as significant. He decides birth is too massive to be shrugged off as something one gets used to, or something that becomes more common with each repetition.

There is a particularly crisp, verging-on-winter feel to the air as he and Moira walk up the steps to the hospital. Laura Marie is staying with Moira's mother. Moira and Ronin were talking about something stupid. About the movie they'd had to leave to come to the hospital. They'd been speculating on the ending, something about a gangster who'd lost his nerve and wanted out. Ronin had been timing contractions and felt very confident that there was lots of time. "We could probably have stayed at home for another cup of tea," he says.

Moira stops halfway up the stairs. "The baby, is coming, now," she says inside an inhalation. He picks her up in his arms, races up the stairs and bursts through the doors.

"Baby now!" he barks. "Baby! Now!" That's enough for three nurses to move into action. They get Moira into a wheelchair and Ronin runs along behind it into a birthing room; twenty minutes later Sarah Jane is in the world. By the time things settle down it's well after midnight.

At 2:00 a.m. Ronin is walking along the corridors of a sleepy hospital with his new daughter in his arms, introducing her to anyone he can find who is awake. He's in a blissful trance and willing to go with it for as long as it lasts. He's chewing a Cuban cigar — savouring the taste.

Moira is not in this bliss with him. She's tired. She watches with weary eyes, almost sadly, as Ronin cannot help his own joy. Giving birth is hard work. Even when it's short work. And there was no time for Ronin to be supportive. He was not able to help with the counting and breathing. There was no counting. This birth was not a long ordeal. Sarah Jane was in a hurry to enter the world. She couldn't wait for her parents to do the breathing exercises and resting and maybe moving into the shower, which is where Moira went through much of her labour with Marie.

2

UNRAVELLING

She doesn't look happy, Ronin thinks.

Moira is sitting on the front step while Marie, Sarah and Ronin try to make her laugh. The three of them have climbed up into the maple and are hooting and yapping like mad monkeys. Moira smiles in fractions of degrees, humouring the monkeys, but she's not anywhere near laughing. Ronin can't remember the last time Moira laughed. Did she begin her withdrawal from laughter before Marie and Sarah were born? He's not sure. It's been a slow unwinding. He thinks she may not be aware of her own darkness.

He looks down from his perch, at her devastating beauty. Despite the sadness that has been rising to the surface more and more often, there are prolonged moments when he cannot take his eyes off her. Everybody should be allowed to get depressed every now and then.

Moira's arms are crossed over her chest, her hands grasping opposite forearms. He loves her hands. They are long, elegant and always soft. But she has stopped touching him, though he still touches her. He can deal with this. It's all right. He gets lots of hugs from the girls. Moira's just going through a phase. She'll come around. Marriages are long-haul journeys.

"You know, I can listen without burdening you with my dick-ass advice," Ronin says. "I'd like to listen to you. Just listen."

"I know you can," she says. "I know."

RONIN STARTS TO FEEL that the Sutra of his life is unraveling, like an old, weathered rope, and he is suddenly doubting everything he once believed was true. All the stones in his life have developed hairline cracks; he knows that moisture gets into those cracks, and it's only a matter of time before it freezes and those cracks split open.

Moira decides that ten years of marriage is enough. She's confused and she's going to fly off to some Vancouver Island retreat to find herself. Ronin believes in the idea of finding yourself; it's a noble thing. But he considers it a life-long goal, a journey. There's something else going on here, but Moira's not saying and she's determined to go.

"I need some time away," she says.

They're standing in the kitchen. The girls are in bed. It's raining. He's just put a pot of espresso on the front burner. "Can you tell me what's going on?"

"I've ... I've lost track of who I am," she says. "I need to find myself."

Find your compassion, Ronin, he cautions himself. Anger is a useless emotion if it's the boss. Oh my God, I sound like a self-help book. "You'll have to move out of cliché land if you want to discuss this," he says. "How long have you been feeling like this? I know who you are. I know where to find you. I love you. Can I help?"

"No."

"Is it one specific thing?"

"It's everything. I'm having doubts about everything."

"Oh."

"I'm having doubts," she says in a listless echo of herself.

"So you think spending a summer on Vancouver Island will help?"

She nods.

He wants to say: *So you think there are parts of you wandering aimlessly on the sandy beaches of Vancouver Island and you're going to go and find these missing bits and reintegrate them into yourself? How do you know Vancouver Island is the right place to look? Maybe fragmented bits of you are actually in Greece, or Italy, or South America. Wouldn't here at home be an ideal place to start looking?*

He looks at her and realizes she's not asking for permission, or even a blessing. This is an information session — he's receiving, she's delivering.

She takes the girls for the summer, and he misses them like crazy even before they're gone. He misses them as if his arms had been removed. But it's only a couple months. That's the deal. They're coming back. They're just nine and ten years old — how are they to make sense of this separation? He'll call them every other day. He's not certain about Moira, but his kids are coming back at the end of the summer. He will not lose his daughters. Moira may be a little lost right now — hopefully it's only temporary — but she's never broken a promise.

RONIN'S WORK HAS LOST its meaning. It seems sudden, but this sort of thing doesn't happen overnight. It creeps away slowly like a retreating glacier — so slowly that it's not easy to notice it moving. A retreating glacier is at odds with itself. It is at once moving forward and also moving backwards, because it's melting at a faster rate than it can advance. Measurement is in centimetres and years.

The sound of water moving under the ice is disconcerting. Perhaps there is only a sensation of melancholy. One morning Ronin finds that the toe of the glacier is a kilometre away; someone has built a highway in between, and he's disconnected. He's no longer part of it. There are huge deposits of terminal moraine between where Ronin is now and where he thought he was.

Did it used to have meaning? Surely, at some point it had meaning. Of course it did. He had stumbled into geology at university and it turned into a full-blown passion. It was the easy science in Arts — a throwaway science credit. But he found he loved it, loved it all. The pure geography — knowing how things were formed and when. Being able to name the types of rock. Maps. Ronin loved maps. Taking a good hard look at how humans interact with the planet. Finally, he landed on paleontology. Fossils, life frozen inside rock, brought back to life micron by micron. Time travel is not just science fiction, he used to say. Fossils allow us to travel through time whenever we discover a new bed. There are amazing narratives suspended inside rock and those narratives are timetravellers.

It wasn't the most brilliant career choice to become a paleontologist, but he found consulting and contract work in the oil industry and some small teaching gigs. Ronin used to believe that his enthusiasm for fossils would never wane.

Last summer he had worked in B.C., scouting a section of land that was to be forested. A high-school friend of his, a guy named Brick, arranged the gig. While it had nothing at all to do with paleontology, it was good work. It felt ethical and true. The forest company actually listened to what he had to say and made adjustments to its cut plan. In fact, it was required by law to make the changes he'd recommended. He was away from Moira and the girls for three weeks, in the bush for most of that time, but it momentarily halted that growing greyness in him — stopped it from opening even wider.

MUSIC USED TO BE VERY IMPORTANT to Ronin, but has become a dull and listless thing in his life. It's been years since he sat in a dark room and listened to something that could move him to tears — apart from rap music. He remembers a long love affair with Samuel Barber's *Adagio for Strings*, and Górecki's *Third Symphony*, and the Bach cello suites. Or Albinoni's *Adagio*. Long lost lovers now. There seems to be no going back, but he goes back and flirts with them and finds a small pleasure in that flirtation, but no spark. The music he once found beautifully sad now makes him sad because he can't find the beauty in it anymore. Perhaps he's heard too much, experienced too much. Maybe he just needs a few years of silence.

RONIN'S FATHER IS LEAVING, slowly becoming a harmless, childlike entity, and completing the circle in a confused haze. His father is drifting off into Alzheimer's. He doesn't remember yesterday. On some days, he doesn't remember the morning. Last night he started to talk about hockey. Most days now he can't remember who Ronin is.

"My son plays hockey," he says, nodding and smiling as if there were a lot of really great memories.

"That's great, Dad," Ronin says. "That's great."

"Yes, he's very good. A rushing defenceman. Just like Bobby Orr."

"Dad, it's me. I'm your son. I don't play hockey. You remember me."

"He scores plenty of goals. He's a natural leader. The team captain."

He's looking right through Ronin, smiling and nodding in agreement with himself.

It's one of those nights when Ronin can't take his father's fabricated memories of his son's illustrious hockey career. Ronin can take almost anything, but not this thing that has been an aching silence between them all these years. Not tonight. But he's promised to come by the home and feed his father a couple of times a week. Ronin has no choice but to listen until it's time for dinner.

There's a box of hockey equipment in his father's garage, almost unused, top of the line. His father pulled strings to get him into a tryout. He could skate as fast as any of the other boys but his understanding of the game was practically non-existent. Nobody had taken the time to explain the rules — even basic things like off-side. He was expected to know and love the game. It was supposed to be in his blood.

Ronin remembers being horrified. He had no idea what he was doing out there. At some point, a coach must have pulled his father aside and said, "Jesus, Logan. The kid's not ready. Bring him back next year." Maybe his father overheard people in the stands talking: *What the fuck is that kid doing here? Jesus, talk about in over his head!*

Was his father disappointed? Hurt? This was his only son. Ronin's father had played this game when he was young and he had been brilliant. Ronin's heard stories about him from men that had nothing to lose by telling the truth. With a little luck, he could have made it to the NHL.

His father used to tell stories about playing in the outdoor rink in Calmar, Alberta, not far from where they first discovered oil. Magazines and catalogues curved around legs and fastened with thick elastic bands as makeshift shin pads. Taping and re-taping broken sticks. Repairing equipment that started out second-hand. Scraping snow off the rink before a game. The cold. The only indoor arenas were in the city and they were few and far between. If you said you thought Edmonton was going to have an NHL team back then, everyone would have laughed, would have patted you on the back as if they felt sorry that your brain didn't work properly. Toronto. Boston. Chicago. Montreal. Detroit. New York. And Edmonton? Completely impossible.

Ronin was out there doing the best he could, trying to be whatever it was that his father needed him to be. Ronin just didn't get it. He never played hockey again and his father never mentioned it. Ronin escaped into school and books. A couple of decades later he finally grew to love the game. All comedy is about timing.

That goddamn box of equipment is still there, one among many in the garage. Eventually, he'll have to sort it all out. There are other boxes of disappointment in that garage. It's not a chore he's looking forward to. Ronin and his sisters keep putting it off, as if there's going to be some miracle cure for Alzheimer's and their father is going to come back, memory intact and not jumbled. His youngest sister, Kate, is living in the house for now. The sorting of artifacts and memories will wait. There's no rush.

When he leaves the home his father is smiling and still talking about his son the hockey player. A small part of him wishes he could have been the hockey player his father wanted. And perhaps he *is* that hockey player inside. In whatever is left of his father's mind, Ronin scored 50 goals one season and went on to play in the NHL. With the Toronto Maple Leafs, his father's favourite team. He loves Ronin and is very proud of him.

What if our disappointments, unfulfilled dreams and wishes start to come true when we have Alzheimer's? Wouldn't that be something? Who knows? Nobody has ever come back from having this disease to report what it's really like. From what Ronin's heard, the human brain is infinitely more complex than we'll ever know. Maybe Alzheimer's is karma — a reward of sorts.

"Three goals" his father says. "He got the hat-trick."

"That's incredible," Ronin says. "Must be quite a hockey player."

"Hell of a shot," he says. "Hell of a goddamned shot."

DO WE REALLY BECOME our parents? Ronin remembers listening to his father screaming at the television on Saturday nights. "Shoot, goddamnit!" "Pass the puck!" "Shoot!" Ronin could not imagine what all the excitement was about. He thought it was ridiculous. He didn't care to try to understand the game. He was kept away from the game because he didn't like the man.

Last night, watching the Oilers beat up on the Rangers, it was Ronin shouting: "Skate you bugger! Skate! Oh my God!!!! SHOOOOT!" Ronin is barely aware he's become like his father in this small area. There are subtle differences. Ronin has a hard time watching three full periods. That's too much time to commit to a game played by millionaire Peter Pans on television. So he might watch the first period, then get up and go do something. Fix a window. Fill a hole in a wall. Read for a while. And then, near the beginning of the third period, he might sneak a peek, sit down again — even if his team is losing.

RONIN SITS UP IN BED in a complete panic: I'm going to lose my daughters! I'm going to wind up being a visitor in their lives. Our legal system is set up to favour the mother and I'm going to be pushed aside. Some other guy is going to wake up each morning and get to see them, hear them, talk to them.

His anger is so intense that he's teetering on the edge of nausea. His fear is linked so closely to this anger he has no idea what to do. Ronin paces the house like a lion behind bars and finally decides on a glass of whisky. Three glasses of whisky later, he's just dealing with fear. It's 8:34 a.m. on a Wednesday and he's quite pissed as he brings the newspaper into the house and tries to focus on the front-page headlines. When he bends down to get the paper, he hears a sparrow singing — the three-note mating call that sparrows perform only in the spring, according to some guy on public radio. Three syncopated jazz notes. Three words. *I'm so ready? I'm so horny? Come do me? I'll do you? I love you?* The bird keeps repeating the riff, and as Ronin turns to go back inside, he notices that no other bird answers.

⌐⌐

"HELLO? MOIRA?"

"Yes."

"Umm, how are you? How are the girls?" Ronin was half expecting a man to answer. He'd prepared himself for that. He realizes he has no clue what she's doing out there, who she's with, nothing.

"We're good," she says flatly. "Hold on. I'll get Sarah. Mare is sleeping."

Ronin never quite understood how Marie could become Mare, but it was something between them and he didn't question it.

"Do you have time to talk for a bit? Hello?" But she's already put the phone down. Finding herself apparently involves a certain amount of hostility toward him. What was he going to say anyway? Was he going to tell her he loved her? Is that it? Is that his bottom line? Is that the plan? Maybe he should ask about her search. That would be fair, but he'd have to keep out any hint of sarcasm and he might not be capable of that just now. He's decided not to tell them he's going to Paris. What purpose would that serve? He's not doing it as a one-upmanship thing. He's doing it because it's a beautiful, exotic distraction and he loves the city. He loves the proximity to thousands of cafés, and great art, and mind-boggling architecture. He loves it that he can walk and walk and walk and never tire of finding new corners to explore. He loves it that people will get in fist fights over the design of a building. The way things look is important. Elegance is important.

Sarah comes on the line and delivers her uplifted hello. Her hellos smile. She can't help it. They are filled with such hope. Ronin is dreading the possibility of the day when her smiling voice is replaced by the nihilistic teenaged voice of raging hormones. He hopes with all his heart this doesn't happen. Of course they have to grow up, and puberty is part of it, but God is a cruel bastard if he takes this away. For now he cherishes each of her smiling hellos.

"I miss you, Sarah. I miss both of you like crazy."

Sarah is quiet. The silence on the end of the line becomes conspicuous. Damn it. He'll have to be more careful. He just told his daughter that he doesn't miss her mother. "I miss all of you," he adds, hoping for a save. "Are you having a good holiday?"

Ronin's life has started to unravel and the first thing he thought of, after walking around the empty house like a stunned automaton for a couple of weeks, is to fly to Paris without telling anyone. Sure it's a bit odd, but he's been there so many times it seems as if he's going someplace comfortable. He could have gone to Montreal, or Toronto, or any number of great American cities, but he has gone to Paris before with wounds that needed healing, so why not this time? Both Ronin and Moira will have moved away from the epicentre of their pain. Perhaps by travelling away from home, the notion of home crystallizes. Well, that's a cliché isn't it? But Ronin is hoping for clarity by looking back across the ocean.

⁓

"I LOOK AT HIM with the kids and every time there is joy in him I grow to hate him a little more."

Moira is sitting at the kitchen table of the cabin she rented in Sooke. She was here once before, with Ronin, years ago. She looks across the table at Georgia, a woman she's taken into her confidence, and then adds, "I can't go on like this."

Georgia is an almost-stranger. She's been the manager of Eagle's Reach Cabins for three years, so she has the comfort of place. She looks across the table and wonders what could possibly be so wrong with finding joy in your kids. From what she's seen, the kids are great. They're polite, they're respectful of others and they seem to like themselves. But it's not the kids. Moira is having a problem with her husband's joy.

Strangers often prove to be incredible sounding-boards because there is nothing to lose and there is no need to lie. So Moira opens up her heart and mind, and spills what is there onto the small wooden table. Outside, the sound of the ocean sporadically crashes into consciousness. That sound has not quite entirely hidden itself in her subconscious, but soon will.

Georgia pours another glass of wine for each of them. "Why do you think that is?"

"I don't ... I don't know," Moira says in a way that makes Georgia think she has a very good idea of what is at the heart of this but she's afraid. Inside that little hesitation after "don't" is the realization of what it could be, but Moira is not ready to go there yet.

"Is he smug about it? Does it seem he's in a secret club of happiness? Is that it?"

"No. Yes. I don't know. He's a father. It's different for fathers. Men love differently. I mean, you know that. We all know that."

"What's different?"

"Love. The bond. Everything. But it's not that. It's not him. It's me. I'm the problem."

"Okay, you're the problem." Georgia thinks about her partner, Rachel. They've had problems with concepts of love. They've had fights about whether love is a form of ownership. Is there freedom in love? And how far do those freedoms extend? Their discussions about commitment and attachment are still going on, even though they've been apart for several years. But they've never had problems about one of them being too happy or too filled with joy.

"I can't seem to shake this sadness. I'm sad all the time."

"Have you told him this?"

"No, but I'm sure he's noticed. He's good at picking up on stuff like that."

"Could it be one of those after-birth things that mothers go through?"

"You mean post-natal depression?" Moira stops over this one. She picks up her wineglass and takes a sip. She always sits up a little straighter when she drinks. At the last second her chest rises slightly, her shoulders pull back and down just a bit and then she drinks. It's a sophisticated movement that brings a serious undercurrent to her drinking. Tonight, she adds to this by turning to gaze out the window at the darkening sea. "No, ten years is a long time to be suffering post-natal depression, and, besides, I think I was sad before I got pregnant."

WHEN THE GIRLS WERE FOUR and five-and-a-half, Ronin went alone to Mountain Park for a few days. He camped at the Whitehorse Creek camp, which was a tiny jewel back then. He took the roomy car-camping tent and packed loose — afforded himself that luxury. A couple of years before, the bartender at the Legion in Mountain Park told Ronin she'd found fossils on a ridge above a meadow on the Cardinal Divide. "They looked like snails and leaves," she said. "Little worms and stuff." That description was enough to cause him to want a look-see. So he filed the little worms in his memory and they eventually drifted to the surface.

The Divide is 15 kilometres from his camp, on a road frequently washed away by any number of the fluctuating streams it crosses. The last time he'd tried driving to the Divide, he was stopped by a metre of ice and snow sprawled across the road in a careless, jagged wave. He's hoping for a relatively clear road tomorrow. He sits at the picnic table holding a cup of coffee and staring into the fire. The constant sound of Whitehorse Creek has moved to the back of his consciousness and there is only the thick darkness and the fire. The clouds are low and heavy above, making the stars a wild story fabricated by a lunatic, and the tops of mountains rich mythologies, and the northern lights only a tall tale told by a con man.

In the fire, he finds a comfort beyond the obvious feeling of safety. Ronin could never explain this feeling of something far back being soothed by his proximity to a fire, especially when his back was to the darkness. He finishes the coffee and pours a generous portion of whisky into the cup as the first few flakes of snow tickle his face.

In the morning, it is suffering to get out of the warmth of the sleeping bag. The tent roof is sagging. As he zips the vestibule open, snow avalanches into the tent. There's over a foot of snow on the ground and it hasn't yet stopped falling. The mountains are always quiet but this is beyond quiet. It's a muffled, beautiful peace, as if each snowflake has the power to remove sound. Starting a fire will be difficult. Ronin has a thermos of coffee planted inside a sweater, wrapped in the canvas tent bag, so he pours himself a cup and crawls back into the sleeping bag. There'll be no searching for fossils today, and no driving. At best, he'll manage a walk, but he didn't bring snowshoes so he's not going far. Ronin makes a deal with himself not to have a drink before noon. It wouldn't be the end of the world if he did, but he really wants to experience this snow before taking the edge off the day. So he hunkers down in his bag, drinks the coffee, reads, and eventually drifts off again.

It takes a couple of days of sun to turn the roads from winding snowfields back into roads that might be passable. He's not worried. He has food and books and coffee, and a bottle of good whisky for the evenings. When the sun comes out it strikes with a vengeance. It eats up the snow on the northern slopes and in the valleys. On the third day, Ronin wakes up and the air is warm and sweet. He takes his coffee to the stream and shaves in the icy water that has risen over a foot in the time he's been there.

He finds himself thinking of Moses and Katya. They were Moira's creation, so he was shocked when Katya, this invented woman, began appearing to him. She's come into being several times, and only when *she* wants to.

"Your kids are great," Katya says. She's wearing small, round tortoise-shell glasses and standing up on the bank smiling down at him. "All that worrying for nothing."

"Well, I do worry. I worry that I'm not teaching them the right things. I worry about the state of the world. I will always worry."

"Enjoy them. Some things can't be taught; they have to be learned."

"I'm wondering how hard I'd have to push for you to bugger off."

"Do you want me to bugger off?" She doesn't seem angry.

"I don't know. I'm not sure I care one way or the other."

Oh, for God's sake. Stop trying to provoke an imaginary woman into a fight.

The sun is warm on Ronin's face and his hands are freezing. It's one of those mountain dichotomies that he's grown to accept. Like being happy beyond comprehension and, at the same time, more uncomfortable than he's ever been. Like being thrilled to be down off the mountain and back at the car, yet feeling sad because the hike is over and he's about to leave the mountains.

The sunlight sparkles on his pots and utensils. It dances in Ronin's eyes — it laughs. He accidentally drops one of the pots and it rings out like a bell. He picks it up and strikes it with a spoon and it gongs through the small valley. He hits it again, then once more. What is it about ringing a bell? A Buddhist thing?

One doesn't ring a bell. One invites the bell to make a sound. As he invites his transformed pot one more time, he holds it up into the sunlight. He listens as the sound begins to disappear, slowly dissipates, diminishes — as it mixes easily into the day.

"What the hell are you doing?" Katya's back.

"I'm listening to the ringing sound dissolve itself into silence. It's amazing. If you really listen, you can't think about anything else. You have to be in the *now*." His back is to her so he can't see her face.

Since Katya is a fabrication, Ronin's mind is imagining this woman, what would he like to see when he turns around? That she'd be topless, with her shirt and sweater tied around her waist, and massaging some sort of lotion on her chest. That would be a very pleasant picture.

Or maybe she'd be seated at the table reading the sports section of the newspaper with her glasses propped far down on her nose. She'd say things like, "What the hell is going on in New York. They've got all this money and they can't buy a win!"

She could be in the tent. Ronin would hear her rustling around in there but won't know what she's doing. She'll have inadvertently created a mystery. What's she doing in there? Is she waiting for him?

When Ronin turns around, Katya is not there at all.

"Do you want to try this?" he says to the trees and the top of his tent.

"Do I want to try what?" She's moving toward him. She's further downstream and is pecking her way up and across the narrow strip of rocky shore, a hunk of real estate that has become much smaller since the water began to rise. She's fully clothed, there isn't a newspaper in sight and she is definitely not creating a mystery in the tent. Ronin probably doesn't have any control over Katya. He's seen interviews with writers who talk about how their characters start to tell them what they're going to do next. They'll protest if the writer tries to make them do something they just wouldn't do. But this isn't even his character. She's Moira's invention. And Moira's not here.

～

THE ROAD IS MUCKY but open. Mercifully, it turns to rock and gravel as Ronin begins to climb out of the valley toward the Divide. He parks his car in the campsite and grabs his pack. This is a barren place but it is not without its beauty. The pines are stunted and wind-carved. The wind must pound down the eastern slopes like a hammer. Vast slabs of scarred granite dot the landscape and there are snowfields higher up. The summit also has enclaves of snow and ice.

The campground is scraped out in the saddle. At one end is a sharp rise to a broken-toothed ridge of rock. On the other side of the saddle is a long steadily rising slope straight up Mt. Deception — no interruptions. He can see his course to the summit. Of course, he'll still have to do all the grunting, and from this viewpoint, near the top, it's a vertical, incredibly technical climb. Without rope, he could probably get to the second ridge of rock. Possibly there's an easier route on the other side. On the west side he'd be coming close to the Jasper Park boundary.

There are ridges of rock on both sides of the saddle. This potential fossil bed could be hidden in either direction. He'll only have time for one exploration today.

Ronin climbs the alpine meadow sections quickly, despite the wet turf and slippery rocks. He tries not to gouge the ground with his boots. He's walking as gently and conscientiously as he can. When he can move laterally to the flat rocks, he does. This meadow is fragile even when it's not wet. He wishes he'd brought the deer-skin moccasins, which he bought exactly for this reason. He never seems to have them when he needs them.

He left Katya back at the Whitehorse Creek camp and he hasn't looked back. She was drinking coffee and Ronin nodded in her general direction as he got into the car. He was focused on the possible *Irridinitus* find, the little worm fossils that might be waiting for him on the Divide. It wouldn't be the first time old *Irridinitus* fossils were discovered in this region. He's well aware of an earlier discovery around Miette Hot Springs, a twenty-kilometre hike.

If their story continued on beyond Moira's initial telling, Ronin would guess that Moses is gone. He left Katya. This removal of himself from a relationship would be the final act of someone obsessed by the idea of simplicity. The simplicity of *one*. What is a Zen Buddhist anyway? Did he remove himself?

"... Moses moved on," Katya says. "I had an abortion."

"He left because of the abortion," he says. It's a quiet statement, not a question.

"Yes, that was at the heart of it."

"Do you have regrets?"

"I have sorrow. The decision was the right one."

"Do you think someday people will look back at our society and shake their heads and say: *They killed their babies when it wasn't convenient to have them.* I'm not judging. I'm just saying this could be the way future generations look at us. On the other hand, they could think it was completely sane, given that there will be 50 billion of them on the planet by then."

"Are we having a debate about abortion, here in the mountains?"

"No. I have liberal opinions that have never been tested. I've never had to — I've never been in that situation. Besides, I'm not going to argue with a lawyer."

RONIN HEARS THEM before he actually sees them. He wasn't looking for ATVs on the side of Mt. Deception. He was looking for fossils. But the whining insect sound reaches him when he is behind a high outcrop. He has no idea that he's going to be moved to violence by that small sound. There are two of them in their little four-wheeled things and they're driving them straight up the mountain toward his perch. Ronin thinks about how much beer he's got. Is it three cans or four? Doesn't matter. Three is enough to share.

He's just left the alpine meadow and he's moved onto rock. Ronin is up a twenty-metre cliff face, which has taken him forty minutes to navigate his way around. There was only one way up to this outlook without using ropes. There's no way they can see him. When they start spinning around and ripping up the turf Ronin feels an anger rising from his gut. It moves into his chest and he can feel his heartbeat quickening. *What the fuck are these idiots doing?!?* They're really working the meadow over. Joyriding around in circles, digging up turf with each turn. He stands up without thinking and throws a medium-sized rock close enough to get their attention. The guy wearing the red baseball cap looks up and says something. He's wearing a sidearm, which is odd. Ronin has no idea what purpose a handgun would possibly have in the mountains, other than target shooting. Not going to put much of a dent in a grizzly bear with a handgun — just piss him off. The other guy who is dressed in khaki overalls has a rifle in a bag strapped across the back of his ATV.

"You're wrecking the meadow," Ronin shouts. "It's fragile up this high."

"Meadow?" It's the guy with the rifle. "We're not in the Park."

"I know. But you're ripping up the meadow. It takes a hundred years for an alpine meadow to heal, if it heals at all."

"Ya, thanks a lot," the guy with the handgun says. *Oh fuck off*, is what he means. He cranks up his machine and spins around a couple of times, spewing turf and loose rock down the slope, no doubt to emphasize his level of disdain. They basically pretend Ronin's not there.

He ducks out of sight. Nothing to be done. He's not going to climb down there in order to confront a couple of guys with guns.

Ronin sits down behind the ridge and breathes. He listens to them ripping the crap out of the meadow for perhaps two more minutes. They're joyriding like a couple of kids in a stolen car. There are options. Either he can sit there and listen, or he can leave them alone — climb further up the mountain to keep looking for the fossil worms. That's the sane thing. Finish what he came here for. But he loses it. Ronin chooses option three, which is to do something insane. In a crazy rage he pushes at the boulder he's leaning against and it barely moves. He puts his back to it and stretches his legs, and over it goes. It drops toward the guy wearing the handgun as if the rock knows to get the most dangerous one first. The rock hits his little vehicle and over it goes. It's pretty well flattened and the guy jumps out of the way just in time. Then Ronin starts throwing rocks — one after another, after another, after another — a continuous barrage of rock. Anything he can lift and throw, or anything sitting at the edge that he can roll. He drops and throws the stones down on them before they can figure out what the hell's going on. He's a crazed Zeus with granite thunderbolts. He's completely insane. He'd have to be in order to throw rocks at two guys who are armed. Ronin hits both guys with rocks and really doesn't care. Something in him knows that he's only got this one chance to stop them. The ATV that's tipped over on its side has smoke spewing from the engine. Once they figure out what's going on, they'll likely be shooting bullets up here. When he stops, Ronin's soaked in sweat. *You've really done it now!* One of the ATVs is done. They've managed to pull the other one out of the way. From a tactical point of view, Ronin is sitting pretty. He's up high looking down. There's just one way up to the ridge. He takes quick glances and then, from behind the outcrop, he lobs more rocks — blindly chucking them over his shoulder. He wants these assholes off the mountain. When he is exhausted, he quietly packs away his gear and looks up at the top of the mountain. He'll have to go up and then around and down. He'll come into the valley on the north side of the Divide. There's no rush. His car is sheltered by a clump of trees and he's parked in a sort-of dip where it can't be seen. Then he'll bushwhack his way up to the saddle and hope to find his car intact. He is emphatically uninterested in meeting up with the well-armed stupid and stupider.

⌐⌐

TWO DAYS BEFORE Ronin leaves for Paris, he goes to the Café Demitasse. He's sitting at one of the outside tables, just out of the sun.

He puts his newspaper on the table and takes a drink of wine. Forget about the news, he tells himself. There's too much news in the world. It can wait; it does not change. Pick up any newspaper. There'll be a story about people killing each other in the name of religion. There will be a car accident or two. There'll be a murder or three. Somebody in the United States will be shot with a handgun. There'll be a story about a corrupt politician. And somewhere in the world, a bomb will explode, and if it kills people who look like us, it will be reported in the news. It's the same every day. What can anyone do to make the world a better place other than changing themselves?

He remembers a scene in the movie *Ghost Dog* where the main character talks about fully understanding the present moment, and how that's all anyone needs. Because life is only one moment joined to other moments, joined to more moments. That's from the *Hagakure*, the book that fell on the floor in front of Ronin in a bookstore a few years ago.

Ronin watches Maurice, the waiter, feeding the birds on the boulevard. He does this every morning. It is his ritual. He comes out from the kitchen with a pan full of crumbs and spreads it under that tree. Is it an elm? A poplar? Perhaps the name of this particular tree doesn't matter.

Why does Maurice feed the birds? Who knows? There may be entire families — generations — of sparrows and pigeons that rely upon this man's generosity, his kindness. This waiter's kindness is the only important thing right now — to the birds that have come to rely on him, and to Ronin, because Maurice and these birds are part of the fabric of this moment, his moment. The fact that he has done this for five, or ten, or twenty years is irrelevant.

Ronin would like to ask Maurice why he feeds the birds, but he knows the answer. Because nobody else does it. It's probably something Maurice feels he must do. The fact that he's kind-hearted doesn't cross his mind.

Normally, Ronin doesn't like it when people come over to his table and want to talk. He sees this place as a refuge — a place to be alone and quiet. Maurice and the other waiters know this and they do everything in their power to protect him when he's reading the newspaper, or working on a presentation, or just drifting. But sometimes they will come with their own stories or because they need to have a conversation with someone they know.

SYLVIE, WHO OWNS the Demitasse, sits at his table one day in January after he's taught a course at the university. Ronin had made good money that day, being a geologist who likes to tell stories.

Sylvie frowns when she smiles. The corners of her mouth move downward. Her smiles take place mostly in her eyes. It's not that one can't tell when she is truly frowning, but her disapproval is also mostly in her eyes. Sylvie is a stocky woman. Ronin does not know how old she is, nor does he care. She wears glasses to read the paper, if that says anything. She can put an apron on and look like an Italian mama, and then take it off and look like a graceful movie star. She always displays the refined warmth of the perfect host, and it is not artifice.

She is not smiling. In fact, Ronin has never seen her look so sad.

"Two weeks ago, my father went to Montreal to see his brother. I mentioned this. I know I did. Anyway, he left me in charge of feeding his cat. Every day I have been going over there to feed the cat. So last night when I was holding the cat, he died," she says quietly.

"He stopped breathing in my arms. He just stopped." She looks confused, horrified, frozen inside this memory.

"I'm sorry, Sylvie."

She looks up and Maurice is there in an instant. "Two espressos, Maurice. And two cognacs please," she says, switching from proprietor to customer. The waiters recognize it immediately. They can all tell when she is still the boss but also no longer the boss.

"What happened? What happened to the cat?"

"I don't know," she says. "Maybe it was just old. Perhaps it was his time. But I do not think the cat was that old. Six years? Maybe more. I don't know. When I arrived there, he was breathing funny. So I held him, covered him with a blanket and held him. I don't know how long it was but eventually he stopped breathing. I knew he was dying. I felt it the second I saw him. But it's as if he was waiting for me to come — for someone to be there." Sylvie is staring into the park across the street. Christmas lights are stranded haphazardly in the branches and there is snow drifting in long swirls through the streetlights.

"I'm glad you were there. Nobody should die alone. Not even a cat."

～

LAST SUMMER THERE WAS a budgie in the tree under which Maurice feeds the birds each morning. A flash of piercing sapphire blue amidst the grey sparrows and the pigeons. A near-perfect anomaly. The budgie must have escaped from somewhere. In the city, a cage was empty. But don't pet shops clip budgies' wings before they sell them? This one could fly quite well.

It would sit in the tree and wait until there was a break in the feeding frenzy below and then dart down to peck at the crumbs. There was a hierarchy — pigeons first and whenever they wanted. They just walked over and dominated with their superior weight and mass. Sparrows and other dull nervous birds dined second. Exotic birds came third.

Amazingly, most people actually walked by the budgie while it was there on the ground under the tree, a lightning bolt of blue, and didn't notice it.

Once the budgie established itself in his imagination, Ronin came to the Café Demitasse every day. It is nothing like Paris but has its own unique charms. The food is as good or better than anything he's ever experienced in Paris. The Demitasse overlooks a park and one entire wall is window, so the light is always good. Most of the wait staff know Ronin, call him by name.

Each day he looked for that flash of blue that was at once a mystery and a small joy. He begins to worry about it. There are falcons and hawks in this city. They nest on top of the tall buildings and feed in the river valley. This crazy blue-coloured bird would make an incredible target. It would stick out. Ronin can imagine a falcon circling above, seeing the budgie and thinking: *lunch is served.*

"Well," Ronin says to Maurice, "is our friend still around?"

Maurice smiles, suddenly engaged at a level beyond the banalities of foodservice. "I saw him early this morning, waiting his turn."

That is the extent of their conversation. To speak at length about the budgie would ruin something. There is magic and awe at work here, something that cannot be explained or examined too much. Questioning the budgie about its history, while quirky and perhaps charming, isn't going to produce any answers.

Ronin looks across the sidewalk at the tree, scanning it for that brilliant dot of blue. He decides this bird represents hope against insurmountable odds.

It's Friday so the café fills up just before noon and stays that way for the afternoon. He orders a bottle of the Mâcon-Villages chardonnay and settles in to wait for the bird. He has the newspapers with him so he can catch up on the world and soften the news with the wine. The people on the sidewalk muffle the impact of the traffic and Ronin can almost hear the music that Sylvie insists must always be happy. "Not stupid happy," she says, "happy but intelligent. This is not a sad café."

Is a budgie flying in the middle of a city a sign of some kind? Ronin tries to find out what budgies mean. They don't appear in any record of native mythology that he's ever read. Bears, mountain lions, porcupines, hawks, eagles, hummingbirds, dragonflies — these creatures all have mythological, archetypal meanings attached to them. But budgies? He may as well have been looking up poodles, or forks, or hair dryers.

He is halfway through the bottle of wine when the budgie makes an entrance. Ronin is relieved and excited. He'd like to get up, run inside and get Maurice, but decides instead to simply enjoy it. It sits high up in the tree surveying the ground. Where in hell does this bird go at night?

At the next table, there is a woman with long fingers. She is smoking with her wrist bent outwards and the cigarette held delicately, like it's a prop, not an addiction. She has her back to Ronin, and she is sitting across from a grey woman. It's not that her hair is grey. It's not. It's a dull brown. There is simply nothing remarkable about her. She has a pleasant, round face. Her hair is mid-length and straight. A simple dress, plain, no pattern. A taupe colour. Ronin looks for the edges: difficult nose, eyes the colour of green pop bottles, strange hair, ears that stick out, tattoos. Anything. But this woman is flat. There are no edges, nothing to hang onto. Perhaps that in itself is enough to make her noteworthy.

The woman who is smoking with a dramatic elegance, whose face he cannot see, says, "Look at the blue jay."

The plain woman nods her head; small looks at the bird, looks at the smoking woman and smiles. She knows.

Ronin smiles back. It seems she wants to roll her eyes but can't because the smoking woman would see. How could anybody confuse a blue jay with a budgie? At least she noticed the bird, Ronin thinks. That's something.

⌒

"I WAS SAD EVEN BEFORE I met Ronin," Moira says in a flat-lined voice. She winces, half-smiles as if something has just hurt her. "That sounds so much like I'm inside a pathetic soap opera and can't get out. But I like it when it rains. And I love fall, when things are dying. Every morning I think about death. I can't help it. That's just how I am."

Georgia leans back in her chair and thinks: *Holy shit! This is way beyond listening. This woman needs professional help. What the hell can I do but listen? If I push her to know what the fuck it is back there that's causing her this sorrow, I'll lose her. She'll shut down. I can't push her.* "Tell me about the moments of happiness, the times when you might have been happy, you know, in the beginning."

"Yes," Moira says. "I was happy. But always there has been this thing — this undercurrent." She raises her eyes from the tabletop, look at Georgia. "He made me laugh," she says. "My husband. He used to make me laugh."

The kids are down at the beach for the afternoon and Moira has brought out a bottle of tequila, which is now half-gone. The girls have taken Georgia's dog, Jake, an arthritic and very protective black Lab, with them.

⌒

RONIN GOES TO VISIT his father before he leaves. He's quiet, sitting in a wooden chair, facing an open, screened window. It's green through that window. There is sporadic birdsong in the trees. Every now and then the sound of children playing slides into the room from across the way. It makes Ronin sad to see him sitting there.

He's stumbled upon a poem by Maya Angelou called "I Know Why the Caged Bird Sings." He'd heard the Branford Marsalis recording — a captivating melody built around a reading of the poem — and that mixture of spoken-word and music had captured him. Only now, when Ronin sees his father so small, diminished and frail in this light, does he associate this man with the poem. That beautiful poem made Ronin think about the prisons we choose to live within. It started him thinking about Moira. He wonders about her prisons, wonders about what kind of song she might be singing out there on the coast while looking for herself. "The caged bird sings of freedom." Is that what Moira wants? Freedom?

And now this image of his father in the window, looking out.

Ronin leans against the door jam and watches him. He is bird-like. A caged bird.

"You used to grab my finger," his father says. "You'd lie on your back in the crib and I'd reach down to touch you — I used to love touching you — just the side of your face, or your arm, or your back. And you'd reach up and smile and grab my forefinger. You had quite a grip." His father does not turn around. He continues to look out the window in the direction of the sound of birds and chil-dren playing. Maybe he sees my reflection in the window, Ronin thinks. Is that it? "That was our ritual. I used to think you were going to be a baseball player. I don't know why." His voice is so soft that Ronin begins to wonder if he's imagining this monologue. Perhaps this isn't his father. He steps backwards into the hallway. Don't be ridiculous, he tells himself, this is my father.

"I used to hold you and carry you everywhere. I loved just hold-ing you. And when you would reach up and hang on like your life depended on it, well, I remember this very well. I'm not losing that part of my mind. I refuse to give that up. I'm keeping that. God is a cruel son-of-a-bitch if he takes that away from me."

Ronin stands there with his heart on the floor, thinking, this is not my father. The disease has loosed this creature that looks like my father but is really a flood of feelings and emotions that have been frozen a lifetime.

"Dad?" Ronin says and his father turns around.

"Who the hell are you! What are you doing in my room? Who are you? Why are you here? Help! There's someone in my room!" It's loud and ugly and three nurses arrive, one of whom is armed with a sedative. Ronin backs out slowly.

"It's okay," one of the nurses says in his direction. "This happens all the time."

"What?" Not to me, he's thinking.

"It happens all the time," she says. "He'll be all right in a minute."

"I'm going to Paris for a couple weeks," Ronin whispers. "I'll see him when I get back."

"Who in the hell are you?!? There's some son-of-a-bitch standing in my room! Who are you!?"

He doesn't have the mettle for calmly reminding his father who he is. Tonight, he can't go there. He can't look at his father's fear, and confusion, and helplessness. Ronin retreats.

In the car he feels very alone. He's not even thinking about it but the car navigates itself toward the Demitasse, parks itself in front of the café and Ronin gets out.

Inside, Maurice delivers his customary greeting. It's a pleasant greeting, both reliable and unwavering. There are subtle variations of intonation that Ronin has only just begun to be aware of after years of coming here. Maurice says hello, calls Ronin by name and then performs a small shrug and tilt of his head, as if to say, sit where you like, life goes on and here we are.

⌒

A MONTH AGO, Maurice had sat down across from Ronin and announced he knew exactly where his life went off the rails.

Maurice is one of the best waiters in this city. Ronin does not know another who is better. There is a serious intensity to everything he does. He does not overly embellish his descriptions of food. He has an excellent knowledge of wine and is not snooty about it. He is a short, well-proportioned man whose clothes are always well-pressed and stylish. He has the practical, French disposition.

"I didn't know your life was off the rails, Maurice," Ronin says.

Maurice closes his eyes and sighs heavily.

Ronin speculates as Maurice fills both their glasses with more wine. Money? Love? Insecurity? Insanity? A death? All these could be derailing factors.

"Yes, yes, yes ... It was just after I met the Artist. I told you about her. She was a rather brilliant painter ... watercolours. She used her watercolours as if they were oils. I thought she was the one, of course. Love. Love blinds you to what is really there. There should be eyeglasses that correct for the condition of love. When you are in love you put the glasses on and you are at least able to see what's going on. You'd still feel fantastic but you'd be able to see ..."

"... ah, but that would take all the fun out of it."

"Perhaps. But perhaps we would be much happier."

"So what did this Artist do to cause this derailment?"

"She had a baby."

"Yours?"

Maurice nods.

⌒

RONIN'S MOTHER, MARY, lives in a gated condo on Saskatchewan Drive.

Every morning, she arrives at the home before her husband wakes. It's a five-block walk and she has never missed a day — not once in over two years. She insists on walking, rain or snow, cold or heat.

"Some mornings it's as if nothing is wrong — we chat, have coffee — read the paper." She stops to have a sip of her coffee. She has always cupped her hand around her coffee mug, as if her hand is cold or something, and when she wants to drink there is a pulling-back motion so that her fingers can find the handle. "On these mornings I feel a guilt more horrible than on the mornings when he does not know me."

It's impossible to look at her with any degree of objectivity. Impossible for Ronin to make his eyes even remotely objective, and find his mother. If he had to describe her, he'd say she is devoutly normal. He might amend that description with the word heroic. Heroic. Maurice would have something to say about this. Maurice is in the habit of correcting the newspaper, out loud. One of his corrections is the idea of what is heroic and what is brave. He says being heroic is a quiet, inner thing. It is done quietly and without fanfare and with no expectation of recognition. An act of bravery is almost always public.

Her early morning pilgrimages are not attempts to come to terms with her own guilt. It is Ronin's father she cares for. It is about him. She has never complained about these early morning visits. They have become part of her life. Like having a shower. Or getting the mail.

"Well, I don't want him to be lonely in the morning when he wakes up. I want him to see something familiar."

"Mom, we must have a hundred pictures throughout his room."

"I know, I know," she says.

"And his favourite chair, and his music is there."

"I know. But I don't mind the walk, and I can go to mass on the way home."

"I'm not saying don't go. All I'm saying is you don't have to go every single morning."

Her skin has begun to acquire the translucence of age. Ronin looks at her and wonders where all the wrinkles came from. When did she become this old? And if she's old then he must be getting old too. She has managed to reach the age of seventy and still be lanky. She wears slacks and looks like Katharine Hepburn. A couple of years back she started wearing Buddhist prayer beads. The fashion of the day was to wear a strand with no understanding of what they stood for. Both Ronin's daughters wore beads on their wrists for a few months. He wanted to tell them it was like wearing a cross simply because it was in fashion but he held back. Some things can't be taught. Gaudy silver crosses are the fashion of the moment. So a bunch of rappers — functionally illiterate, violent and rich, devoid of anything resembling a moral fibre wear chunky silver crosses around their necks — meaningless, egocentric and ultimately insulting to anybody who happens to be Christian. Ronin's mother never takes her mala off. When he'd asked what they were, she said Richard Gere wore them and she thought he was very handsome.

"I know I don't have to go every day," his mother says. "But I don't want him to ..." Tears stream down her cheeks and then her talking is muffled in Ronin's chest as he wraps his arms around her. "I think if I'm there every morning, by some miracle, he won't forget me."

A COUPLE OF MONTHS AGO, Ronin had found a rocking chair for his dad in an unfinished-pine-furniture shop in the west end. Once Moira left for the Island with the girls, he had time on his hands, so he painted the chair a moss-sage green and began three days of coat after coat of Varathane, with fine sanding in between. By the time he was done, he was quite attached to the chair and almost did not want to give it up. In fact, it hurt a little to think about leaving it in his father's room.

Now, he puts the chair into the trunk of the Plymouth and bungee-cords the trunk lid down so it hits a blanket that's wedged in between the edge and the chair. His father is sleeping when Ronin arrives. He places the chair near the window, not facing directly outward but more at an angle between the room and the outside. The soft green colour is a perfect link between worlds. Then he tries it out for the first time. The arms feel smooth and cool, and the rocking motion is gentle.

Before he leaves, he goes over to the bed and puts a hand on his father's shoulder — not to wake him up — just to connect. Ronin closes his eyes and immediately feels that tingling at the back of his neck, as if somebody just blew very softly on the nape.

Just let go for a second, he thinks. Breathe. Let it happen. And there his father is on the other side of the yard with a hardball in his hand. He's throwing it to Ronin. There is the slapping sound of the ball coming home into the pocket of Ronin's glove. He throws the ball back. Not too hard, but not a weak throw either. No competition here. Just two guys playing catch. Two men connected by an invisible trajectory, and velocity, and time. Two men in an almost holy silence. There's a rhythm to tossing a ball back and forth that can become almost meditative. Ronin is happy in this memory. It's such a stupidly simple thing and he's disproportionately happy. And his father is woven into this happiness.

In the car, before he twists the key into the ignition, he experiences a tremendous rush of missing for his girls. He wants to have a catch with someone right now. Moira is in Sooke. His daughters are in Sooke. He calls Sylvie. "I feel like having a catch," he says.

"What? What is a catch?"

"Throwing a baseball back and forth. Do you have a glove?"

"I do not think so."

"That's all right. I have an extra."

"Are you all right?" she asks.

"I will be after we have a catch."

She agrees to meet Ronin in the park across the street from the Demitasse and it turns out she's got a hell of an arm — a great throw.

"Four brothers," she says.

3

CATS COME, AND CATS GO ...

Paris is a horrible city in which to be alone. Even with all the art, the cafés, the museums and people, Ronin feels the loneliness begin to seep into him. He does not unpack and settle. If Moira were here, she would have done it for him. Moira liked to nest in hotel rooms. But that is not Ronin. He prefers to live out of his suitcase. He hangs up a couple of shirts and a suit coat in the closet, and moves his toiletries into the small bathroom. That is the extent of his Paris settling.

It is his first night in Paris, and while it is not his own bathtub he is comfortable. He's downed a bottle of wine and there are three more bottles in the other room. Ronin is not a big drinker. Frequent but not big. It's not in his nature to be severe. Tonight, it seems that he arrives at the bottom of this bottle without thinking about it.

He's brought three books with him. He picks Gao Xingjian's *Soul Mountain* out of the bag and begins to read.

PARIS IS A HORRIBLE CITY for cars. Ronin remembers a ride to the airport a few years ago. He was staying at the airport hotel for the night so he was not in a hurry. He communicated this to the driver several times but the driver still persisted in driving over 180 kilometers an hour. Apparently, he was under some time constraint that he shared only by the speed with which he guided his vehicle through narrow streets and finally onto a sort of highway. Ronin had just closed his eyes and hoped to live through it.

He's been in Paris four days. He had too many Air Miles. More Air Miles than he knew what to do with. So he had booked a flight to Paris. Booking a free flight meant flying to Calgary, then to Toronto, then London, and finally Charles de Gaulle airport. It was a hellish day of travel, but to be in Paris, even for a few days, was worth that hell and probably more. Paris was always interesting in the summer months because there weren't many actual Parisians. Ronin's not sure where they all go. At the airport, the glass-enclosed uniformed man who checked his passport photo seemed almost pleasant. Normally passport checkers are grim and they have become more so over the past couple of years.

RONIN IS SITTING BY HIMSELF at one of the inside tables at Café Deux Magots. It's been raining on and off all day. There are people smoking all around but here in Paris it doesn't bother him. People should be smoking in cafés in Paris. Two women are speaking French at the next table. Ronin understands perhaps every third word and only when they slow down. They don't slow down much. This conversation comes to him as poetry — cryptic fragments with much white space. From the fragments he manages to hear, he understands a cat is missing. At least, he thinks it's a cat. The woman facing him, who has her hair pulled back and is wearing a cotton scarf loosely around her neck, has lost her cat. It went out the window as usual but she has not seen it for days. She is obviously upset. She drinks two glasses of wine to every one of her friend's. She looks tired. Maybe she's been up all night wandering the streets looking for the cat. Regardless, she is trying to be nonchalant about it. "Les chats viennent, et les chats vont," she says.

Cats come, and cats go? Did he hear that right? Is that correct?

Ronin orders another Ricard. This woman reminds him of a black-and-white picture, by Robert Mapplethorpe, of a woman standing at a balcony railing, with the Eiffel Tower in the far distance. She is wearing a housecoat, and is preoccupied with something going on in the street below. She might be angry. Is someone leaving her? A hand rests on the railing. Her right arm seems unnaturally outstretched, as if old Mapplethorpe has asked her to extend her arm along the railing a little bit more than anyone should. Or maybe she was going to wave but then stopped, and instead, clung to the railing. The sky in that picture is composed of ripped layers of charcoal. For Ronin, that sad sky is Paris.

It starts to rain again — a gentle soaking rain, causing fog on the insides of the café windows. This pleases Ronin. It automatically draws attention away from Paris-the-city, and refocuses it on Paris-the-people. The two women with the missing cat get up to leave and he realizes they are both strikingly beautiful. They are beautiful but they seem not to be fully aware of their beauty. He'd like to think neither of these women cares very much for fashion or cosmetics and that this indifference causes them to have style.

On the day he arrived in Paris he saw a beautiful woman sunbathing nude beside the Seine. It was a hot day. He'd looked over the wall to see if he could spot the saxophonist who was playing with his own echo — sending out riffs like birds to tease the air currents. This guy would play a line and then enter the echo of his own melody with a new melody, which would curve over the top of fading echoes of the previous riffs. Ronin was fascinated by the music and pleasantly surprised by the naked woman. He remembers the small details of her body clearly. She had hairy armpits.

When they stand up he can see that both women are tall although neither is model-skinny. They have lovely curves. The missing-cat woman has a slender face and the line of her jaw is soft. Her eyes are dark and questioning. When she looks around the café, it is with a bemused curiosity. The other woman, who spoke very quickly — and as a result, he has no idea about her life except that she has a deep voice — is wearing a vest and no bra. He'd like to think he was drawn to her eyes first, or her face, but that is not the case. She displays her breasts with a casual recklessness as she turns and bends over to pick up her bag. That is where Ronin looks. How could he not look? She leaves nothing to the imagination for a couple of seconds and then just as suddenly takes away this view. But the image of her dark areola and the liquid fullness of her breasts attaches to his memory. She is completely nonchalant about this exposure. She is very comfortable with her own body. Or this sudden exposure was planned to titillate every man within a certain radius. Ronin is definitely titillated.

But this is not the one who captures him. The lost-cat woman produces an umbrella. Just for a second, as she turns to leave, she finds Ronin's eyes. Did she smile? He cannot discern the colour of her eyes. She's a bit too far away. He looks across the room and slowly lets his gaze move toward the door. That way, they will walk into his view and it will not appear that he is looking at them. He watches them outside, unfurling the umbrella. The woman who is not shy about her body kisses the missing-cat woman on each cheek, then walks slowly into the crowds of people moving past the café. She walks as if the rain does not exist. As if it is a common thing for her to get soaked to the skin. As if it does not matter. And disappears into the rain and the fabric of Paris.

BEYOND THE PEOPLE on the sidewalk, the cars zoom at stupid speeds along boulevard Saint-Germain. The sound of car tires shushing along the street and the pin-prickly rain walking across the awning of the café insists on a space in Ronin's consciousness. But there is nothing special about the sound of traffic. Ronin begins to think about the cat woman. He's wondering if she'll come back inside the café. He'd like to look at her again. She stands in the rain under the purple umbrella for a long time. Maybe she expects to see her cat. Something in Ronin is saying: get up, go out and stand with her. Offer to help her look for her cat. Say something like, he's sorry for overhearing but he knows what it's like to be worried about a missing pet. But suppose she does not speak English? Pretty ethnocentric to assume she can. He is not the kind of traveller who expects the whole world to speak English. Ronin can see himself stumbling through in his fragmented French and looking like a completely incompetent idiot. Maybe she'll think it's charming.

But he doesn't listen to that voice. Well, he listens, but he doesn't act. I love my wife, he tells himself.

Of course there have been temptations. But Ronin knows his life would be very different if he listened to that voice instead of just being sort-of interested in its directions and tone. It is a self-centered voice with no regard for consequences. That's not him. Not now.

Ronin does not exactly wish for the cat woman to come back and sit at his table. He hopes she'll stay inside this movie scene of his, just continue to linger at the edges.

A blue Mercedes pulls up and stops in front of the café. Cars behind the Mercedes begin to honk almost immediately. She climbs in and gives the man a kiss on each cheek. Then the car is off into the idiot traffic. The potential of meeting this woman is gone. He finds himself thinking about cars. He starts a litany of the cars he's owned. Mercedes Benz is not on this list, and likely never will be. He thinks about the cars his father drove over the years. Ronin doesn't care what his cars look like, and someday his daughters will be old enough to be embarrassed by this. They'll want their car to look as nice as their friends' parents' cars or vans. They're probably at that point already. Ronin will do his best to teach them about the many things in life that are more important than the way a person's car looks, or the clothes they wear, the toys they own, or the house in which they live. He'll probably use words like honour and integrity.

His father was one of those people in Ronin's life who spent a great deal of time making sure their cars looked nice. They'd clean and fuss, wax and shine, stand back and look and then begin again.

SOMEONE IS TALKING TO HIM. She sounds very much like Moira. But this voice is recent. It's the woman with the missing cat. The one who drove off in the blue Mercedes. She's come back into the café.

"I like your eyes," she says. "There is a kindness in your eyes."

Ronin stands up, bumps his knee on the table, jars the glasses. She's here. It's her. How did she know he spoke English? Was she listening to him order his drinks?

"Oh. Hello," he says. "Um, bonjour."

"Hi," she says, and then clears her throat. "Perhaps I am a mistake, but I think to me you are attracted?"

Ronin can't help smiling. "Your English is better than my French, and yes, to you I am attracted." He motions for her to sit down and she does. He tucks her chair in as if he's in a forties movie, and sits down across from her.

"I am called Claire," she says.

He mangles an introduction of himself in French and then gives it up. He switches to English. Tries to speak plainly. "I was just thinking about you."

"Really? What?"

"I, I was hoping that you might come back ..." Is that true? He'd been eavesdropping on a private conversation. Best leave it at hoping she would come back. "... and I was thinking it would be pleasant to drink almost too much champagne with you."

He can see the wheels turning. She's thinking about things. Perhaps she's trying to figure out what *almost too much* means.

"I couldn't help overhearing that your cat is missing," Ronin adds. "I'm sorry."

"Ah, my cat. Yes, she was a good listener."

"That sounds final. You're certain the cat is gone?"

"No, we are not certain but it is Paris and there is much traffic. It has been four months."

Four months. That's what he'd missed by listening like skipping a rock on the surface of a lake.

"So, I am curious," she says. "What would you enjoy to do about this mutual attraction?"

"Could we stay here a while? I would enjoy that." He reaches across the tabletop and places his hand in hers. He's not sure why he does this, why he's flirting with danger. Maybe he just wants skin on skin with a woman. Touch is important and this sort of touch is lacking in his life.

She inhales quickly. She smiles and Ronin is instantly, stupidly, in love. There is a small unfurling of vulnerability in her smile. Her eyes are a deep navy blue. He knows he's in love and this does not dismay him. He wants to devour this woman. Consume the minutiae of her life. This is the kind of in-love-ness that is mixed together with lust, and accepting, and sorrow, and a potential for absolutely anything. Endless possibilities. Ronin catches the waiter's eye and asks for a bottle of good champagne. He could have ordered a specific bottle but instead, he entrusts the waiter to use his own creativity and make his own interpretation. Ronin only hopes the waiter understands that he doesn't want a bottle of *great* champagne. Over the years, Ronin has noticed a romantic intuitiveness in his experience with the French. There is an extraordinary respect for love and romance in this culture. They notice when there is love and they honour it by giving it space and weight.

The waiter returns with a bottle of Veuve Clicquot Brut Carte Jaune. He makes the opening of the bottle special, yet very efficient and understated. It's as if he has picked one of his favourite wines. He understands this play. He saw this woman leave and now she is here. He seems happy to be part of the unfolding story. He plays his role flawlessly. The flutes sparkle as he fills them. "L'ambroisie pour deux," he says with a conspiratorial silkiness. "Pas comme si vous en avez besoin." He slips the bottle into an ice bucket and disappears.

"To love," she says, lifting her glass. Her eyes find his across the table because, for her, it has always been important to have eye contact when toasting. Ronin begins to remember the simple pleasures of touching skin, of smoothing hands and being lost inside a secret bliss where there is only skin, touch, taste. He remembers moving his hand over the topography of a lover, of wanting to know the landscape so well, of needing to pay attention to every minor perfection.

How can he drink to love? Here is a beautiful woman who still believes in love. She wants to toast love, with him. But he loves his wife.

Be in the moment, he tells himself. Don't think about anything but the woman and the champagne. I do not have to fly away home because my house is *not* on fire. My children are safe; they are with Moira and I love my wife. I love my wife.

⌒

IF MOIRA HAS LEFT FOR GOOD, then he should not feel guilt about Claire. But what if she does just need to find herself? What's Moira doing on the Island anyway? He thinks about what it was like to stay in that cabin on the cliff near Sooke. He and Moira spent a week there. He remembers walking along the beach with her and feeling oddly disconnected. He didn't exactly feel alone but he'd thought maybe with time together and no kids they would naturally come together again. Perhaps they should have been looking for the lost bits of Moira. With the two of them looking, it would have been easy. Ronin imagines walking out into the ocean up to his hips and then reaching into the water for something — pulling out a small, dripping television screen with one aspect of Moira showing over and over again. Maybe it would be a character-changing scene — one of those life altering moments. "Is this what you're looking for, honey?" he'd shout above the sound of the waves. "This looks like your Grade 9 graduation picture."

He has a hollow echo knocking around inside his head. It keeps repeating the line: *Moira is not coming back.*

Nobody gets closer to someone by moving away from them. She's not trying to find herself out there; she's gathering speed for an escape. She's withdrawing for good.

～

WHEN RONIN FIRST ARRIVED in Paris, he rented a GSM cell phone for a couple of weeks and call-forwarded his home phone so nobody would know where he was. He didn't bother to ask the guy at the counter what exactly GSM stood for. He was just grateful the guy spoke a little English. The nine-hour time difference was a strange adjustment. When it's nine at night in Paris, it's only noon in Sooke. He's been waking up at 5 a.m. to talk to the girls, so that for them it's around 8 at night. There was no need for them to know he was really calling from Paris. He felt a bit guilty about this. He's supposed to be at home, standing with his feet on the ground holding tightly to the kite string, while Moira drifts around up in the sky like a lost little fairy.

～

"HELLO? MOIRA?"

"Yes."

"How are you?"

"We're great," she says. "I'll call the girls ..."

"... wait. No. I wanted to talk to you. I wanted to know how *you* were doing."

"Where are you? Is everything all right? You sound far away."

"I'm on the cell. It's a lousy connection." Big breath. "Listen, I want to ask if you're figuring things out but perhaps that's a moot point? Are we going to be okay? Our family?" Ronin's hoping this doesn't sound condescending or glib.

There is a long pause. "I don't know," she says finally.

He'd like to ask her if at some point she is going to tell him what the fuck is really going on. But instead, he says, "Obviously if you were great, we wouldn't be talking long-distance."

"I'm not happy," she says.

Well that's a start. He immediately wants to do the guy thing, which is dive in and determine the problem, come up with solutions that might work, and then derive a plan of action. In fact, he'd probably come up with a list of pluses and minuses and an outline of several potential solutions. But he knows Moira's likely not looking for solutions. There's a value in just talking.

Shut up and listen, he tells himself. He'll ask her why she's not happy. This is Moira, his wife. They've shared a great deal of life together. This shouldn't be difficult. He knows what she needs.

Well, apparently he doesn't. Apparently he does not know her as well as he should. He's off balance.

"Why?" he asks. "Why are you unhappy?"

⌒

RONIN'S SISTER, KATE, is on the phone. She thinks he's still in Edmonton. "Dad's not good," she says. "He seems to be shutting down."

"He what? But I was just there," he says. "He was talking up a storm. I actually wanted him to shut up and he wouldn't. What do you mean shutting down? When did you see him last?"

"He's retreating. He barely talks. Barely moves. I'm worried."

"What do they say at the home? Did they call you?"

"Nobody called. I was just there. I'm in the car."

Ronin doesn't know how to respond. He feels a sudden panic. Would it do any good to sit across from his father and speak his heart? He knows his father loved him. But his father's not going to remember who the hell Ronin is. He thinks his son is away playing hockey in the NHL. It's the off-season. Hockey season is months away.

⌒

"HELLO, MOIRA?"

"No, this is Georgia. Hang on, I'll get her."

Who in the hell is Georgia? Ronin's thinking. But what does it matter? She's probably a friend. It's not easy caring for two kids 24/7 by yourself. But he doesn't remember Moira ever mentioning a Georgia.

"Hello."

"Moira, it's me. How's it going out there?"

"Oh, good."

There is a distinct upward inflection in her voice. A tenor not there before.

"And the girls?"

"The girls are having fun but they miss you."

"And you? Are you okay?"

Ronin listens carefully, let's himself sink into the silence and waits for a curt, pat answer. But this pause continues longer than the pauses he's come to expect from Moira. This is it, he's thinking. She's not coming back. He can feel his heart beating and he's bracing for whatever dark news is about to be delivered.

"I love you," she says. "I hope you've never doubted that."

This sober statement slips him into an unexpected awkwardness. It's an assumed intimacy that has been absent for some time.

"Listen, I'll get the girls," she says.

He missed his chance, an opportunity to say something loving — to let her know that he feels the same way. But he was out of practice. And then the girls are on the line. They bubble over about the beach, about Georgia's dog and Georgia — she sits around without a shirt on, they say. Sarah says she saw a seal. Marie insists it was a walrus. They both agree on having seen a bald eagle although Sarah calls it a "bad" eagle. After he hangs up he wonders if perhaps the eagle was doing something Sarah disapproved of, or if she just got it wrong. Or is bad good?

THE CHAMPAGNE IS COLD and smooth and dry, with an almost buttery aftertaste. There is no bite. It tickles the throat and then rollercoasters in a cold thrill toward the stomach. Claire makes her living writing technical manuals but has published a few short stories. Ronin asks if she knows Mavis Gallant. A whimsical question grasping for a common touchstone. She not only knows her but has had coffee with her several times.

The waiter brings another bottle of champagne and asks if it would be okay if he lit the candle on their table now.

"Non, merci," Claire says. "Not just now."

She turns back to face Ronin.

"The light is beautiful," she says. "The diminished light. Crepuscule, yes?"

"What?"

"Crepuscule. What is the word? Night coming but not quite yet."

"Twilight?"

"Oui. Twilight. *Crepuscule*. This is a time when one can see hidden things. Things are written on the skin. Truth is visible."

Ronin has consumed just enough champagne. The benefit-of-the-doubt line has been temporarily misplaced. This is a beautiful woman, and this is Paris. He's willing to entertain wild notions of crepuscule. He can imagine faint words just under the surface of his skin. Sentences. Fragments of sentences. Words and letters drifting to the surface. An elegant, sloping script. A shifting kaleidoscope of unspoken desires. He makes mental calculations of how much he's had to drink. He does not want to see the truth right now. He prefers the truth of haziness. He wants the illusion. He wants the lie of romance. He's had enough of sober truthfulness.

"My mother used to say there was magic in this time. It is a very special light." She half smiles. "Perhaps you will discover why you have such sadness in you."

I am not sad, he wants to say. But he is sad. She's right.

"Not sad entirely," she says. "But there is sadness in your eyes. I am sorry. It is only something I noticed. I ..."

"... No. Don't apologize. You're right. But this is not a discussion for crepuscule. Let's talk about happy things."

He looks at her and realizes she's not feeding him a line about the light, there actually is a subtle deepening. The café seems to close in on itself. They have become part of the throng, they are no longer just visitors. Claire is being filmed with a soft filter. The small lines under her eyes disappear. Her eyes glisten. Has she been crying?

They sit there in this eldritch light and he does not know what to say or do. Ronin's sober enough to understand that anything could happen. He's old enough to want to bathe in that feeling. No rushing, no running away, just to be right where he is.

"What are you thinking," she says.

"Strawberries." He's grasping. "I was thinking about eating strawberries."

"Shall I order some strawberries? Are you hungry?"

"No, I'm fine with this champagne and your company."

"Hmmm, and now I think we will sleep together? We will make love, yes?"

A straightforward question to which he only smiles. Why is it that he feels like crying? What the hell? She reaches across the table to touch his hand. Her fingers are a sigh on his skin and it seems as if he's known this touch for a few hundred years. This feeling of knowing is combined with excitement, with too much champagne and it all scares him a bit. But he does not move his hand away from her touch. That connection becomes his breath. Steals his breath, becomes his breath, steals it.

⸺

THIS COULD BE THE MOMENT when my life goes off track, Ronin thinks. Now, I will truly be lost.

Claire comes up to his room and they fall into each other at the doorway even before he produces the key. He disappears inside a rush of warm, rising music and then he is lost within the feeling of being lost. The sound of a saxophone wends its way through the hall, from the club two doors down. Christ, it's sweet! It's a Paris soundtrack if ever there was one. This is a dream in which she is naked except for her shoes. Long legs pushed up into pointed, sexual weapons. He barely manages to unlock the door. Now she is clawing at him. She begins to need like a crazy vampire and he finds that he wants to give her his neck with an equalled desperation. Clothes are strewn everywhere — kicked inside the room in order to shut the door. Hands on skin. The flesh. Consuming. She pulls him inside. There is so much to discover. It's all there for the taking. Her smells, the sounds she makes, the things she insists upon. Does she talk? "Your skin is so soft," she says. "Your skin is soft." Why is she saying that? How does she let him know when something he's doing works very well? Is it a "hmmm" in the back of her throat?

This is a brand new landscape. Claire becomes the distant hills, hazy with the curvature of the Earth, suddenly touchable, real and responsive. The curves and scars and crevices become his tactile experience. Claire has scars on the back of her right leg, Braille that speaks of some past event. His hand lingers on the tiny ridges, a timid question. "Not now," she says. "Those are healed, but there are other wounds, inside me — these need time. I need time before I can tell you." She pulls him back to the dream with a kiss, then a long slow bite at the back of his neck. Her kisses move across his back and then pleasure is unfolded into something other than itself. It becomes a hedonistic feast of letting go. Release. A guttural grasping for life where it's all right to rush. It's all right to want too much. They stuff themselves on loving. For a few sensorial hours there will be ample opportunity to go slower, to try older methods of loving, they will have this night to shock each other with what they remember of loving. Because this is likely only once. This becomes sheer delirium. A memory unfrozen from some poetic, romantic and ultimately foolish archive. And then they are exhausted on the bed, but he is determined to stay with Claire. He will not drift to anything or anybody but Claire. He begins to memorize each molecule of her skin. Outside, a police car with the siren honking like a runaway donkey. She slips out of bed and opens the window, pulls the curtains aside. Streetlight crashes through the stylized metal grating and sprawls swirling shadows across the floor. Look at her! Look at the way the light touches the curves of her buttocks. See the careful slope of her lower back. They are suddenly in a black-and-white film where everything is grainy and beautiful and no one speaks English. And the subtitles consist only of poetry.

⌐═╝

THE NEXT MORNING, in a crowded café, Ronin can just see the top of the Eiffel Tower. This means he's probably going to pay twice the price he would be paying elsewhere. But he doesn't care. He's hung over. He's drinking the good strong coffee and he's got the *International Herald Tribune*. Claire is on her way home in a taxi.

Ronin smiles, places the paper aside. He needs a version of reality in which he is not a scoundrel. In that version, he would only have held Claire. The night would have started out as one long scene from a Cary Grant movie, in which nobody kisses with any passion, and certainly nobody removes clothing for the purposes of sex. She would have come up to his room. They would have talked until the sky became pink at the edges. Claire would have stripped down to her bra and panties, and crawled into the bed. "Hold me for a while," she'd have said. And so he would. He would crawl in next to her, on top of the sheets and hold her as she drifted off to sleep.

In this new and guiltless reality, Ronin would be holding a woman, a stranger with soft skin, a woman with some interesting scars below her buttocks on her right leg. He'd be thinking about how holding this woman, in a hotel room in Paris, as she falls asleep, is enough. He hardly knows anything about her. Her cat is missing. Twilight is a special time for writing on the skin.

Just before Ronin drifts off, he'll think about Moira. She's not coming back. Moira's not coming back. I can't feel guilty about this. I'm in Paris with a beautiful woman and, right now, to hold her is enough. He has no idea what the hell is wrong with Moira. He'll probably get a phone call, or better yet, a letter, from some dickless lawyer out on the coast wanting to discuss how much fucking money he'll have to pay Moira, and when he'll get to see his girls.

This is not what happened. This is a version of events that makes it easier for Ronin to look himself in the mirror in the morning and not fall apart under the weight of guilt. It would have been more dangerous not to make love with this woman. She would have become a nagging mystery. Every time he'd notice it was twilight, he'd have drifted toward the memory of the thing not experienced. The wine not tasted.

THE GIRLS ARE SLEEPING. Moira is sitting on the deck, feet up, looking at the world over the top rim of her sunglasses. Georgia's gone
into Sooke for groceries. For just a brief moment, halfway through
her third Caesar of the morning, Moira's mind wanders to Ronin
and she finds a rich tableau of memory, but nothing current. When
she left for the summer, they were having sex twice a year. It seemed
she'd slowly lost interest in it. They've got two kids. It became a duty.
Not much fun. This lack of love life was causing tension. She knew
Ronin had had more than enough rejection. He'd stopped coming
to her. He'd retreated into a perplexed silence. She wasn't sure what
he was waiting for. Things to change? A sudden and profound
horniness to reappear in her? Stupid really, but she hoped that their
love life would come back. Not the same as it used to be, different,
but just as satisfying. They needed to connect at that physical level.
But she did not know how to begin to make this happen.

When did I get so damned serious? Ronin's thinking. *I used to be
funny. I used to laugh a lot more. What happened to that part of me?*

Ronin thinks he should call Moira in Sooke and ask her if she
can find his sense of humour rolling around in the ocean froth. Is it
having children? Is that what does it? Is it worrying about his girls?
Is that why he's become so serious? Ronin reads the newspapers
and sometimes watches the news on television. Even though television news, in his mind, has become a farcical, semi-entertaining
joke, watching it still makes him anxious for his daughters.

RONIN ORDERS ANOTHER overpriced coffee. He does not want to
rationalize — he will not make the reality a dream. He prefers the
insane lust. Of course he made love with Claire.

4

OPENINGS

Georgia is worried. She may have heard too much about Moira's life, or not enough, and she senses an incredible repression going on just under Moira's skin. The woman is drinking like a big sloppy fish. It starts in the afternoon with cocktails. She doesn't do any serious drinking until the kids are in bed. Then she goes at it pretty heavily, will even zone out and not hear her kids at times. They have to repeat things three and four times, or touch her arm to bring her back from where she's gone. Other times, her focus on the girls is incredible. There's a communication that verges on the clairvoyant.

The weather has socked in with grey upon grey rolling in from the Pacific. A steady drizzle has developed but there is an awning on the cabin, so they stoke the fire inside and sit out on the deck. It is not cold but sweaters take the chill off.

"What a beautiful light," Georgia says. "Even in the rain, twilight manages to be beautiful."

"The gloaming is an honest time of day," Moira says. "I've always liked it for its honesty. Here's to the gloaming."

Jesus, she's drunk already, Georgia thinks.

"I don't want to talk about my life tonight," Moira says. "I don't want to be sad. I'm through with that. No more sadness. Let's talk about your life shall we?" She reaches over, her arm extended in a wobbly, insistent offering, a tilted wine bottle in her hand. She fills Georgia's glass and then leans back in her chair.

"What do you want to know?"

"Your life," Moira says. "How did you come to be here? I know things about you. I know your name. I know you're probably a little lonely because your partner is teaching English overseas. Ummm, you've been here almost three years. You're good with kids but don't have any of your own. But there are things I don't know, like your dreams. What do you dream of doing? Things like that."

"I don't have a partner. I should have said *ex*. I can't seem to face up to that one just yet. I don't want to face that failure so I ... I've been drifting, you know, here by the ocean."

Moira squints over at Georgia. "Listen, it doesn't mater a rat's ass to me but are you gay?"

Georgia smiles. She always thinks it's blatantly obvious that she's not interested in men. "I prefer women," she says. "I have always been with women."

Moira's been toying with the idea of sleeping with a woman — to feel what it would be like, to experience breasts that are not her own, to taste another woman. She thinks she'll start dropping subtle hints that she'd be interested in bedding Georgia because here is an opportunity. Moira has never been one to let an opportunity slip by.

MOIRA KNOWS. She is well aware of what it is back there that rears up ugly and fetid. Repression can be hard work but Moira has been diligent. She watches as the lambent shadows of trees sketch themselves across the window blinds. The wind has picked up now. The intensity of the rain increases in gusts, as if the droplets are not falling but are being thrown against the window. An ugly darkness is out there, hunched and lurking amidst the trees.

For a long time she sits and listens to the conversation between the ocean and the storm. Everything seems so angry out there. In her mind it seems to be repeating a single message: *I don't care about you. I don't care about you. I don't care about you.* But here, with this lovely woman beside her, there is only gentleness, warmth. Being inside, sheltered and loved, is a blessing. There's an empty bottle on the floor, and a half bottle of red on the bedside table. She drinks from the bottle. Pouring, she decides, is an unnecessary gesture, a movement that could wake Georgia and she is sleeping so beautifully. When the wine is gone, Moira will cover Georgia with the quilt and tiptoe down the hallway to check on the girls. She will kiss each of them and make sure they are not cold. She'll say a quiet, *I love you*, to each of them.

Back in bed, she will make a decision. She will decide that her separation from Ronin has gone on long enough. It's been two months. It's time to stop being ridiculous. It's time to shine a light into the dark corners. Time to act.

"Is everything all right?"

"Everything's fine. I was just checking on the girls."

Georgia slips her hand along Moira's waist, slides it above her belly and upwards to cup her breast and then she is asleep inside her own elongated breathing.

Good night, my love, Moira thinks. She lifts the bottle again. *Here's to one more gaudy night, filling our bowls, mocking the midnight bell.* She shakes her head at the absurdity of bringing these lines to the surface. Surely there is a better play from which she could have lifted a line.

I've suddenly become ridiculously romantic, she thinks. But perhaps these lines are not so romantic. She left out the bit about the "sad captains." Who are they? Maybe *Antony and Cleopatra* is the perfect play. Moira props herself up a bit and realizes that she's a sad captain. This is a quote from an evening before battle.

She'll lie there and mull this over for a while but the wine pulls her back, stops her from going into a zone where only sober thought can make sense.

When she is through with trying to make assumptions on the intricate meanings of Shakespeare and how they might apply to her own life, Moira experiences a peace that she has not felt for a decade. This feeling has been away so long that it has become new again. She doesn't really know what to do with it. This is what she has been missing. Perhaps it is because she has finally decided what she is going to do. She is able to lower her guard as she closes her eyes and drifts on a rising wave of contentment into a dead sleep.

Georgia wakes up in the middle of the night to pee. She comes back to bed and in a stunned, semi-drunken state she looks at Moira. A small, dreamy-child smile. Innocence. Moira's face is relaxed. Her breathing is quiet and slow. Georgia knows they were both drunk but she also knows there will be no remorse, or embarrassment, or awkwardness about this loving.

~

THE STORM CONTINUES ITS ATTACK throughout the night. It presses even harder the next day. The girls play inside and Moira spends the day locked in her room, writing. "Just catching up on my correspondence," she says. The girls could hear the ice cubes in there. They knew she was drinking.

Nobody catches up on their correspondence these days. We send e-mails. We fax. We call each other on the phone. Nobody corresponds. Not today.

Georgia knew. She knew Moira was a loose cannon. She knew the literal ramifications of a loose cannon on a wooden ship at sea with three-metre swells. She knew the possibility of damage. Georgia did not think for a second that sleeping with Moira would offer her any kind of salvation — not the kind Moira needed. Georgia was only an inadequate salve. She could lay her body over the parts of Moira that were hurt but it was more than that. Georgia was in love. She was able to overlook Moira's loose-cannon potential and open herself to love regardless of the risk. People like Moira, people who seem to be dancing very intimately with their own fate, are very, very attractive.

*

MOIRA IS PROPPED against the headboard with Georgia's head in her lap. It's not clear who seduced whom but it doesn't matter. It's an appropriate meeting of skin and fingers, longing and lust. They lock the door and pull the blinds. They light a single candle. When they kiss they are filled with a tactile awe. But at first there is a horrible hesitation, an insecurity like bunched up snow clouds and then all of touch becomes a flurry of erotic salvos. The small candlelight softens, smooths away any imperfections.

Georgia is sleeping. Moira is listening to the concussions of slow thunder and the wrecked ocean. Perhaps she is thinking that inside this sound there is life, and death — so quickly, in a white froth across the small, rounded stones of this jagged beach. The ocean keeps coming on relentlessly. Night huddles like something dying. The stars are exercises in faith, trapped beyond the heavy clouds, and all ideas of perspective must be dismissed until tomorrow.

Maybe she is thinking this is it. This is as far as she can physically and spiritually be from her own life. She is with a new lover, sexually beyond where she has ever been. She is at the edge of the land with this new lover in her lap and her children asleep down the hall. This is a soft distraction. The physical pleasure becomes all of life. But it has nothing solid at its base. It beguiles all her sensibilities. Her husband is inland, on the high prairies, too many kilometres away. The monster that chases her through the night is temporarily at bay. But keeping it at bay is like trying to stop a wave from coming ashore.

GEORGIA OPENS TO MOIRA. These openings usually coincide with one of Moira's intense states of inebriation. Whether Moira remembers these cracks in Georgia is uncertain. She says things that make Georgia believe Moira doesn't miss a thing, even a very intoxicated Moira.

Georgia knows quite a bit about depression. She shot out of university with a massive debt load, a unicorn tattooed above her right ankle and a modicum of sexual confusion. Add to this, a car accident on the Trans-Canada near Hope, in which the driver of the car that crossed the median died. Georgia crawled away from the accident with a punctured lung, a fractured bone in her leg and the remnants of the windshield in her face. Her dog of eleven years became a small German shepherd torpedo as he shot through the windshield and died thirty metres down the road. When she could finally walk without limping and half smile without wincing, Georgia didn't care much about anything. She didn't want anything, didn't need anything. Maybe there just are times when we are scheduled to be down in the dumps. Georgia's time began with the accident and ended six years later.

She spent these years in a dark cave, struggling for a smile. She wallowed inside a whisky bottle, floating around in golden liquid. Or maybe it was vodka, the supposedly undetectable spirit: silent, tasteless and odourless. The constant application of alcohol to staunch the melancholy gradually became a bigger problem than the depression itself. After this, she tried antidepressants, which simply replaced one drug with another. She never felt depressed when she was on antidepressants. But she never felt truly happy either. It was a weird trade-off. In the end, she found that hanging out with her sister's kids was the organic cure she needed. It was close to impossible to be depressed around children. They need you to be present, in the moment. So, Kara and Morgan and Emma saved her from sinking. She stayed and worked in her sister's day home for a year. The three girls were joined by four other kids every morning. The routine of being present in her own life helped Georgia stay afloat. She endured. She pulled it together.

Her mother and father believe her life is a waste because she's done nothing with her education. All that studying and fretting, time and money. "You should be working for a big firm," her father says almost every time she calls. "You'll never get these years back. Nobody wants a middle-aged rookie lawyer. You're better than a motel manager. You're smarter than that!"

"But I'm happy doing what I'm doing. Dad? Do you get that? I'm happy where I am."

"That's great but you have to think about your future. What about children?"

Georgia's father is either in denial about her gender preference or he figures it is a passing, thirty-five-year phase. The fact he mentions children every other phone call hurts her. She struggles with the idea of children. She has been struggling with it for about twenty years.

"Is Mom there, Dad? I'd love to talk with her for a minute ..."

"... I can get you an appointment with Robert. He's in a big firm. He asks about you all the time ..."

"... just get me Mom, Dad. Thanks."

"Okay," he says, resigned. "Well, you keep an open mind about this ... don't rule it out completely ... and listen, I'm glad you're feeling better." Then he's inside a pause where neither of them knows what's going to come out. This is too much for Georgia and so she fills the uncertain space with certainty: "I love you too, Dad."

"You take care," he says. "I'll get your mom."

Georgia's mom has always been quietly accepting and supportive of whatever direction Georgia's life has travelled. Georgia had been sick for a few days, and her mom tells her about Mrs. Rubins, across the bay, who died from complications from the flu. Of course, the fact that Mrs. Rubins is ninety-seven years old doesn't come into the story as a possible factor in her death.

Georgia will now automatically pick up a pencil, or a pen, whatever is available ... and start doodling on whatever piece of paper she can find ... circles, squares, filling in circles and squares ... doesn't matter. She'll scratch her absent-minded patterns on the backs of envelopes, newspapers or advertising brochures. It's habitual and persistent and, for the most part, unconscious. She's chatting with her mother, and for this, she needs to doodle.

GEORGIA AND MOIRA are at the beach. The girls are playing in the surf, letting the incoming waves chase them up the shore and then running after the retreating water as it pulls away. Georgia's dog sits and watches them. The two women are sprawled in canvas chairs, reading. The sun is strong enough to neutralize the cool sea spray that hangs over the beach. So they are in a sort of equilibrium. The sun is pounding down hot, and a cool mist rolls in off the ocean.

"I don't like drinking when the girls are around but I think we're entitled to a little snog of something, don't you think?" Moira has a habit of peering over the top of her sunglasses like an old schoolmistress.

"Isn't snogging the same as fucking? Isn't it slang for fucking?" Georgia is topless — her breasts are no longer perky but still attractive.

"I mean drink, of course, what do we have?"

"I rolled a bottle of the chardonnay in a towel."

"And do we have something to smoke? I'd love one of those little Padron cigars of yours, Georgia."

"I happen to have a couple with me. I was saving them for tonight but if you'd rather smoke now, I'll join you."

So they clip and light their cigars, and pass the icy bottle of wine back and forth while the girls play at the fringes of the waves.

"What are you doing?" It's Marie, who's come out of the water's edge.

"Mommy's having a cigar."

"Why?"

"Well, I enjoy the taste."

"Oh." Then she's off to tell Sarah that their mother is smoking a cigar and it smells yucky.

Sarah comes back and looks at the two women. She smiles. Then her small narrow face darkens.

"I wish Daddy was here," she says.

Moira immediately wants to make some gesture of kindness — she wants a physical connection, to soothe that feeling in Sarah. "Do you need more sunscreen?" Sarah lets Moira slather it on her back. Moira is fighting a welling up of tears, determined not to let them escape.

⌁

GEORGIA'S VERY FIRST MEMORY is of rain and the colour green. She thinks she remembers being propped up, with a view of cedars and undergrowth and a thousand shades of green — and all the shadowed hues painted on the forest floor by the shifting boughs above. There may have been music too, something classical, sad. Schubert? Some adult — her mother? — propped her up in front of a window with a glorious view of a forest, and played something sad by Schubert. Years later, that same parent, or aunt, or uncle, talked about how Georgia would sit and look out the window for hours at a time, listening to the music. The kaleidoscope of green, clouds and sunlight flashing through high branches. Then the rain would come and make the colours razor-sharp. So Georgia believes this is her first memory. But it is a told story as well. She remembers the telling of it. So she is not sure if this memory is hers or if it was manufactured inside her.

GEORGIA DOODLES. Sometimes she drools too, inside a particularly heavy sleep. And when she shifts to her side in her sleep, she will often release gas. But her doodling is the most interesting of these personal behaviours. It is comprised of various geometrical shapes and squiggles. Never recognizable images — she doesn't believe she has any artistic talent whatsoever. If somebody thought she was actually drawing something, she would be horrified. Although, there was a man once, when Georgia was twenty or twenty-one, who got her to paint and sing and dance with only a hint of inhibition. He worked on an orchard in the Okanagan, in southern B.C. At the end of the season he knelt before Georgia and presented her with a lovely ring, a plain silver band, which turned out to be titanium. Georgia laughed out of nervousness and because she'd never really considered any man as a suitable sexual partner, let alone a marriage partner. The ring was a gift regardless.

In a small one-bedroom flat above a barn, he'd encouraged her to use colour and stroke to express not what was really there, but rather, what she felt about what was there. Even her stick people had an innocent simplicity that was never judged or assigned explanation. She made her paintings and sketches fearlessly. Water colours. Acrylics. Ink. Her art was without hesitation. It was innocent. It was unpolished.

They would sing, for the pure and simple joy of making music with their voices, and because they were too poor to have a radio or a stereo. They drank wine and danced to half-recalled melodies. And for months, in the darkness of 3 a.m. they touched one another. They became each other's paintings. Fingertips lingering in the darkness. Hesitant tongues making brush strokes. Breath and inhalation giving life to skin.

But something in Georgia knew this was only a gentle dalliance. For her, the real thing was yet to come.

He wasn't proposing marriage. "Come with me tomorrow," he had said. "Got a job to do in Oregon. I love you. Come with me. We'll live a day at a time for a while. See where we land."

When she thinks about it now, it takes her breath away. She remembers his sincerity and the timbre of his voice. And it pains her to remember her nervous, stupid, reflexive laughter. It hurt him, and once in the air, there was no retrieving this laughter. There was no fixing the hurt.

Georgia slips her fingers between the buttons of her blouse to feel the ring, hanging there on a chain around her neck, a steady reminder of her own stupid capacity for cruelty. That night, being young and stupid, she applied her sex like a salve to his wound and learned that, even though he was a decent human being, and she had fun, and manufacturing this pleasure was a simple thing, he wasn't a woman. And he wasn't for her.

GEORGIA LOVES THE MOVIE *Vanya on 42nd Street*. The movie based on Chekhov's *Uncle Vanya*. The actors in a movie rehearsing to do a play inside the movie flit in and out of the play and the movie and their own lives. It's a beautiful labyrinth in which the lines between realities are blurred.

And she loves the movie *Solaris*, the slowness of it, the long, silent pans. The stillness of it. A movie in which nothing really happens. There's just the slow unravelling of characters in some strange order of time and space, life and death. Sometimes, Georgia will turn the movie's sound off and play her own music — Bach's cello suites or Shostakovich's piano preludes. The cinematography in *Solaris* is that beautiful.

⁀

IN HER THIRTY-SIXTH YEAR of life, Georgia discovers several grey pubic hairs. Her hair has always been the colour of the absence of light. Jet black. Crow's wing. And then one morning, sitting on the toilet, she looks down and there are the first overtures of middle age.

These few grey pubic hairs have a freeing effect on her. She becomes more outspoken, less forgiving of blatant stupidity, more aware of small beauty, very intolerant of television.

⁀

MOIRA HAS A NIGHTMARE. She is standing in a field that is completely covered with babies. There are babies as far as the eye can see. But there is something wrong. These babies — not one of them makes a sound: not a cry, or a whimper, or a moan. Just silence. Perhaps the sound of wind. There is just the sound of the wind, which starts to grow, until it sounds as if there is a very high waterfall nearby. The roaring, thundering, grows even louder. Moira's first instinct is to run, but nothing works. Her legs and arms are useless, numb pieces of flesh. The babies are not afraid. Either they can't hear the roaring or it's of little concern. She tries to bend down and make sure the babies are alive but cannot do this either. At the edge of the field, a darkness slowly begins to consume the babies. The devouring darkness is moving toward her. She wants to run and save the babies, but she can't move toward them. She is only able to make sloth-like movements away from the sound — her painfully thick legs take halting, stupid steps.

"That is not a happy dream," Georgia says.

Moira nods. "Definitely a nightmare. Sometimes the babies talk. Nothing I can understand. Like it's a different language."

"Do you have any happy dreams?"

"Sure. Sure I have happy dreams," she says, her voice defensive and pulled back. "But I don't remember them."

"I'm not suggesting that you don't have happy dreams, it's just that this nightmare is so awful."

"It's only awful when it follows me into the day."

"What?"

"Sometimes, I wake up and I can still feel it coming after me. I sense it. I'll be making dinner and I'll get a cold shiver and there it is right behind me, waiting."

No wonder she drinks like a son of a bitch, Georgia thinks.

5

THE MEAL

Rigoletto's Café has only one booth and an expanse of tables and chairs. Sitting at the bar is another option. It's a dark-grained Italian restaurant in Edmonton's downtown core. Early in the spring, Ronin and Moira come to Rigoletto's for dinner. Ronin's sister, Kate, is babysitting. They do not get the booth. There's a group of four women, all smoking, sitting there already. Ronin walks back into the kitchen to say hello to Stephano and to ask if he'd surprise them with one of his creations — something not exactly on the menu. This is something Ronin has done perhaps a half-dozen times in five years. Stephano is a sober and serious chef. He's a dark-haired, high-strung Mediterranean who is shaped like a brick. He seems to be almost constantly worried about some-thing. Ronin has noticed that he rarely smiles. But tonight, when Ronin offers him this challenge, he performs a rare smile. It's a remarkable thing to see Stephano smile — like seeing an eclipse, or a shooting star. "Leave it to me," he says in his gravelly throated voice. "It will be beautiful." He nods in Ronin's direction — a tacit but graceful dismissal.

Moira orders wine, a Bordeaux. When the first glass has been poured, Ronin looks at her.

"Let me tell you a story about glaciers," he says.

"That's not a story," Moira says. "That's a lecture you've given a hundred times. It's not fair that I make up stories and you get to give lectures."

"I'll put some characters in it for you."

"Really? Glaciers, characters and a story? This ought to be good."

"Okay, I have a story about a guy who comes up to a high camp that is three kilometres away from a retreating glacier. He goes there to heal because his actions have caused damage to himself and those closest to him. He takes his dog, Karma."

Ronin stops and looks for Moira's approval. She is listening, which is something of an endorsement from Moira.

"Am I allowed to use technical words? Just a few?"

"Just as long as you provide definitions."

"Let me offer one to begin with. Firn. Firn is the part of a glacier that consists of the partially compacted snow carried over from previous seasons. The firn limit is the boundary where loss from melting and evaporation is the same as the annual accumulation of snow. It's the balance point of a glacier."

"This is a story about a guy named Baltesson who wishes he were a bear. He comes to a high campground across from the Columbia Icefields to hibernate. He really wishes he were a bear. He wishes for the simplicity of bear existence. The long, beautiful hibernation each year, the ravenous waking up. His full name is Sven Baltesson but all his friends call him Baltesson."

Ronin takes a sip of wine. "How am I doing so far?"

Moira nods her approval. She leans forward, elbows on the table, her chin resting on her hands.

"Baltesson believes he's there to heal, or at least, to think about things and hibernating is not a viable option. While there is still a great deal of snow — enough to burrow out a cave of some kind — it's melting quickly. Each day, the sun peels away another few centimetres of snow. Even though he is completely surrounded by mountain peaks, the sun works hard at bringing life back to this place. Willow shrubs, flattened by the weight of snow, begin to arc back into shape. Birds around the camp weave through the pines like death-wish daredevils.

"This guy doesn't know if healing is possible. He doesn't know where to begin. He would have to understand what went wrong and why. And he has only theories. Thinking about things seems to be the most plausible exercise. But he's always thinking about things.

"He's tired, a weariness of the heart. He feels at the end of something. Well, that's an understatement. When he started out with his wife, he believed he'd be with her for a very long, very beautiful time. He had romantic notions of growing old with her, of still loving the feel of her skin when he was seventy."

He pauses and looks around the room. It's early. The restaurant is half-full but people are drifting in steadily through the front door.

"I'm going to tell you the ending of the story," he says, "and then if you have questions I'll supply the details."

"Oh. Okay," she says inside a questioning hesitation.

"He comes to the Icefields with his dog because it's the breakpoint for him. He's been fooling around on his wife for so long, the act of adultery has become an addiction. He is baffled by his behaviour. What it was that started him down this path he really couldn't say. It took away the energy he needed for his wife. Eventually, he had nothing left to give."

～

THE SALADS ARRIVE. They both get the Caesar salad, which comes in generous portions and is rich and spicy and saturated with garlic. The anchovies are lost in the salad and, in Moira's mind, this flavour ought to be more present. "The anchovies should stand to attention at the edge of the garlic," she says. "These anchovies are slouching. But it's not bad."

～

"ONE DAY," Ronin continues, "while Baltesson and his wife are in the mountains, up at Lake Louise, on a weekend excursion, his mistress decides to drive up to Kootenay Crossing. She'd called him up at home and invited him there for a weekend of debauchery. But he wasn't there to answer her call. She never makes it to the Kootenay Crossing. Her car skids off the road in an attempt to avoid a couple of elk and flips and lands in a river that holds the same green, emerald-turquoise shade that imbues the water in Lake Louise. The police say she died instantly.

"This is the great part. Baltesson goes on a hike above Lake Louise and meets up with an elderly Japanese man who is in some sort of distress. The Japanese man draws attention to Baltesson's compassion, his honour and his kindness. With a very small number of words, he draws Baltesson's courage and grace and integrity to the surface. And Baltesson comes down off the trail *not* thinking about himself anymore. He comes back with his eyes and heart opened to others, especially to his wife."

～

FOR AN APPETIZER, a bowl of the steamed mussels arrives, and then the Spicy Feta plate. These choices prove to be incredibly delicate counterpoints to each other. The zest of the feta, sweet gherkins, olives, crisp-but-not-too-crisp tomatoes placed beside the subtle flavour of the mussels in a light tomato sauce. Lots of fresh bread for dipping. The butter is the perfect temperature. This is a very good start. Moira believes the butter is too warm but by only a few degrees. She reminds Ronin that although it is very good, the feta is not quite the right temperature, and that it is probably a problem of the restaurant itself being very hot. It is also a bit too peppery. But it is very good, regardless of these minor indiscretions.

⌇

"BALTESSON CARRIED NO YEARNINGS or desires with him to this stranded camp — only memories. He doesn't know what's going to happen. This camp, for him, is barren and well-loved. He has to scramble over a metre of packed snow blocking the entrance of the cookhouse. The water is barely running. In fact, there is no water out of the tap until after noon each day. It takes that long for the pipes to warm up. Mice have found their way into his car so he's resorted to hanging the food bag from a tree at night.

"There is barely enough space in the dried grass beside a snow-covered tent pad to pitch the tent. He uses a rock to pound in pegs. He's in a hurry to be settled, and in his hurry, he whacks his hand, catches the edge of it with the rock.

"He's brought Karma with him. It's a German shepherd, a good steady mountain dog that doesn't chase every little movement in the woods but always lets you know if something's there.

"After dinner, he takes the flask of whisky and a cigar, and begins his nightly custom of walking to the glacier. Half-a-kilometre to the highway, perhaps two kilometres to the turnoff, and another klick along a winding esker to the toe of the glacier."

⌇

THE ORANGE SHERBET ARRIVES. It looks like nothing special, but the first bite! The piercing, frozen-orange flavour explodes in Ronin's mouth. Not too sweet but not tart either. There is a delicate hint of another fruit ... lemon? Tangerine? Mango? He holds that first bite on his tongue for as long as it will stay. It takes a long time to melt and as it does, the flavours unfold. The burst of orange now calms itself and lets the other flavours seep in ... it's mango, and a hint of nutmeg, and something else. He decides not to ask. Mystery is not a bad thing.

Moira says the sherbet is wonderful but she tastes something peppery. "Apart from that offensive pepper taste, it did its work. My mouth is refreshed. But it really is too bad about the pepper."

⌒

"AT DUSK, BALTESSON WALKS the highway to the Icefields. Sporadic cars zoom past. He hopes these vehicles won't straddle the shoulder, but he's never going to be sure that he's seen. Karma doesn't like this walk; he stays in the ditch — keeps an eye on him from a safe distance.

"When a car is coming, there is ample warning. A haze of light like an approaching comet can be seen nearly three kilometres down the road.

"As he turns toward the glacier, there is barely enough light sifted into the sky to make out the road. It humps its way over and around deposits of terminal moraine. The air becomes warmer as he approaches the glacier. He cannot see the signposts but knows he is moving past points where the glacier's terminus used to be. It has been retreating for at least several hundred years. Not very long ago, it would have covered the highway."

⌒

RONIN ORDERS MORE WINE, a Guigal Côtes-du-Rhône. It is a few degrees too cool. Moira insists they have tried to compensate for the room being too warm by chilling the wine slightly before serving and they have obviously overcompensated. She adds this can be solved by simply waiting for the bottle and its contents to slowly warm up. It's nothing really, just a few degrees. The glasses are spotless fishbowls, a fourth of each glass is filled to allow for swirling. This is not the best wine in the world, but Ronin releases the bouquet and sticks his nose into the glass anyway.

Stephano's creation finally arrives. He watches from the kitchen entrance as the waitress brings the two plates to the table and places them with no small degree of elegance. Stephano has prepared triple-A beef tenderloin medallions slathered in a mushroom, brandy, red wine sauce on a bed of angel hair pasta. It's amazing. The beef is melt-in-your-mouth tender. The pasta is perfect. Stephano nods as Ronin waves the fragrances from the plate toward his face and smiles at him approvingly.

Moira suggests that the sauce is excellent but if the wine used for the sauce had been matched to the wine they were drinking it would have been so much better. Of course there was no way they could know we switched wines, she says. Also, the medallions are perhaps a shade too rare. Nothing serious, she says — perhaps just twenty or thirty seconds longer on the heat would have done it.

⌒

"BALTESSON STOPS ON THE SMALL metal-grated bridge that crosses the glacier's meltwater birth canal. He stands on this bridge with the fast, black water flowing beneath and finishes his cigar.

"This is a new valley. The landscape is so raw it could well be another planet. A desolation of rock. The only life is brought by tourists, seeds stuck to the bottom of hiking boots, miniscule flowers edging pathways. But Baltesson prefers the esker. It's lonely and cold. Tonight he feels more than physically cold. Perhaps his grief, which is immense and unruly, should remain frozen for now.

"Comedy is all about timing. Both his wife, who finally saw his litany of infidelity, and his mistress are gone from his life. And his timing has been beautifully ironic. He pulls out his flask, raises it in a toast to comedy, then sucks back a healthy portion of the whisky.

Karma is drinking from a melt puddle. Baltesson can hear the lapping sound overtop the flowing water beneath his feet.

"Now there is the walk back to camp, a walk that can seem very, very long. He'll climb out of this glacial dip to the highway, then walk the road, in the dark, to the turnoff to his camp. The smell of smoke from his dinner fire will be a welcome sign. A few coals will remain — enough to get the fire going again — but tonight he wants sleep. Inside the womb of a tent, he will fall asleep. He'll lie in his sleeping bag looking at the roof of the tent for a good long time. The cold air under the pines will work its magic. He will be held in the arms of these mountains and the turmoil in him will be lulled. In the morning he will begin again to attempt to untangle the events of his life.

"But he does not turn back yet. He thinks about all the women he's been with in the mountains. Only a few remain clear and pure and untouchable.

"At the base of this retreating glacier, he now realizes he's made an error. In all his contemplations, he has left out the one constant woman, the one he always returns to, who accepts him as he is regardless of his many faults. The one who challenges and comforts and sometimes heals, is unpredictable, always changing. Who soothes and startles, and exists as a trinity of granite, pine and icy water. The one who is an entirely different reality of truthfulness, space and time."

⌒

MOIRA SITS UP, wipes the edges of her mouth with her napkin. She tilts her head ever so slightly, about to ask a question. "Does it turn out that Baltesson's mistress was really his daughter and they weren't lovers after all?"

"What?"

"Is there a count somewhere, singing?"

"A count? Singing?"

"Does Baltesson have a little bit of a hunchback thing going on?"

"No, but aren't you clever. That would have been an appropriate deviation of the story, given where we are." Ronin is a little baffled by these questions, until she mentions the hunchback. Ronin used to have seats at the opera. *Rigoletto* was one of his favourites. But *Dialogues of the Carmelites* killed opera for him. It was the only one he ever left in disgust before it was finished. He remembers thinking that if they'd killed all the nuns in the first scene and had some guy come out and tell the story, it would have been far more entertaining. Ronin never went back.

"Your story was interesting, but there was only one name," she says.

"Yes, it was an abbreviated telling. I have sympathy for this guy. I feel for him."

DOES MOIRA THINK RONIN was trying to tell her something? Really, he was just telling a story. He had no idea it would become a sort of harbinger. He was working around a glacier — weaving a sort of tall tale.

He was remembering what it was like to stand at the toe of a glacier at dusk and look up. He was remembering how lonely it felt to look down the valley at darkening clouds and the colour grey everywhere — beautiful beyond words, but a cold, divine beauty.

THE COFFEE IS SUPERB. Moira says the beans were probably the wrong grind for espresso. The silt in the bottom of her cup proves her point. They were overground. It wasn't Greek coffee, but regardless of this error, it was quite delicious.

Their waitress orders a taxi, tells Ronin it's going to be twenty or thirty minutes. He orders a triple scotch. He leans back in his chair and takes a good long look at Moira. The scotch is exquisite, flawless. Ronin smiles at the mother of his children. How the hell did it get to this point? It used to be so easy, so natural and wonderful. It seems they are not only on different pages — they seem to be reading different books, by different authors.

6

THE CALL

THERE IS NO MALICE nor kindness in a ringing telephone. Phones ring with a blanket of equality, the same for bad as for good news. They ring the same for all people no matter how rich or poor. Human beings assign meaning to a ring. Is it irritating? Is it welcome? Is it a friendly sound? A dreaded one? Who is it? What do they want? What the hell do they want now?

⁓

RONIN FINDS A GROUP OF CHAIRS inside a small park under the shelter of trees. He's been walking around for a couple of hours and he's not entirely certain where he is. He knows Paris has twenty arrondissements, and that he is somewhere inside the sixth. The guidebook said the sixth arrondissement used to be a hangout for bohemians and intellectuals but that recently it was transformed into something chic. Upscale boutiques, art galleries and restaurants are everywhere. Ronin could care less what the guide says. Paris is a good city in which to drift aimlessly.

Five men are playing boules at the far side of the park. A small table with a bottle and several glasses on it sits not too far from the action. They stop the game occasionally in order to have a drink. They are not playing on the grass, but on a sort of gravel-sand mixture. Ronin has noticed that not many people actually step on the grass in Paris.

He's not really following the game, but occasionally he'll notice the arc of the dull silver ball against the far trees. He's read some-where that when the balls are new, they are shiny and when they are well-worn, they resemble old cannonballs. The men are silent. Whenever Ronin has played boules or bocce, there has been much shouting, cries of excitement and disappointment, even arguments. These particular men are quietly focused on their game. Two of them are much older. Their movements have a careful solemnity the others do not yet possess. Both are wearing caps. Their pants are baggy and their shirtsleeves are buttoned at their wrists. There is something brittle and unmoving about the way they bend to check the position of the balls. The other three are middle-aged. All three have rolled their sleeves up. One of them is wearing dark suspenders.

They call Paris the City of Light. Ronin begins to understand what that means as he sits there on the bench, half-watching a game of boules. The light is diffused, amazing. The day is overcast but not cloudy — the sky is painted a damaged grey. Maybe Paris should never be seen in clear blue daylight.

"Which one was I?" Katya says, appearing suddenly beside Ronin, in the park.

She is wearing a loose, pale-grey dress with a silky, tan trench coat over it. The dress reaches to her mid-calf where it is met by the tops of her boots, which then arc downward into black points. A scarf is wrapped tightly around her neck. The boots give her three inches. Katya has the look of a great many of the women Ronin has seen on the streets. Except today. There is an implicit care in the way Parisian women present themselves to the world. Regardless of Katya's clothing, there is something off about her. She seems distracted, haggard.

"What do you mean?" he whispers.

"Your story. The one you told Moira. You know, the fellow who has the affair."

"Baltesson?" Ronin says.

"Yes," she says. "Which one was I?"

"You aren't in that story."

"But if you were to put me into the story?"

"Well, my first inclination would be to suggest that you're the mistress."

"The mistress who dies in a car crash?" She's not happy about this. She looks like she's going to cry. Her bottom lip quivers. Ronin wonders if all women practise this.

"Well, yes, the one who dies. Look, it was just a story."

"Why did you tell it?"

"I don't know. I suppose once I started I just couldn't stop. I wasn't trying to stir things up. I wasn't trying to drive her away."

Ronin walks away from the boules game toward the river. Katya is beside him. One of the old men says a quick *Bonjour, Monsieur* as he walks by. The guy probably feels sorry for Ronin — the lonely guy, the crazy person talking to himself, but who appears to be harmless.

Why would Katya show up here — now? Is it that Moses, the phantom husband, was reading a Hemingway short story to her and Paris is one of Hemingway's old haunts?

"I feel odd," she says. "Something's wrong, very wrong."

"SO, DID YOU REALLY SLEEP with that woman?" Katya asks this question in a way that says she doesn't care one way or the other. But it's too casual. It's a forced indifference. With most women, in Ronin's experience, the right response to a question like this is a definitely stated "no."

Claire was a lovely surprise but it may just have been the pleasure of being for a few hours with a happy woman who loves to touch. His heart is still tied to Moira. She has always had his heart. Ronin is very likely drawn to Moira's melancholy. It's true that her emotions roller-coaster — making it a constant challenge to live with her — but he found a way for his heart to love that about her. She could spin out a beautiful, touching story on a whim. Her stories always capture him. Also, she's a good, steady and loving mother.

"You don't have the right to ask that question. Besides, you already know, and I am not accountable to an apparition, no matter how attractive."

"You're right," she says. "I am stunningly attractive, and besides, I already know."

But Katya is not attractive today. She has not been attractive for days. In fact, Katya looks worse every time Ronin sees her. There's a bruise on the side of her face, as if she's run into a wall or somebody's hit her. Her hair is greasy and hangs in limp strings across her face. She is constantly pushing those loose strings of hair off her face in increasingly flustered and choppy movements. She seems on the verge of cutting off the offending hair instead of having to carry on this way.

～

GEORGIA'S IN THE KITCHEN, standing beside the table in Moira's cabin. She sits down and picks up the telephone, dials the number. Hangs up. Dials the number. She holds her breath. Keep breathing, she tells herself. Breathing is a good thing.

She pours herself a drink. Picks up the telephone. Dials again. Hangs up.

My name is Georgia. I was a friend of your wife's, she thinks. Georgia swallows — tries to draw some moisture into the desert her mouth has become. *Look, there is no easy way to say this ... I knew your wife ...*

"Hello? Yes. My name is Georgia. I was a friend of your wife's."

I was a friend of your wife's. It's a dry, lifeless statement that says too much. The sound of something metal being dragged through endless sand. Ronin doesn't need to hear any more. That's enough. "My name is Georgia. I was a friend of your wife's." It's passive language — meant to be soft. Don't analyze this. It means something. These words mean something.

Everything beyond this initial foray becomes farcical white noise.

PART TWO

7

FALLING

YOU HAVE TO BOOK A FLIGHT. You have to make sure your daughters are safe. You have to get to your girls.

There are no skid marks. There is no note. What was her intention? This is a quandry only Moira could devise. The absence of written confirmation is a missing detail that points to the absence of further details. So you are alone in Paris and she has offered no explanation — she has created a mystery of herself. She takes her darkness with her. You thought you were in a crisis of doubting before. Now your doubt moves effortlessly through flesh and embeds itself in the bone. There is Katya saying over and over again that she doesn't feel right and that something is wrong. She doesn't look well. There's something wrong with her. And there is Claire, in her underwear, singing something quiet and soothing in French. She is holding you like a baby, in her arms, rocking you. And there is a cat. Her cat has come home. *The cat came back*, you giggle. *The cat came back and we thought it was a goner.*

"What?" Claire says.

"Forget her," Katya screams. "She's a distraction you don't need. You don't know her."

You begin to imagine Georgia. You see her as the kind of woman who would describe herself in a dating advertisement as queen-sized but happy with her weight. This would be a gross exaggeration. She is probably slender and tall and has no clue as to how beautiful she is. You imagine Georgia has blue eyes. All this from an ocean-removed voice on the telephone.

You think of your kids. What the hell are they feeling right now? They sounded all right on the phone but how could they be? You should phone them again. What time is it in Sooke? It's 3 a.m., no, 4 a.m. Ridiculous to call and wake them if they're sleeping — and why? — because you feel guilty for not being there, because you lied to them. You let them think you were at home when you were really in Paris. But you are going to be there.

Moira and the kids are coming home. Did Moira say that? Or did you assume this after she said to remember that she loved you? Moira gave you hope and that is something she never did lightly. In her mind, hope was not to be fooled with. What happened to her hope? That's a question to which you already know the answer. Lost. Gone. She became a person with no hope. The *why* was a bit more problematic. Why understate something that is a hugely infuriating mystery? You are stumped. You are not beaten yet, but you are baffled. How anybody with two beautiful daughters could turn so inward is very far beyond your understanding.

It's very important for you to make sure your daughters are safe and sound. Well, they're not going to be sound. Their mother just died in a car crash. But safe. Yes, they can be safe. You talk to Georgia for over an hour on the phone. You find out about her friendship with Moira. You find out about her schedule. She is able and willing to look after the girls. Your daughters know Georgia.

"You know that Sarah has a peanut allergy," you say.

"Yes, I know," Georgia says.

"When Marie is sick, she likes tomato soup with ham-and-cheese sandwiches," you say.

"And she likes the crust of the bread trimmed," Georgia adds.

"Marie is quiet. It doesn't mean there's nothing going on inside ..."

"... she's just quiet. I know. They're going to be okay."

"Of course they're going to be okay. It's just that I'm not there and you are, and I've never met you and I need to be so incredibly certain that they're safe ... or I'll ... stop breathing." Hold it together, you think. You need to be steady and strong.

"Okay," Georgia says, "keep telling me things about them and I'll listen. We can talk for as long as you want."

"Sarah loves the rain, loves walking in it, loves getting cold ... well, not too cold but cold enough to have to warm up ..."

You go on blathering for over an hour. You assure her your mother will be there that night and you'll be there the following day.

Your flight to Victoria departs tomorrow night. Your daughters are safe. They're with Georgia. You have over twenty-four hours to be whatever you need to be, to be enraged, to make wild stabs at understanding. But you only have this weight, this confused, swirling weight. Remember her? Remember Moira? That is all you have now, just memories of Moira. There is only the past now, and whatever remnants you drag along with you into the future. Paris transforms into a city of grief, your city of grief. The trees are black and dead. There is dirt and dog shit and garbage everywhere. People become gargoyles. Gargoyles crawl down from their soot-stained perches and slouch along the streets spitting up gobs of green phlegm and growling at everything that moves. Do not think for a second that this is the first time sorrow has been tied to this city. But you claim the city as your own and hold it up as a symbol of misery.

Georgia was surprised you were overseas. Moira had told her you were home. There is an implied intimacy in those shared details and certainly a trust. The girls are with Georgia — not a stranger to them. The girls are safe but your heart has imploded. "I need you to be strong for a little while longer," you tell them. "I need you to listen carefully. There is no easy way to say this. Your mom had an accident — a horrible accident — and she's not coming back." Silence. More silence. "Are you still there? Listen. I'm coming to get you tomorrow and Grandma will be there tonight. Georgia isn't going to leave. She's going to be there until Grandma and I arrive. I love you."

You leave your hotel, which had started to vibrate, and you start walking. You are walking the streets of Paris, the air feels cool and clean and brushed by pines. That can't be right. You are remembering Pyramid Lake, and the walk with Moira. Did you take a walk with her that morning? Well, it's there in your memory, you walked together and Moira continued her story ... she told you Katya and Moses had the baby, and everything was all right. Katya was fooling around on Moses, with a woman, but the baby was fine. Moira got angry because she assumed you'd think two women having sex was less adulterous than if it were a man and a woman engaged in sex outside their marriages. All these things are in your memory. You are looking for clues. You remember Katya telling you she aborted the baby or did Moira tell you that? But Katya, the idea of Katya, is from Moira, which you adopted and then carried within you as a dim reflection of something Moira started. If Moira created Katya, does Katya shine a light on Moira?

You are walking along Pyramid Lake Road, in the Rocky Mountains, toward Pyramid Island. Moira is telling you about Katya and

Moses. Moira is radiant. She is pregnant with Laura Marie. They say pregnant women glow. They say a lot of stupid things, but Moira proves this one: her face is a source of radiating gentleness and it creates new definitions of loveliness. It's fall. The light is kind and lingers half-heartedly in the narrow sky. There are long waves of golden aspens tucked in amongst thick pine forests. The clouds seem to want to sneak down into the valleys, but they hesitate. "I was worried about Katya's baby," you say. "I don't know why." "The baby was perfect," she says. "I told you it was perfect." "Nothing is perfect," you say. "Perfect is an idea, like democracy, or communism." "Look, just leave it alone. Leave the baby alone. I told you it was perfect." "Why are you calling the baby an *it*? Why not he, or she?" "Because it's perfect," she says. "If you're going to keep pushing this baby thing, I'm going back to the hotel. It's just a story anyway. Katya has an affair with a woman. Talk about that."

"You know what really happened don't you?" Katya is beside you, walking on the road. Faint shadows of trees stretch out across the asphalt. She clops along in three-inch heels. The boots, which crawl up her calves and stop just under her knees, are stylish but stupid for the mountains. "You know the truth. I told you what really happened. I stopped the pregnancy." She's walking as if her feet are already sore. "Yes, I know what a fabrication told me." Katya smiles, a devious and sexy upturning of her mouth. Her lips are bright red. Such a profound knowing in this smile. "A fabrication that gave you a killer blowjob. How do you explain that? What if Moira is the fabrication. Did you ever think of that?"

Well, Moira is certainly going to be a fabrication of sorts from now on. She'll be on an equal footing with whatever demons you might have running around in your head. The reality of her has stopped somewhere on Vancouver Island against some unnamed tree. From now on, you will be making her up. You will fill gaps in your memory with preferred, enhanced memory. Not on purpose, but that is the way of memory. When you arrive in Sooke, you should remember to ask what kind of tree it was. Go back, for a moment, see if Katya could be real, and Moira a character you created long ago who plays a part in some crazy narrative. It could make sense. Don't be an idiot. You know exactly what the reality is. Moira is your wife. Is she still your wife now? Katya is a character from a story that Moira made up as a way of telling you she was pregnant. You were having a debate about raking leaves. Moira loved to rake leaves in the fall. Before that fall day in the front yard of your house, there was no Katya.

"You know what happened. You're just like her. You don't want to admit it." Katya is hurt, angry. She's leaning far too close to your comfort zone, twisting her body as she walks, pushing her face toward yours. "Look what happened to her! Why can't you see what happened? All the pieces are there!" Are you in Paris, or is this Pyramid Lake Road? There are too many cars for the mountains. But once, you remember … cars were everywhere, stopped, looking at something black moving slowly through the pines. Everyone was trying to see. Some were snapping pictures. The park wardens call them "bear-jams." The girls wanted to get out. "No! Absolutely not," you remember barking. "Bears can move at the same speed as a race horse. They're fast and unpredictable. These people trying to get closer with their cameras are idiots; dangerous, they're going to get this bear killed." There was a fairly long pause. "Daddy, how will the idiots get the bear killed?" You remember how much you love Sarah. Her compassion became visible at such an early age. When she was two she asked what a scratch on the wall was. "What dat?" she said, pointing at the wall. And Moira told her the wall was hurt. "It's an owie." Sarah spent the rest of the day walking around the house kissing any scratches or dents, trying to make them better. "If the idiots get too close and the bear feels threatened, it will attack and hurt them, and then the Park wardens will have to kill the bear." But no, this is Paris, nothing big and black is moving through the pines. Maybe something big and black is moving through your subconscious.

You start to look at cars. You try to imagine what 170 kilometres per hour might feel like. They were guessing; there was no way to know for sure. Airborne off the embankment. Did it come off the ground and begin to roll in the air? When it hit the tree was there an explosion like on television or in the movies? What kind of tree? You are having a hard time picturing the tree. It had to be pretty big.

Back up. How did she get away from the cabin? She would never leave the kids alone. Georgia was there. Maybe Moira said she was going to get the newspaper. Or milk. Maybe she stood in the doorway with those streams of murky-river mascara running down both cheeks and said: "Listen, I'm depressed. I'm tired of being depressed. I need a good long rest, a permanent rest. I can't reconcile my life right now. There is no fucking reconciliation. No salvation. Nothing. So, listen, I've got this tree and this car and, well, goodbye. Call my husband. The number's there. He'll come." Then out the door she went.

No, she wouldn't have had time to say all that. Besides, when Moira was decided, she became downright cryptic. More than likely she looked at Georgia and said, "Gonna get the *Globe*. Back in a flash." Maybe she lingered a bit too long in the doorway, the final nail in her resolve, so that when the police called, Georgia remembered that lingering and even before she picked up the phone, she knew. You wonder if there was music playing as she stomped down on the accelerator? Was she drunk? The girls think it was an accident. A horrible accident. You start to imagine the car folding in half at the base of some tree. What kind of tree was it anyway? Why the hell couldn't they goddamn well tell you that? It's the least they could do. You can hear the goddamn car horn screaming against the sound of the ocean — screaming against the sound of the wind in the trees. There's a lot of screaming. Someone is touching you.

There are car horns blaring all around you. Someone is taking you by the arm. Claire? It's Claire. "What happened? You look horrible," she says.

"Are you real?" You place your hand gently on the side of Claire's face. She feels real.

"Yes, I am real. What happened? What are you doing wandering around in the street? Are you drunk?"

"I'm looking for a tree," you say. "There was a tree, a big tree but all I can find are these bloody chestnut trees."

"Do you remember that we were to meet this afternoon?"

"Yes, Claire, of course I remember we were supposed to meet. But there is a tree and I don't know what it is."

Claire knows about Moira. There was no reason to lie. She takes you inside a café and the two of you become enfolded into a scene, a new scene in which a distraught man is talking to a slender woman who appears to care about him. They are sitting in a café. It's not a famous café but it is a stone's throw from Notre-Dame Cathedral.

People who see you will think she has broken up with you and that you are desperately pleading for one more chance. This is not you wandering around by yourself, caught inside a delirium. You're in Paris now. Look there, you know that street. That's ... well, you've been here before ... several times. Claire sits you down and when the waiter comes, she orders two coffees. "And two cognacs," you add. She glares at you but nods to the waiter. "I'm not drunk," you say.

"But I took you from the street. You were in the traffic, in the cars."

"Yes, it's a good thing I came by so you could save me."

"Paris is not famous for pedestrian right-of-way. It is a concept, I think, that does not exist here."

"That was becoming apparent."

"Really? You were slowly beginning to comprehend that you could have been killed?"

"Yes, I could have been killed. That would have been real."

You start to spill out your fragmented understanding of what happened. You are like a naked man wearing only oven mitts trying to piece together a broken mirror while blindfolded and drunk.

"There's been an accident," you say. "At least they think it's an accident, but ..."

You become a cameraman in a movie that is directed by someone you don't know. The camera zooms in on the man who is talking slowly, as if in a trance. He is talking to a woman who sits across from him but he seems to be looking over her shoulder. The camera moves to her face, which fills the screen. As the scene progresses there is only this woman's face and music — you begin to hear a solemn and drawn-out string section. The music has its own unsentimental integrity. There are no words, but it is clear that the man is continuing to speak because the woman's face slowly becomes sorrowful. But mixed in with the overwhelming sorrow, there is kindness and compassion. "You can pull back a bit now," the director says. "It's over. Let's see what happens." You do not want to pull back. You want only this face. The director places a hand on your shoulder and you stop the camera. You take a few steps back and make adjustments to the lens. "Cut!" the director says. The man and the woman continue to sit and talk. The man finds relief in this talking, his face begins to relax — the furrows between the eyes smooth out. He takes big extended breaths ... holds ... exhales in long sighs. His shoulders begin to sink into his body.

~

THERE IS A GREAT COMFORT in being taken care of, especially when the caring is as protective as Claire's. She makes space around you and guards it with the ferociousness of a pit bull. She makes phone calls, rearranges her day, and night, and the next day. You don't remember the cab ride, or walking up to her flat. There was a red door, a beautiful, red door. And an inner courtyard, a small space that felt peaceful as you drifted by on Claire's arm. An oak tree, there was an oak tree. It wasn't in the middle of the yard.

Claire sends someone to your hotel to get your bags, clear out your room, and pay your bill. These are kindnesses that cannot be repaid.

It's not a feeling of being tilted but rather it's out of phase with time and reality. You feel as if someone loving has just sucker-punched you in the stomach. Breathless. You've not had a full breath in hours. And now, you're exhausted, worn-out, but also wide awake — buzzing with anticipation of something that's about to happen. You lie there in the bed and listen to the braying donkey sounds of French police cars in the distance, chaotic car horns and the kettle in the other room. You smell the shy scent of vanilla. That mildly erotic smell of vanilla.

Someone has given you two small pills. You take them without question. Nothing has an edge anymore. There are no sharp corners, no harsh sounds.

It's dark when she comes into the room and sits in the big armchair beside the bed. You are in the netherworld between awake and asleep — suspended, weightless, and conscious of the fact that you are only conscious enough to realize you are adrift between worlds. The floor creaks as she moves toward the bed. Her perfume is pleasant and simple. It reminds you of a garden in which there was thyme growing between the stones of a sidewalk, and the plants would release a gorgeous delicate scent when anyone walked here. You only sense that she is there beside the bed, watching over you. Perhaps you are delusional. Still, you fall asleep feeling grateful. *Thank you. Thank you.* Did you say it? Whisper it? You don't know.

In your dreams, Claire turns up the stereo, lets Mozart twirl and throb in the corners of the room — she opens the windows and invites the sounds and smells of Paris inside — she opens a bottle of champagne, carelessly chugs from the bottle, giggles, and passes it to you with a bubbly lava froth erupting out of the bottle's mouth. You open another bottle of champagne, and suddenly the smallest details become necessary for your survival. It is as if you are on a mission to capture everything about this woman and this lovemaking. The flat space nested below the small of her back and slightly above her buttocks. A mole inside her right armpit. The back-of-her-throat mmm-sounds she makes as you move together. The round throw of her breasts. A breeze blows sunlight into the room and across her body. She becomes too innocent, gleams in the brilliant sunlight. White light pools on her body and then is whisked away as the curtains fall back into place. Claire's skin is cool as she folds herself into your back, presses skin against skin. Once you are over the surprise of her being in the bed with you, you expect her to lie still. But she does not. Her hands begin to caress and smooth. You are literally in pieces. There is no blood but nothing of you is attached. You are separate from the bits of yourself. There is a pulled-back hesitation in her touch. She is testing to see if this is welcome. You sort of grunt-moan your appreciation and she begins to shape you into something alive. She becomes a powerful goddess who finds the mud of you and forms it into the shape of a mostly whole person. You back up into her touch, let it wash over you, drift face-up in warm, salty water. And in the end, you are whole again. You sink back into a dreamless sleep ... just darkness ... a vast blackness.

In the morning, you open your eyes and half-wonder where the hell you are. There is a note on the pillow: Come on the balcony. And then you think only about your daughters. Your panic to be with them, to hold them, rises up. They woke up today and their world was completely changed. You pick up the phone and do the calculations. What time is it? You brain is sticky and sluggish. Coffee. You need coffee. You put the phone down. You're going home today.

There is a housecoat on the end of the bed and you stagger onto the rooftop balcony wrapped in a blue robe. You're not quite sure how you got from your hotel to here, and you certainly do not know where exactly here is, except that it is in Paris and the Eiffel Tower is not in view. You see other buildings and the streets below, a park farther along the street.

"Here is new coffee," Claire says. She folds, then places a newspaper on the table. The day promises rain. It smells heady and thick, and the clouds concur. There is a shifting state of grey behind Claire, and for you it seems to be moving more slowly than it should. She wears a thick, white robe with a collar that folds luxuriously at her neck. You would have expected her to have slippers but she is wearing only woollen socks on her feet. You don't know why you looked at her feet. She is more beautiful in this light. But everything is more beautiful in this shadowless light.

You'd like to ask Claire what the hell happened but it's all starting to drift back into place. Claire is sitting at a small wooden table. It is set with a coffee pot and cups, a basket of croissants, and utensils. There are flowers in a vase, placed slightly to the side. Daffodils.

"Yes," she says. "Daffodils."

"Did I just say daffodils? Did I say it out loud?"

Claire nods.

"Well, that's not a very good start is it?"

"I think it is to be expected. You had a horrible day but now there is much to do, yes?" She drops the "h" in *had*, and in *horrible* and also makes it a distinctly three-syllable word: You 'ad a 'or-i-ble day ...

"My plane leaves ..."

"... everything is arranged. It has been taken care of. A car will pick you up."

"Oh ..., I ..."

"Come, she says. "Sit. Have some coffee and croissants. Perhaps you will have something stronger? A cognac? It is early but exceptions must be made, always."

GUILT RISES UP LIKE GORGE, and you are overwhelmed by it. You feel guilty being with Claire. Because of Moira. Because of your daughters. Because of the lie of being in Paris. Because what's left of Moira is lying dead on some metal tray in a morgue in Victoria and you're with another woman. Just a couple of months ago, you held Moira, woke up with her, loved her. You loved your daughters together. You watched her do that stupid pantyhose dance that women do. You showered together — washed her back with the yellow scrubby thing she liked so much. You watched a movie together. The one with Julia Roberts where she whispered throughout the entire movie, and in the end you both wished someone in the movie would kill her. You want to remember everything, every little detail. Her smell, the way she brushed her teeth. How did she brush her hair? How did she hold hands with you? God!

Your daughters need you — what are you doing here? You should be at the airport, waiting, scratching the ground like an angry bull. It's just past noon but you don't really have to think about time. Your plane leaves at six. You've already talked to the girls, said goodnight and reassured them you will see them when they wake up. Now there is an enormous guilt pressed down on you like the lead apron at the dentist's office but tripled. You are with Claire, and the guilt attached to her is not easily pushed aside. There is nothing to do but wait. There is comfort and kindness here. Your capacity for feeling seems short-circuited. There's a creeping numbness in you.

If you do not feel all you can feel right now, you will regret it. There are no hard edges here. Can you feel that? Claire is a near-stranger who is displaying a profound, unrequired kindness. You push Moira away only for short bursts, like sweeping water uphill.

You begin to talk about Moira, about the girls blurting out everything in a long-winded stream. You talk of the girls' births, of how you met Moira. You tell absurd stories about your marriage. This one-sided conversation is a monologue really, an antidote to your guilt. You only stop for a few moments to ask Claire a couple of basic questions.

"Where are you from?"

"I am from Mâcon. It is south from here."

"I know Mâcon. I was there once when the temperature was in the mid-forties. Do you have family there?"

"Oui, my people are there. They are making wine. Winemakers." She smiles shyly, embarrassed. "My English is down the drain, I think."

"Do you have brothers and sisters?"

She returns your blather by asking how old the girls are.

"Nine and ten. Ten-and-a-half," you say automatically.

But your heart is not in these questions. You're not listening. A very small part of you wonders if you will ever see Claire again. You do not allow yourself to take it beyond that. You let the question linger on the surface of your frazzled mind.

At one point in the afternoon, Claire puts something by Bach on the stereo and comes back out to the balcony with a bottle of cognac and two snifters and sets them on the table. A severity comes into her face — her eyes lock onto yours. This look penetrates your baffled monologue with a desperation that demands you be present with her only. "You will give me a number where I can telephone you?" Her voice is even and only becomes hopeful inside the word "you."

"Yes, of course, I'll ..." You're off-kilter. Why would she want your phone number? Your kids are alone with a woman named

Georgia. Moira is dead. Your wife is dead and Claire wants your number. Who wants your number?

"... in one year from now I will call on you. Not before. And then we shall see, yes?" She leans forward and cups your face in both her hands. She kisses your lips so gently you could weep. Then she sits down and begins to pour. She does not smile but her voice is filled with resolute hope. "Now, tell me more about your girls. How it was watching them grow?"

8

IN FLIGHT

CLAIRE'S FRIEND, who works for an airline, booked you into Business Class. You're sitting in a vast leather seat. You can drink pretty well whatever you want. You do not want to think about what this ticket cost. The flight attendant, a narrow brunette named Miranda, brings you a pillow and a blanky. She actually says "blanky," a particular linguistic tic, that, as far as you can tell, she only uses with you. Everyone around you gets a blanket. You chalk this up to the bags under your eyes, or maybe you appear lost and she has a need to mother. You're going to see your girls, soon. They've lost their mother and you will do anything for them. *Relax*, you tell yourself. You'll be landing in Victoria. You're going home and you are in flight. The clouds are far below and the stars are a beautiful churning chaos above. You order a glass of champagne.

The first time you can remember seeing stars this clear was in Cadomin, a small blink of a place at the edge of the mountains. Your father had driven you there. He was long gone, back to the city, when darkness fell and the stars began to appear; you thought they'd never stop: the sky was ablaze with them — they burned in your eyes and into your memory. How long ago was that? Four hours, it took. It was the only time you needed him to drive you anywhere.

Your father is driving you to the mountains, a four-hour drive that includes a last fifty-kilometre stretch on a horrible, dusty, pot-holed sorry excuse of a road. Your father does not like to drive his car on gravel roads like this. You only want to arrive at the end of that road where your friend's family has a cabin in an old mining town.

Before the turnoff, there is a three-and-a-half hour drive on a pretty good highway but that drive is unimportant compared to these last fifty kilometres. There is a left turn toward Cadomin, a welcome mat of perhaps a kilometre of partially paved road, and then the road goes to hell.

It is a snaky, ugly road. The man does not want to be on that road yet he is driving it anyway. The kid wants to be at the end of that road — he wants to arrive. You might believe that good stories almost always have beginnings, middles and endings. Perhaps this fifty-kilometre stretch of pothole after pothole and these two characters is the beginning of something — the answer to an unspoken question that goes like this: *How the hell did I get here?* Well, it's as good a place as any. It's a small memory fragment from your past. This is not the only story here. It's not even the main story. It just happens to be the place you begin. There's an epiphany buried inside the swirling, omnipresent dust of this memory. There's something you're supposed to understand.

THERE WAS A ROCKING CHAIR at Cadomin. It's the only one you can associate with your father. You were just a kid and your father drove you to Cadomin to be with your friends, because, silently, he understood that you loved the mountains.

You get out of the car and try not to be too excited about being there. You try to be business-like about it. You don't want to hurt your father's feelings. You want to appear grateful and not too excited. You can be excited later.

"Thank you," you say quietly to him, as you unload your bag. He is standing at the back of the car, ready to shut the trunk, get back in the car, and drive off. There is a palpable awkwardness between you. Then Elsie has your father by the hand and she guides him gently inside the cabin.

"Shouldn't I lock ..." your father starts to say, and he turns back toward the car, starts to fish for his keys.

"Don't worry about that," Elsie says. "We know everyone in the town. Sam's a member of the volunteer fire department. How's Mary?"

"I can't stay long ..."

She settles him in the rocking chair beside the stove and puts the kettle on. "I'll make some tea," she says, so subtly insistent that even if you don't like tea, you want to try this particular one. Your father does not drink tea. He likes coffee, instant, with thick, canned evaporated milk. But this day, he is going to have a cup of Elsie's tea.

Elsie is afraid of Millar moths. You and your friend, her son, were always killing moths for her — often tried to make a show of it. Especially at night when the moths were drawn to the light on the back porch. She called you two her knights in shining armour. She got you reading the Arthurian legends. She taught you about selfless behaviour. About honour. About putting others before yourself. She taught you the absolute joy of giving with no thought of recognition.

Elsie was your friend's mother. She was a big woman, a woman who got so big she was eventually confined to a wheelchair. You do not use the word *fat* — not even in your mind. It seems disrespectful, though that's what it was. *Obese* does not sound right either.

When you arrived with your father that summer, she was still able to walk, although with considerable pain at times. Elsie's size did not matter. She was your friend's mother and possibly the kindest person you knew, next to your own mother.

Your father sat in the rocking chair and had tea with Elsie and Sam Grant. You've no idea what they talked about. Your father was so buttoned-down and the Grants were practically bursting with a sense of adventure. Maybe they talked about the weather.

Later, you thanked your father for the ride again, and then he was back in his car, driving through the scattered houses and cabins, and onto the dusty road toward Hinton. From then on, the rocking chair was called after your father: "That's Mr. Bruce's chair," people said. "Sit in Mr. Bruce's chair why don't you?"

―✺

DUST IS A STRANGE THING to remember on an airplane. But there was so much dust on that road. You're not saying you remember even a third of the drive into the mountains with any accuracy. You have no idea how this small act of kindness played out so many years ago. You were too young and you weren't really paying attention. You're not even sure how old you were. *Roll up the car's window, tight, so the dust doesn't get in.* Every time a car or truck passes in the opposite direction your vehicle is bathed in dust. Even with the windows rolled forcefully, you breathe it, taste it, and it settles silky smooth on the surface of your skin.

You only have snippets of memory-shards stuck in your hand from a broken window. But you'll fill in the missing facts with memories of other trips on the same road. There are some things you know. It was you and your father in a car driving toward the mountains, the road was a two-lane highway, and passing other cars or trucks was an exercise in judgement. You can't remember if your father had business in Jasper. Was he going that way anyway? It isn't pertinent. It's those last fifty kilometers, the left turn — there's the story.

At the time, this event had no depth. It was simply a ride to the mountains. You were grateful, and then your gratefulness was quickly distracted by hiking and climbing. Your father was meticulous about his car. He bought the especially durable and efficient back-seat floor mats. He washed it on a schedule. There were garbage bags on every window knob. There were no dents or scratches, and when parking the car he always put it in an isolated corner of the lot so nobody would scratch the paint while opening a door. He carried this obsessive carefulness into all areas of his life. But he drove all that way on that gravelled, pot-holed, snaky, goat-trail of a road to deliver you to a friend's cabin in a small deserted coal-mining town at the edge of Jasper National Park.

Here you are, 35,000 feet above the planet, and you're just beginning to understand the ramifications of this childhood journey. You were thinking about your father because he is not well. You were thinking about him and you suddenly wound up in the car with him. There was something important about that ride to the mountains and that trip comes sharply into focus as you tilt your third flute of champagne and drain it. The cold liquid touches your stomach as the buttery taste nestles in the back of your mouth. Miranda is there, smiling and quietly saying, "Another one, sweetie?" and efficiently filling your flute again and again.

YOU BARELY UNDERSTAND your father's obsessive drive to keep things looking new and shiny, apparently unused. It doesn't go with having children. They break things, scratch things. They're messy and clumsy by nature. You have to be able to say: "Oh, well," or "Don't worry about it," or "These things happen." Remembering your own youth, and what it is like to be a child, you think of your own daughters who are nine and ten-and-a-half, Sarah Jane and Laura Marie. Sarah and Marie. Marie goes by her second name and this already causes her grief in school, because each new teacher tries to call her Laura.

You've driven that same road for so many years the trips begin to meld together. At first, intermittent farms, small towns and clustered communities. Then, just farms. Evidence of civilization becomes much less frequent, and soon, there are only stands of dense pine lining the highway. Road signs begin to point to distant places with exotic names. Carrot Creek. Entwhistle. The hotel and bar in Nojack. The wooden train trestle at Marlboro. Niton Junction. Cynthia. Robb. Sounds of the highway. The hum of the tires on the road becomes the grounding note inside the absence of dialogue.

The tall grass at the highway's edge; the way it bows and sways and just doesn't give a damn. Dusty willows encroaching on the cutback. And the air that is already noticeably fresher, even inside the isolated cavern of the car.

Your mother packed a lunch. The sandwiches are wrapped in waxed paper and secured with elastic bands. There are carrot sticks in a small, circular, Tupperware container. A bag of potato chips, two bananas, a thermos of coffee for your father and a bottle of cola for you.

"Be careful with that pop. It'll stain," your father says. You probably just nodded. Of course you're not going to spill the goddamn pop on the car seat. Not on purpose. Inside your father's voice is another, silent one, saying: *You're stupid.* An insinuating, always judging voice that curls at the edges of what should be a normal conversation. What you know is that if you did spill something on the car seat, you would never hear the end of it. He would rant for days: *It's ruined. Money doesn't grow on trees. You have to take care of things*. The active logic is that a week of constant ranting, belittling and assurances that you're stupid, will somehow prevent such an incident from ever happening again. You don't remember ever hearing anything encouraging come from your father. The truth is, you grew to dislike and finally despise him for this.

Your father insisted on leaving early in the morning. You're headed west and the sun in the rear-view mirror is easily dismissed. Perhaps the son in the rear-view mirror is easily dismissed too. Don't believe for a second that he doesn't think about where the sun will be when he goes out on the highway. With the sun pushing the car down the road, it's only a small adjustment to move the blinding light out of his eyes. Driving toward the sun is a different, more difficult, matter.

You are sharing a journey. There is a hesitant gratitude in you. A small recognition and gratefulness. But you do not know how to communicate that gratefulness. You are afraid if you say something wrong, the spell will be broken and your father will stop the car, turn around and take you home. Ridiculous, really. But that is the way of it. You are both trapped inside your own silences.

What is going through your father's mind? What does he fear? He is going out of his way to do this. Perhaps it's just what fathers do. Is he thinking about money? You know he plays the stock market. Is it going badly? Is he worried about something else? Maybe there is an illness in the family and he does not know how to speak about it. Is he lonely? Is that why he listens to radio stations with more talking than music? Is there comfort in hearing the voices from the radio? Is he unhappy? Consumed with fear? Maybe he wants desperately to speak his heart but does not know where to begin.

Does he remember being a small child in Poland, being hungry, and living through the Depression? His mother sold everything they had, travelled across Europe, and Britain, and then the Atlantic Ocean by boat, with two young children. She travelled across most of Canada by train, to arrive in Alberta with money still in her pocket. She never learned English. She remained isolated inside her language. Maybe what he remembers most clearly is that things can go terribly wrong, that people can go hungry and then die. You've never lived through a war or a depression. You've never been hungry.

But you aren't thinking about what might be going through your father's head. You are thinking about your arrival in the mountains. You likely didn't care for this journey. It was something you had to live through in order to arrive. Make it short, you're wishing. Make it fly by. You'd like to fall asleep and wake up already there. Surely your father knows where the turnoff is. Of course he does. He knows what he's doing.

⌒

YOU ARE AROUND ELEVEN years old. You're sitting in the passenger's seat, your face downcast and sullen. You are wondering if this trip is worth the price. Normally, you would have to sit and listen to your father go on and on about life, about saving money, about education, death, sickness. It seems there is no love of life in this man, no joy, no laughter.

You can't remember ever hearing your father laugh. Not one memory of him laughing. Isn't that crazy?

Inside this car there is no escape. Your father is mostly silent. You become apprehensive, edgy. You love being with the Grants. They are a family who like to take left turns into the unknown. They do it as a group. *Where does that road go? I don't know. I don't remember seeing it before. Well, let's see where it goes ...*

Cadomin is more of a summer cottage type of place, where folks came to nest in small, old houses. Sixty years ago it was a booming small city. Now, there is no burrowing under the ground like blacked gophers; the coal is stripped away from the surface and then hauled in huge trucks. On the road in, there is an open pit canyon, a gaping wound. Most of the inhabitants have tried to keep their places in good shape, but there are a few completely deserted houses. Cadomin is nestled at the eastern border of Jasper National Park, in the mountains. Mountains. Rock. Icy streams. Hiking. Bears, deer, sheep, goats, lynx. Eagles. This is where you cut your mountain teeth. You loved the open and seemingly endless possibilities of being at the cabin with this relaxed family. Every day was an adventure. Snow in July. Ferocious winds that blew through the "V" at the end of the valley and were strong enough to flip a motorhome across a meadow until it became pieces of aluminum and engine chunks. Bears scratching around the back door at midnight. Horses. Throughout the valley there were horses let loose for the summer months to fend for themselves, and rounded up in the fall. You dreamed of one day getting close enough to get up on one of them and take a little ride. And there were always new cutlines to explore. These straight and narrow swaths, carved through forest, allowed access to potential forest fires but they were also great ways to get far back into the dense pines and very quickly up on the side of a mountain.

PROBABLY HALF THE MALES on the planet are uncertain of their father's love. Your father wasn't exactly your favourite person as you were growing up. A difference in world view is normal. You spent a few decades being angry at his clamped-down, silent, controlling way. You never tried to understand him. You never thought about what his dreams might have been, or what he gave up for you. Maybe kids aren't supposed to think about these things. If he had been a different person, some of these things might have come up in conversation. Did he dream of playing in the NHL? Did he want to go to university? When your daughters arrived, your anger started to soften but you carried remnants of it in you. That's why this sudden memory of his act of love is more than an epiphany.

You have to reconstruct your entire understanding of what it means to love.

Because what your father did, he did for *you*. He drove those four hours into the mountains and then, without hesitation or complaint, without a word about it, he drove the remaining crap road to Cadomin.

It has taken you almost twenty-five years to unravel this memory and connect it to your father's obsessively careful attention to his cars. For you, he had risked a broken windshield, any variety of dents, flat tires, and pounding the hell out of the shocks over those final kilometres. He never drove on gravel. *Never.*

Only now, on this airplane out of Paris are you able to begin to see that there was sacrifice in that journey, and understanding, and love. You begin to think about what dreams your father may have given up. What sacrifices? Was he really good enough to make a run at the NHL? What stopped him? What did he really want to do with his life?

9

PYRAMID LAKE

You've got your blanky and you've had several flutes of champagne. You're floating. Memories drift in and out. Some, you discard. Others you entertain.

You and Moira are in the mountains, at Pyramid Lake, just west of Jasper. You've wrangled a good off-season rate and have one of the upper-level rooms. Laura Marie is not due for another six months. The snow is reaching down the mountain slopes into the valleys with elegant fingers. The upper peaks are already socked in for the winter. The lake is not yet frozen over. Nobody goes near it. It feels icy, beyond cold even from a distance. It seems wrong for it not to be frozen over yet.

It's a short hike up the road to Pyramid Island, a small dot of land joined to the shore by a narrow footbridge. She likes the walk. When you have been walking for about ten minutes, you ask her what happened to Moses and Katya.

"They have the baby," she says.

"Everything worked out okay? It's a happy ending despite the cat dying?"

"Well, something odd happens."

"The baby's fine though, right? The baby's healthy?" One afternoon, you looked up Down syndrome on the Internet and spent a few hours scaring yourself into a frenzy.

"The baby is great. Her name is Sidney and she's one of those kids with a positive energy about them right from the start. An aura of peacefulness. She smiles and seems to welcome everybody she comes across. So, Sidney is like this little Jesus-Buddha and her parents are happy as hell with her."

"But?"

"There's no but. It's just that Katya has an affair. It's stupid really. Another lawyer. A woman."

"Oh." You didn't expect this. *Where in hell is this going?* you're thinking. "That's an interesting turn."

"You mean interesting as in uninteresting, don't you? Katya begins to think she might be in love with this woman. This woman is her body opposite. She is tall and full-figured and fair, which is sort of what Moses is actually. Katya doesn't know what to do. She should probably be focused on her baby but she can't help herself. She is with this woman every chance she can get. They make love under the desk, on top of the desk, in motel rooms, hotel rooms, bathroom stalls." Moira stops to catch her breath.

"Are you all right?"

"I'm turning you on aren't I?" She looks at you with a weird intensity. "The idea of two women making love. It turns you on doesn't it?"

"A little."

"Can you see them playing with each other in the bathroom? Going painfully silent when they hear the door open. Taking each other's scents on fingers and faces into boardroom meetings? Does that turn you on?"

"You know it turns me on."

"But you don't really consider it adultery do you? Don't answer that. I already know the answer. But Katya is falling in love with this woman, which has some pretty sharp-edged consequences for Moses and the baby."

"Yes, quick fucks are one thing. Falling in love is something quite different."

You pull the whisky flask out and have a swig. It's loaded with the cheapest single malt you could find. It's been a rough few months for geology. Moira looks at you. "I miss having a drink every now and then," she says. "Come over here, you." So you move in close. And she grabs you and kisses you. Her tongue searches your mouth for the pockets of scotch taste.

"Oh, my God. That's so good, and I am so horny right now it's unbelievable."

How is it that Moira has become more beautiful with each passing week? You find yourself caught in a lovely whirlpool — getting closer and closer to her with each loop. Of course, getting physically closer to her will become less and less realistic.

At the far end of the island she draws you in and kisses you again. This time she is not searching for the aftertaste of scotch. You are standing on a thick moss bed — hundreds of years of pine needles make a cushion of the ground. Even though it is chilly, she slips her boots and socks off, and stands barefoot on the moss. She drops her pants and uses the tree to push her bum into you. You join with Moira in the ancient dance, under the spreading arms of a pine and the steady gaze of Mt. Pyramid. Then you are curled on the ground, nested in your coats and clothing. You pull a blanket from your pack and cover up. There are the beginnings of stars in a thick indigo sky. "I'm still horny," she whispers.

The next morning you let Moira sleep. You walk down the hill to the shore with your coffee cup steaming in the cool morning air. Ice along the edges is getting thicker by the day. There's open water further out.

Moira was sleeping so beautifully, like the baby inside — curled on her side, adrift.

You head for the island, and while you are walking you start to think about Moses and Katya. A bend in the road offers up a partial view of Mt. Pyramid. It's difficult to understand its name from this angle. You have to know where to look when you're approaching from the east. If you come at it from the east and look up over a large hump of sloping land called Pyramid Bench, you can see a pyramid of rock. From that angle it's clear how this mountain got its name.

"We didn't have the baby. I had an abortion," Katya says. She has a walking stick in her right hand and her cheeks are red.

Okay, this is breakpoint. Do you acknowledge this imagined person or do you keep walking in silence?

"I was worried that there was something wrong," you say.

"Oh, I'm all right." She looks up into your face. "We're all right."

"Why am I not entirely convinced about you and Moses?"

"Really. We're fine. We had no idea what we wanted. Didn't know where we were going."

"Where's Moses?"

"How should I know? I'm not really here."

"Then he's back at the hotel. You two had a little spat ..."

"A spat?"

"Yes. He's not paying enough attention to you. You're high maintenance, Katya."

"Or maybe you wanted to get me alone on Pyramid Island." There is a soft straightforwardness to her statement that is neither invitation nor discouragement. Does she have a little bit of an English accent? How could she? She was born and raised in Saskatchewan. In a small town called Lytton.

"Lytton is in B.C., dumb-ass. I'm not a daft hallucination."

"You know what I'm thinking?"

"Tit for tat."

"Will you walk with me to the end?"

"To the end of time?" she says. "Life? This road?"

"To the end of the island for starters."

The silence becomes a long, dripping icicle. You become aware of your footsteps. You're alone for Chrissake. Your wife is up in the room. You haven't been drinking. You've got the narrow thermos, filled with fresh coffee from the lodge.

But I create myself every morning when I get up, you think. *I have an entire scenario of possibilities and assumptions that allow me to make it through the day.*

You begin to hear Katya's footsteps joined together with yours and you are happy. You are happy to be walking with the clouds thick above you, with the air sparkling, the pines along the road, and the thousand hues of brown that colour the grasses.

"It's your business, but I'm wondering why you had an abortion?"

"It probably seems selfish to you. But we weren't ready. And I wasn't entirely certain about Moses. I'm still not certain."

Is anybody ever ready to have a kid? Or absolutely certain about somebody else — even somebody they love? Half the time you think Moira is a flake, with her incense and meditating and that hideous statue of the female incarnation of some Indian god she loves so much. The other half, you think she's a brilliant anthropologist who knows people so well she's able to sell a lot of very expensive cars to a lot of very rich people. Other times you just love her for putting up with you, the idiot-paleontologist, lost and wandering through life looking for peace — struggling to find that slippery balance of passions.

You've been worrying about strange things. Can you make enough money to support a family? What if the baby has Down syndrome? Would you love this child any less?

You're on the footbridge, which reaches over half-formed ice and scant open water to Pyramid Island. Katya is there. Mt. Pyramid rises in all its orangey-grey-tinged glory behind her. You are drawn toward this imagined woman.

At the far end of the island she pulls you in and kisses you. She kisses like a woman who has nothing to lose. You know in a second that you will make love to her there on the island. Katya takes you in her mouth and slowly and methodically begins to suck. From across the lake, a raven makes its rasping caw sounds that reverberate sharply in the still morning. There is an absence of any other sound, and that sound becomes forever a reminder of this particular moment.

You need to snap out of it. You are walking by yourself on a small island, in a lake, in the Rocky Mountains, on a grey day, early in the morning. Only the hardiest winter birds remain. Chickadees, sparrows, dippers. You have been thinking about a woman named Katya. Who is not real.

Have some more coffee. It's still hot in the thermos. You went for a walk and had a little fantasy. You're acting like you're lonely or depressed. You're not, not really. It's so beautiful here and you want to share it with someone. It's not good to be alone in the face of such beauty.

You leave Katya, naked and lying on her side on top of the table at the far end of the island. Her body is one more layer of landscape amidst so many layers of cascading trees and rock and sky. Her hip makes a luscious curve against dark green, a smooth cresting microcosm of a line of pines rising up a mountain. Her breasts are fallen angels, toppled mountain peaks, swirls of heavy snow, and water around a rock in the stream that feeds this lake.

You take that image back up the road toward the lodge. You are still imagining Katya when a white-tailed deer skitters across the road in front of you, as it moves from the lake to the forest. Once it is safely far back among the trunks of pines, the deer pauses to turn and look at you. Meeting deer always means something. It's an injection of grace and softness into your life, and it makes you happy.

⌒

YOU PICK UP A CUP OF TEA from the restaurant and trudge up the steep road to your room. Moira is still asleep, so you take the lid off the tea and place it beside the bed. The scent of the mint will wake her. That's a good gentle way to wake up. While you are filling and fussing with the stovetop espresso-maker, you wonder if Katya is still on the island. She may become the ghostly waif of Pyramid Island — the patron saint protector of lonely souls in the mountains.

IO

FIELD

Paying attention to the smallest details helps you survive your flight. It keeps you focused and helps you gather strength for your girls. You land at Edmonton International Airport, 2,373 feet (723 metres) above sea level. YEG. YEG is the code for Edmonton International Airport. You don't care about your luggage. Sylvie is there. She pulls you in and guides you to your next plane. You walk to a different gate and board another plane headed for Victoria. YYJ is the code for Victoria, British Columbia, Canada. The runway in Victoria airport is 63 feet (19 metres) above sea level. Did you thank Sylvie?

Hours before, you took off from a runway in Paris, France that was 292 feet (89 metres) above sea level. CDG is the code for Charles de Gaulle airport in Paris.

You register sporadic things — the plane's tires hitting the ground, the sudden slowing down, the warning not to undo your seatbelts until the plane has come to a full stop, and the one not to forget your overhead luggage.

You feel your ears pop on the way down to Victoria. Moira would have thought to bring some gum.

You're sitting in your seat, barely contained, waiting for the plane to stop completely, when a flight attendant with very dark eyes touches your shoulder and scares you. She says your name, and then whispers, "Come with me." She unfastens your seatbelt and pulls down your carry-on bag, and then you're walking toward the front of the plane. The second the doors swing open there are two more women from the airline waiting. Kind faces. The short one inflects your name up into a question and you nod. Then you're off down a long carpeted stairway to your girls. Perhaps you hugged them a little too hard and a little too long when you got to them. This is your family now. Even before you reached them, you could see they were holding it together, and that gave you more strength than you knew you had. This is your family now.

YOU DO NOT GO TO THE SITE of the accident. You don't think it's important to see where she died. What does it matter, really? Stop. You just called it an accident. That's interesting. Something in your gut says it was on purpose but your subconscious says *accident*. When you got to Sooke you were only interested in your daughters and arranging for Moira's return. You made a dozen phone calls. Moira's father wanted to come and make sure she got home all right. While you are not quite able to understand your own grief — every time it raised its head, you whacked it down — you certainly understand his. You imagined how you'd feel if Sarah or Marie died. This heartbreak was monumental and transparent.

He comes to the Island to take his daughter home. You meet him in Victoria.

IT'S RAINING AND DREARY when you pick Moira's father up at the airport.

"I'm so sorry, Frank," you say.

"It's horrible for all of us. How are the girls?" His face is drawn, ashen.

"They'll pull through all right. Not now I'm worried about. Couple of months, a year, two years ... that's when it's going to be tough."

Frank nods his head. "Do you think she ..."

"I don't know. Lots of things point in that direction but there are things missing. It's not a complete picture. We might never know for sure."

There's nothing to do. The casket is already at the airport. Moira and her father will go home later that evening. You and the girls will follow tomorrow. You find nothing irrational about him wanting to be on the plane with his daughter. You take Frank into Victoria and find a nice, quiet bar down by the harbour. You both order Guinness.

You look for Moira in Frank and, perhaps, she's there. Around the eyes. The same delicate chin. Frank is diminutive, perfectly proportioned, with white hair and old hands. You notice the age spots on his hands. That, and they seem frail, as if there's no strength in them anymore.

"My memory has been doing strange things lately," Frank says. "Last night, for some reason, I remembered a race she ran. I think it was the 400-metre. It was the city championships, anyway. In the hurdles. She was fourteen. I went to that meet, of course. It was her first race with a starting pistol and when they fired it, it scared her. She stood up. She didn't know what the hell it was. She was used to someone shouting a percussive *Go!* preceded by *On your mark, Get set ...* In the meantime, all the other kids were off down the track."

Frank takes a long and careful sip of his Guinness.

"Once she realized the race was on, you could see her anger turn into this wild energy. Maybe she heard some kids laughing. Maybe she felt embarrassed. Anyway, she took off down the track and slipped over those hurdles like they weren't even there. It was beautiful to watch. Moira was like a sleek hunting animal. And the girl leading the pack was her prey."

He's looking at you, but not. He's inside your body with his vision, moving through molecules and corpuscles. Then his vision is into the wooden bench behind you and through the wall, out onto the wet street, through the rain, and across the dark grey-green harbour. His vision surprises the glide-path gulls, and eventually you realize he's not with you but in another time, watching Moira run inside a crystal-clear memory. You're not going to be the one that brings him back. No way. You'd love to wave a magic wand and let Frank be inside that happy moment for as long as he wants. A month. A year. A decade. For now, you'll protect him by glaring daggers at anybody who approaches, by not moving suddenly, by not speaking, by not doing anything jarring. So you have a slow drink of the good dark beer and you wait. You wonder about the details. You go to the same place where Frank is, except you're loaded down with questions. You can visualize a steely-eyed fourteen-year-old gliding across hurdles like a sleek hunting dog. Moira's long legs. Her determination. But what was the sky like? Was the sun shining? Was it a hot day? What was she wearing? How long was her hair and did it fly behind her as she ran? What happened in the race — how did she do?

"She won the race," Frank says, causing you to jump. "By a nose. I've never seen anything like it. I was so proud of her."

He's looking right at you. His eyes in your eyes, and the sadness you see in him is filled to overflowing.

Being so close to Frank's grief starts to cause problems with your own sorrow, which you've pushed aside and pushed aside in the last couple days. You want to tell him to please not cry because you're just barely holding it together right now, but how can you do that?

You want this, and you do not want it. You want to ingest every syllable and every fragment of a story about her, no matter how dumb. Whatever Frank can muster, you want to hear it, and at the same time, you want him to shut up. You need to be in life, here, in the present.

After several more stories — you never knew that Moira took violin lessons when she was four — and two more pints, you both head off in different directions. Frank insists on getting to the airport on his own. So you go for a walk in the drizzle before driving back to Sooke. God is making a movie, you think, to mirror this sadness and he's arranged for the perfect, solemn weather. You understand this bleakness is normal for this time of year. You'll drive back for supper. You should have sobered up by then.

The harbour is unsettled. Its stomach is churning and miserable; it feels nauseous. The rain descends in random sheets of cold as if it's trying to hurt you. You pull your collar up and around but you don't really give a shit about the rain.

~

GEORGIA SAID MOIRA spent the day before her car crash locked in a room, supposedly corresponding. To whom did Moira write? Or was she just avoiding the girls. How can you wish to kill yourself when you look at your children? You wonder how much more difficult it was with the girls there.

For a few weeks, you expected something to arrive in the mail. But nothing. Every day you approached the mailbox with heart pounding, filled with dread. After three weeks, you accepted the nothingness. You grew accustomed to the hollowness of the empty mailbox — the cranky lid, the scraping cold metal sound.

Maybe she was drinking in there. Maybe there was no correspondence. Nobody you know got a letter from Moira, but the world is a big place and Moira had a life before she met you.

~

TWO MONTHS LATER, with everything essential to your life packed into a U-Haul trailer, and your daughters in the back seat, you drop down from the high mountain passes into a small town called Field. You're also carrying a triple scoop of grief. You're not sure how the grief is going to come into play but you know it's there, and at some point you'll have to deal with it.

In Field, there is a line of large poplar trees near the railway station, close to the river. These are pretty big deciduous trees for the mountains. You descended into Field with no feelings toward the mountains. They neither thrilled nor disappointed you. They were not sad; they were not happy; they were merely veiled with cloud. Snow was visible in the high gaps and folds. And the trees were thick on the mountainsides. There was a long steep drop into the valley where the town nested just above the flood plain. One bridge. A train station, a government-run information centre, a few hundred people. The river, and the mountains looking down on everything.

Both the girls fell asleep as you passed Banff and you drove alone past Lake Louise, the provincial border, and then over the high passes until you reached Field. By the time you arrived it was very dark. But you've been here before. It's a smidgen of a town, a small grouping of buildings, very close to the rising spines of granite. You have arranged to stay in a house that belongs to a friend of Moira's mother. You have enough money. You've told the girls it's for a couple months or so. You hope this secluded retreat might heal all of you, or at least prove to be a fresh-air salve for wounds, visible or hidden. The girls are not exactly thrilled about this. They will be going to a new, very, very small school. You want to just be with them. There is no mall, no movie theatre, and hardly any people in Field. This is no Cockaigne. A word-of-the-day website delivered the word Cockaigne, meaning an imaginary land of ease and luxury, a week ago. It's pronounced "kah-KAYN."

~

"WHY FIELD? Why such a small town when you have a great big house in the city?" Your mother sounds exasperated. Now, it's a long commute to see her grandchildren. She is torn between you and your father.

"I've always liked Field. Backyards that scoop themselves up into mountain peaks. The proximity to rock. It's uncomplicated here."

Your mother sinks into silence and it does not make you uncomfortable. There is no arguing that there are profound reminders of Moira in the city house. It's not that this is a bad thing. You want to be reminded of Moira.

"What about the girls?"

"The girls are fine. They're grumpy about the size of the school but they're fine." Marie's bad dreams are between you and Marie.

"Do you know anybody there?"

"Not yet, but there are good people in this town. I just feel it. I'm not exactly sociable right now."

"Do you have everything you need?"

"We're fine, Mom. Tell me about Dad. How is he?"

"He's the same." She pauses. "A little worse, maybe. The periods of silence are getting longer and longer."

⌐⌐

WELL, YOU'VE BECOME a very good liar. One of the main reasons you picked Field was because of the Burgess Shale. The fossil beds — one of the richest, and a world heritage site — are right at your doorstep. The opportunity to poke around up there on a daily basis had a lot to do with your decision. It's late in the season. The snows have come early and by the time you're settled, it'll likely be well past the closing date for the Shale site. There might be work here for you. But you'll have to bide your time over the winter. You need to make the right connections. They wanted you once; why wouldn't they want you again?

⌐⌐

IT'S NOT THE MOST IMAGINATIVE name for a town. Maybe the first expedition named it for the flat field they found in this valley bottom, after weeks of slogging through forests of pine and mountain passes and fording too many rivers. Suddenly, here was an expanse of flatness in the middle of so much vertical landscape. *Well, there's a field here. Let's call this here place Field.* Could it be that simple? Perhaps these men and women struck an impromptu baseball game in that field. Is that how it got its name? That's like calling a place "Steep Incline" or "Ocean" or "River" or "Shrub."

You just picked it as a good place to live for a while.

SARAH IS SITTING ON ONE of the stools in the small kitchen. Her back is to the window, to the rising mountain, grey-white stranded clouds, and descending fingers of snow. Now this mountain scene has a narrow-shouldered girl with shoulder-length brunette hair and dark eyes. This girl is wearing a white T-shirt and jean coveralls. There is a small gap between her two front teeth — something Moira wanted to fix but Sarah said she wanted to keep. She is precocious and vocal, and never afraid to ask questions. You have begun to see profound strands of Moira in Sarah and this makes you happy.

"I feel like I know this place," she says. "Like I've been here before. Have we?"

"When you were very young, you might have been three, I used to make up stories about a little girl who lived in a high mountain town with her parents. You probably don't remember. The little girl always looked like you. It was always a story about this little girl who was befriended by a Buddhist monk."

You've never met a Buddhist monk and probably wouldn't know one if you saw one. At the time it seemed perfectly exotic and strange and no three-year old is going to question your knowledge anyway. You know very little about Buddhism. You know about compassion and being in the moment but the being-in-the-moment part might be from Taoism. You're not sure.

You fill a pot with water and place it on the stove to boil. Slide the cutting board out from beside the toaster and pick the best knife. Pull vegetables from the crisper.

"You see, there was a monastery at the edge of the town. And there were these two monks who were moving a rather large statue of the Buddha. I often thought it might be made of wood, but a very heavy, dense wood. They definitely had their hands full. They were struggling. One of the monks gets an itchy nose and along comes this little girl. The little girl had her dog, Rufus, with her, and her walking stick. They were just out exploring."

"That's a funny name for a dog," Sarah says.

You begin to slice a white onion. You don't actually recall what the dog's name was. "He was a big German shepherd who was very protective. The interesting thing is, Rufus didn't growl when they came across the monks. He usually growled when he met people he didn't know. So the monk with the itchy nose asks the little girl if she would please scratch his nose for him. The little girl has to think about this. Her parents told her never to talk to strangers, let alone scratch their noses. But she looks at the monks, wearing their orangey robes, and realizes they've both got their hands on the Buddha and they would have to drop the statue in order to grab her, if that was their intent."

"Saffron," Sarah says. "Buddhist monks' robes are saffron-coloured."

"Yes. The monks were wearing saffron robes. This little girl was pretty darned smart. Actually, she was a lot like you, Sarah. So, after careful consideration, she reaches out her hand and scratches the monk's nose.

"That's the beginning of a long friendship between the monk and the girl. Then I'd start to tell you about how they would watch the seasons. I'd describe the mountains in the summer and the fall and the winter and so on. It was at this point you would drift off to sleep. I always imagined Field as that small town. Your mother and I used to come here quite a lot, before you girls were born. I know there's no monastery here, but there could be. It seems like a natural place to have one. You seemed to like this story when you were three. Maybe you remember a bit of it?"

Sarah smiles. It's Moira's smile. "Maybe," she says.

"It's a silly story, really. I made it up very quickly and desperately, and then you kept asking for it. You wouldn't let me change anything."

"It's not silly," she says. "I like it." She scrapes her chair back from the table and stands up. "When's supper?"

ROUTINES BECOME IMPORTANT. You never used to believe this. But you fall into a small series of necessary, life-saving routines. Getting the girls up and off to school. Making breakfast. Coffee. Making lunches. More coffee. Laundry, cleaning, chopping wood. Various phone calls. A daily walk to the Troubled Pig for a mid-morning coffee with Carl — he's one of the chefs at the café. A nightly walk down to the river after dinner. Being there if the girls need help with their homework. And you begin half-heartedly to look for work as a paleontologist. You put out some feelers. You don't have a lot of hope for a job right now but at least you're in the right spot to land something with the Burgess Shale folks. These are the daily events that glue you together in the daytime. At night, you're a bit less structured.

The girls begin to enjoy school. They make friends easily. Though Marie punched a girl. You're thinking it's because she's tired most of the time. Her bad dreams have started to escalate. She's been waking up in the middle of the night, trying to shake the dreams away, and quite often she comes to you. Marie and the girl she punched are the best of friends now.

Roughly every two weeks, you drive to Golden to buy groceries and rent movies for the girls. The one store in Field, which serves as a restaurant, liquor store, café, deli and quick-fix grocery store, rents movies but the girls were able to move through that collection fairly quickly.

It's only late at night, after the girls are in bed, that you can let your sadness visit. Some nights you play the Górecki symphony, his Third, which almost matches the intensity of your own grief. You don't know how much grief you have. Inside that symphony, you slip back to your Paris state, where nothing makes sense and there are no answers. There never will be answers. The only gods are the ones you've created, derivations of Guilt, Sorrow, Self-pity and Despair, and they're not a kind bunch. There is no Claire to save you. Only the morning and your routines offer small salvations. But at 3:42 a.m., a very long way from sober, and lost in fragile memories, that tree, Moira's tree, looms up dark and tall. You have no idea what kind of tree it is. It stands there like a holy icon for a religion you don't understand. You don't know the password. You can't break the goddamn code.

You stoke up the fire and pour a whisky. You notice there is a direct and clear correlation between the type of drink and the flavour of your sadness. A single-malt scotch, for instance, brings clear memories that are bold and brash. Cognac, on the other hand, brings a haze to the proceedings. On the nights you drink wine, you remember Claire, and Moira is always there in the background, trying to be noticed. All of your late-night reveries lead to one unavoidable crux: why did she do it? Once you get there, you drink even more. It's stupid to smash your head up against this wall but you always had a predilection for hopeless causes. You and Saint Jude. One of these nights, you'll have to have a long conversation with old Saint Jude. Only part of you understands that drinking into the early morning in front of the fire, in the big upstairs room, in a borrowed house, in the mountains, is not going to solve a god-damned thing. Is there a patron saint of self-pity?

⌐

THE GIRLS TRUNDLE OFF to school and you step out into the side yard with your French press of coffee wrapped in a thick towel, and a bottle of cognac. It's cold this morning and the forecast is for more snow. You pour out a mug of coffee and a snifter of cognac, tighten your steel-toed workboots and pick up the axe. You've had two cords of wood delivered and now you're going to chop it up. You have to smile at the optics of what you're about to do. You're not exactly the macho stereotype. You know how to chop wood. It's something you grew up with. But you haven't had a lot of practice lately.

This morning you are angry with Moira. You are pissed off that she could be such a self-centered bitch and you decide to take it out on the wood. You pull on a pair of leather gloves you found by accident in a drawer in the kitchen and start swinging the axe. The work feels good in your bones. The sound of wood being chopped is pleasing. You have on a wool sweater and a down vest, but the vest likely won't last long.

With each inefficient swing of the axe, you release a sliver of sorrow. This morning, you are not sorry for Moira. You are angry that she wrecked herself, and now you are left with her ruins and with the responsibility of cleaning up her mess. You have become one of Moira's ruins.

The deep barking sound of the axe forced abruptly through wood is made slightly bigger by the cold day. There is clarity around that sound — a percussive focus.

⌐

YOU REMEMBER BEING IN EDMONTON on one of those rare spring days when the weather is ahead of season. There's snow everywhere, but the air is sweet and warm. You had a meeting downtown but stop at Café Demitasse and use the house phone to cancel your appointment. You'd parked a couple of blocks away, and found yourself walking closer than normal behind certain women trying to see if you could catch a scent of perfume, or soap, or something real. You wanted to steal their smell and carry it for a while, just because. You watch women as they walk. Find it fascinating the way their bums move. The loose swaying hips, the clip-clopping small steps, the leaning-forward women with elongated heels, those that slouch like rag dolls, and the painfully tight-assed marchers. Right now, you love them all. Skinny, medium, large ... it just doesn't matter. There's beauty in every butt, every scent — no matter how acrid or flowery, every face, and hairdo, and every shoe and boot and ankle. Maurice overhears your phone conversation and brings you a Heineken, hands it to you even before you sit down.

After a while, Maurice sits at your table. He looks at your beer with the determining eye of a waiter — discerning, *Is it time to offer another?* Maurice decides no — there is sufficient beer. Then he nods his head and says he knows exactly where his life went off the rails. Perhaps he doesn't remember telling you this story already, but what does it matter? Maybe the spot of this derailment has changed since he last told it.

"Your life went off the rails, Maurice?" you ask, as if this notion is unthinkable.

He closed his eyes and nods gravely.

"Of course it was just after I met the Shopper. She was the tall brunette who went to mass every day and who had all the credit cards. In the end, we counted fourteen cards. Not all in her name, but they were all hers."

"She had fourteen credit cards?"

"All pushed to the maximum amount. Over $100,000 in debt. It was amazing."

"And this is where your life went off the rails?"

"No, no ... it was after the Shopper. The Shopper was a lovely woman who started to steal from her work in order to pay for her massive debt. I was sorry to see her go. She had begun to gamble in order to recoup money. The gambling pushed her further into debt. She went to prison for stealing from her workplace. It was then that I met the Nymph. That's when my life went off course. The Nymph had gorgeous breasts — they were swollen honeydew melons — they were beautiful and liquid and ... before I met her, I was getting ready to go back to school. I'd gathered together enough courses to get into university. But for three-and-a-half years, the Nymph caused those plans to come to a grinding, incredibly erotic stop." Maurice smiles, a slow lifting. "The Nymph is one of those women I will remember as I am nodding in my deathbed with tubes stuck into me and beeping noises all around."

"I've noticed your past loves, umm, these women from your past, they don't have names."

"Really?"

"Yes, they seem to have titles as opposed to names."

MARIE IS FINALLY ASLEEP — her emotions rubbed raw by the dream that persists and haunts and threatens to ruin her. She is exhausted by the repetition. You've come out into the backyard to stand at the edge of a starry night with tears in your eyes, because this is your daughter and she is in pain and you feel responsible. Your failure as a father, as a husband, as a human being is wrapped up in your daughter's horrible dreams. Somewhere along the line you made a mistake. You could have loved harder. *Something.* You want to scream into the night — a scream so awful and filled with anger that grizzly bears up on the mountain will cower and whimper. And bears that are in deep hibernation will lift their drowsy heads, shocked by this sound.

Marie's night terrors put a damper on your nocturnal drinking. You slow down. You want to be sober in case she needs you. You don't want to send her into adulthood with the memory of a father who always smelled of booze.

~

THE GIRLS STILL BELIEVE IN THEIR HEARTS it was an accident. Do you tell them the truth, the assumed ugly truth? You don't want them to be playing with a cousin at some point in the future and have that child blurt out: "Your mommy killed herself! Your mommy killed herself!" That would be a cruel surprise. It's not a scenario you want your daughters to live through. At the very least, they have to know what people are thinking and why. There's no way to contain that now, it's too late for that. Too many people are already muttering and murmuring, and quasi-secrets like this always come home to roost.

There were so many sad and silent faces at the funeral. Your mother, your father — who looked more confused than ever — Sylvie and Maurice, various uncles and aunts, the owner of the car dealership where Moira worked. Moira's parents looked completely, utterly lost. In fact, most of the people who came to the funeral looked like your father, in shock, and confused. If Moira had died of some actual disease, or had definitely been in an accident, there might have been a different feel to the service.

The idea of tragedy is split into camps. This particular one falls into the befuddled camp. It's not an easy tragedy to understand, or accept. Difficult to celebrate a life with such unspoken sadness at its core. Difficult to celebrate a life that ended in this way. Everyone stood around trying to make sense of Moira's decision. Nobody was really certain. They all had strong ideas, hunches. The Medical Examiner's Office called it an accident but they didn't poke around very much. They asked simple questions. They got simple answers.

She was estranged from her husband. They were getting back together. She was drinking a bit more than usual but she was on a holiday of sorts. She loved her children. She'd never been on medication for depression. The booze in her system was negligible — not enough to nullify the insurance.

During the funeral, halfway through one of the hymns your father stands up and shouts: "I like this goddamn song!" and his words echo through the church.

"Why did grandpa say that?" Sarah asks.

"Because," you whisper. "Because ..." *Because he's losing his fucking mind*, you think. But you leave it at "because."

Sarah and Marie stand their ground, chins up, even-keeled. You are proud of them. Marie doesn't cry. "It's all right to cry," you say. "If you feel like it."

"Not right now," she says and then moves close to your side, slips her hand into yours.

You begin to feel an enormous guilt. Imaginary whispered voices echo in the back of your mind. *You were the one who was closest to her. Why didn't you see she needed help? Why couldn't he prevent it? Why didn't he try to help? He's a bad husband. He's a bad friend. Look what happened.* The voices get so loud you purposely seek out Moira's Uncle Bob, renowned for his whisky flask. The last time you saw Uncle Bob was over a year ago. He'd come into town for a curling match, and was so drunk at dinner that he dropped an antique serving platter bearing the roast. You wound up ordering Chinese. He was horribly apologetic and pathetically contrite, but not enough for Moira. She was pissed off and good old Uncle Bob more or less disappeared from your lives. He sank back into the Saskatchewan prairie. He returned to Regina where he was a partner in a small publishing house. The prospects of his visiting in the near future became hazy at best.

You two have a drink together in the basement bathroom of the church. There is an overwhelming pungent smell of urinal disinfectant cakes, but you don't care. "To better times," Uncle Bob says. "Happier times." He's wearing a brown tweed jacket, a white shirt that's likely never been pressed, and a dark blue tie. One of the buttons on his jacket doesn't quite match the others. His glasses are scratched and blurry, and the thick black-plastic frames are not subtle.

You take a good swig from the flask. "I knew she was depressed," you say. "I knew it. But didn't know it was so bad that she would do this."

"Not your fault," he says. "You never truly know a person. All sorts of hidden alcoves, dark nooks and crannies."

"I could have ..."

"No, you couldn't," he says. "If she chose to end her life with determination and careful planning, it wasn't a cry for help. She was, she was resolute. Nothing you could do." He winces at this word as if the thought of that kind of resoluteness hurts him. "And if it was an accident ..." He closes his eyes and shakes his head.

Uncle Bob and you drain the flask. Then he gives you an awkward hug. "Your daughters need you to be strong right now, and you are. You are. A lot of people love you." He takes his glasses off and unabashedly wipes the tears off his face. "A lot of people are thinking about you right now. Nobody blames you." You walk out of the bathroom feeling closer to breaking down and thinking that the beginnings of absolution can come in the strangest places.

↔

YOU WILL HAVE TO TELL the girls the underlying story, the assumed truth, but first, you must believe it yourself. You'd like there to be no doubt. But without the tree, you don't have the whole picture. Are there any other details missing? It seems the tree is the only thing. You're starting to believe you need to know the tree — the tree is the key. But you can't bring yourself to ask anybody who might know what kind of tree it was.

SHE HAS BEEN FEEDING this fire for half an hour — keeping it steady and obedient. When she came into the room there was only a faint blush in the bottom of the fireplace. Now there's a steady, orangey glow, but it does nothing to succour the remnants of nightmare in her head. The heat from this fire is of little consequence. She's wrapped in a down quilt and still stuck inside the horror of her dream, a dream that started pleasantly enough but quickly slipped into nightmare. This is a dream that becomes more intensely horrific with each repetition. Marie has started to dread the thought of sleep.

It's 2:16 a.m. when you notice the crackling sound from downstairs and sit up. You silently curse the fact you know it's exactly 2:16 a.m. instead of about quarter past two. You curse the damned inventions of clock radios and digital time. You much prefer the continuum of a clock face, which includes past, present and future, as opposed to the now, now, now — *the exactly now* — of digital time.

You'd left the fire when it was a perfect coal bed and there was a fair chance there might be something there in the morning. That way you wouldn't be starting from scratch. This crackling sound can mean only one of two things: the house is on fire, or someone is down there putting wood into the fireplace.

You see Marie on the couch in the living room, wrapped in her quilt, rocking back and forth, staring into the flames. She's strangled inside a dream she can't shake, even though she is mostly awake. She places another chunk of wood onto the fire, just as she's seen you do. She watches as the papery bark-edges catch. The flame jumps and multiplies, orange and yellow, and then she sinks back into the sofa.

Her nightmares have become yours. Your heart aches for her. She's too young to have this. Why should your daughter be haunted when you are able to sleep? You wish you could trade places with her.

You sit on the top stair and push away your own sorrow before descending into the living room. This has to be part of grieving but how much longer can it last? Three times a week, sometimes four, Marie wakes up inside this horror. Some nights you find her on the couch curled into a tight fetal position, whimpering. Other nights she will come into your bedroom.

Downstairs, you sit next to her on the couch, slip your arm around her shoulders and let her breathe into you. She has become a clenched fist and it takes time for that fist to uncurl.

"Same dream?" you say, and Marie nods her head. You don't call it a nightmare. You call it the bad dream like when she was five — Marie used to say she had the growing pains.

You hold her until one of you has to put more wood on the fire. Then you get up and make a pot of herbal tea, with milk and honey.

You feel completely helpless in the face of this suffering, and it appears there's nothing you can do. How do you control your dreams? Is that even possible? Marie says she will not talk to a psychologist. You are getting close to insisting.

"It's just a bad dream."

"It's bad enough to wake you up."

"They'll go away."

"If they keep waking you up like this we'll have to go and see someone. There are people who do this for a living. They unravel dreams, especially bad ones. It's not a big deal to see a psychologist. I'll go with you."

"I'm fine."

Gradually, you can feel her begin to relax.

But these middle-of-the-night interruptions are starting to wear you down. For two months now, Marie's bad dreams have been increasing. Rarely does she go three nights in a row without waking up in a terrified sweat. Some nights, she is close to hyperventilating. It takes two and sometimes three hours to get her back to sleep. And then your own sleep is fitful and worried. But this is what parents do; they have restless nights of worry. Perhaps this almost constant state of exhaustion is part of the package. Marie needs you to be there. She needs you to be solid and together and grounded, and so you are. You just are.

When she is sleeping soundly, you slip from the couch and cover her up. You stoke the fire with three more good-sized hunks of wood and pull the glass door across. You stand there and watch her sleep. Just for a minute or two. You wish with all your heart that there will be happy dreams in her, or no dreams at all.

Tonight, you make a mug of instant coffee, pull your parka and boots on and step outside into a cold mountain night. The stars are arrogantly luminous, as if they know how brilliant they are compared to anything you could offer. But this is not a competition. You offer your awe, and an overwhelming feeling of humility, smallness and insignificance. And perhaps for the stars, this is enough.

Ah, but you know this sky. The stars were like this the night you arrived at Cadomin. How long ago was that? It was the one time your father drove you up there. You were just a kid and his hair was still black.

The stars were like this when you were at the coast, in Sooke, on Vancouver Island, for the first time with Moira, before the girls were born.

Were the stars like this on the night Moira left? Isn't that interesting — the word *left* as a euphemism for *died*. She *left* life. She *left* her family. She *left* work.

⌐⌐

YOU SHOULD CONSIDER THE IDEA that you'll never know for sure, start to accept this option. The reason Moira was so unhappy doesn't matter. Why she drove into that tree doesn't matter. Accept the mystery and move on; it could have been an accident. It was pure chance that she was at that level of depression, that she had the opportunity, that you were not there, that the girls would not be in danger by her leaving. Perhaps the moon was in transition. Maybe she was pre-menopausal. Or a goddamned butterfly in Taiwan flapped its little wings and caused a chain of chaotic events that eventually lead to Moira's *accident*. The one thing you know for sure is that Moira's dead. You have to deal with what you know.

FOUR YEARS AGO, you had a job offer that would have put you in the Burgess Shale. It was a dream job for you and you turned it down because Moira was making great money and your father was starting to lose it, and you didn't want to uproot the girls. It would have meant moving to B.C., or at least Banff, or Canmore. Field would have been the likely destination, as it's the starting point to get to the Shale.

It could have been the opportunity to poke around in a Cambrian fossil bed that was basically a snapshot of what life was like over 500 million years ago. That opportunity excited you more than you were willing to admit. There was a massive explosion of life around this time and the Shale contains the fossilized remains of creatures found nowhere else on the planet.

"About 500 million years ago, most land on the planet was barren. Life was basically all in the oceans. The land had all sorts of things happening to it. Erosions and massive mudslides were common. Sediment would roll into the sea and bury creatures. That's a good thing. That's how fossils are able to tell a story about life back then."

You point up toward the Burgess Shale and Marie follows your finger.

"A guy named Walcott found these 500 million-year-old fossils up there. For a long time scientists defined all these fossils into groups they already knew, but eventually somebody took a closer look and realized that there are creatures up there like nothing alive today. There's a fossil of a creature with five eyes and a snout like an elephant. Can you imagine?"

"That's great, Dad, but I just wanted to know why they called it Burgess Shale."

"Oh, I think it was named after Burgess Pass but I'll find out for sure. And Burgess Pass was probably named after the guy who first discovered it. Well, the first white guy who saw it. It probably had a perfectly fine Indian name for hundreds of years. We were pretty full of ourselves to come along and start renaming mountains and rivers and passes after ourselves."

"Great. Thanks, Dad."

"I thought the three of us could go up there this fall, but the snow came too fast." Okay, you think, you'd better shut up right now because your daughter thinks this is just a couple of months and the dig won't open again until spring. Deep down, you'd like to be here in the spring. You have to keep operating like it's only a couple months. Let the girls grow to love this place. Give them time.

Marie makes a quick escape into the kitchen and you smile. You just gave a lecture on fossils to an eleven year old. She must think you're a complete geek.

‌⌐

"WHY DON'T YOU AND I TRY to figure out what your dream is about. We're pretty smart people. Maybe we can, you know, make it go away."

Marie has come down the hall to your bedroom and you've turned on the bedside light. It's about half-past three. You sit up. She crawls up on the bed and pulls your arm around her shoulders. You're not quite awake.

You lie there for perhaps two or three minutes in silence. "Is this dream about your mom?" you say finally.

"I don't know," she says. "No. I'm in school; I'm always in school. Not the school here. The school back in the city. It's really bright at first, like the lights are on high or something. It always starts the same. And then the lights go off, one by one. I can't move. Sometimes there are faces. I just stand there until it's really dark. I can't move, and there's something there in the hallway with me. Something big. I can't see anything. I can feel it breathing and then I see hands reaching for me ..." She stops and takes a big breath, deals with a shudder that you see twitching in her shoulders. "... and then I wake up."

You pull the quilt up under her chin, tuck it in around her shoulders.

"Is it always the same?'

"Not always."

You hold your daughter until it is after four in the morning. You listen for her breathing to become long and smooth. You listen for a train at the station in the valley bottom, or one coming in from the spiral tunnels. Eventually, you feel her relax.

When you're sure she's asleep you carry her back to her own room. She rolls to her side immediately. You say a silent prayer to whatever force is out there — that she have a peaceful sleep, that this thing not haunt her anymore, that this is the last time.

Then you hesitate. You look at her — this miracle in your life. You have always loved this moment — the hesitation before leaving — the pause to gaze upon a daughter, to know that you have done your job — she is warm, and safe, and loved. You know she is suffering with these nightmares. But right now — right now, at this exact moment — she is safe and loved and nested in sleep. This is the easiest time to love them — when they're asleep. Not that it's difficult to love them ever, but in sleep there are no masks. No barriers. There's just the honest, beautiful and innocent face of sleep.

IN 1886, OTTO J. KLOTZ — a Dominion topographical surveyor — named the Shale after Alexander M. Burgess, who was Deputy Minister of the Department of the Interior in the late 1800s. So the pass, the mountain, and eventually the shale were named after some bureaucrat who likely never even saw a mountain in his life.

Paris and the Burgess Shale are both made up of layers of history. You're into the whisky and water pretty heavily one night when you make that absolutely genius observation. The layers of Paris-the-city reach back over two thousand years into the history of mankind. The layers of Burgess, 500 million years into the Cambrian period, into the history of the planet.

⌒

ON YOUR WAY TO GOLDEN, you have a sudden realization of where you are in your life. You do the math, add up your years and your daughters' years, and you know instantly and all too clearly the age you will be when they are thirty, and forty. Perhaps you will not be there beyond that. It becomes incredibly simple and crisp in your mind. It rips your heart out to think of it. You can't see them as adults. Not yet. You start to panic. But you're driving and this is a tricky road. You look at the narrow mountain sky. A hazy wisp of cloud cowers in a flawless, cold blue. The insides of the windows need cleaning. Moira used to smoke in the car — the only place she could do it with impunity. She didn't smoke much really, only when she was stressed, or angry.

You wish you could go home and shake Moira, insist she tell you what the hell is wrong, that she speak the horror haunting her subconscious. You'd like to get married all over again and begin to forgive. Forgiveness is what marriage is to you — a hundred thousand forgivenesses starting with yourself — and it's an every-day occurrence you'd gladly face. But Moira's not at home. You want to hug the girls, kiss them, hold them. Have Sarah curl up beside you to watch a hockey game. Go for a walk with Marie in the cool, dusky air along the river. Be quiet with her in one of her extended silences.

You push the gas pedal and speed the car into a curve — enjoying the sense of power and the feeling of coming out of the curve.

In town, you want to smile at that woman in the car next to yours stopped at the red light. She is smoking and talking on her cell phone. Her hair is pulled back through the slot in the back of a black baseball cap. You love it when women do that with their hair. She looks angry, or hurt, on the edge of some emotion and about to teeter into whatever it is that's waiting down at the bottom. She glances your way and you smile at her — you attempt a smile, something resembling kindness — but you're not sure how it comes out. She pulls back a bit, stops talking. The light turns green and you are quick off the mark into the traffic. You roll down the window and take what's there, exhaust mixed with the fresh air and the wind at the edge of your hair.

II

CHRISTMAS ALWAYS COMES

I<small>T'S MID-DECEMBER WHEN CARL KNOCKS</small> on the door and announces that he and his brother have reclaimed the floor of a school gymnasium in Golden. You bring them into the kitchen and offer coffee. Tom pours five heaping tablespoons of sugar into his mug. Both you and Carl watch in a stunned silence. Tom doesn't miss a beat, he doesn't notice you're watching him. He goes for a sixth spoonful of sugar.

"Any minute now, he's going to have a diabetic fit," you say.

"We'll have to drive like demons to the hospital in Golden."

"It's sad really. He's so young and probably quite healthy."

"What the hell are you guys talkin' about?" Tom says.

"Your habit of having a little coffee with your sugar," Carl says.

"'s just a little sugar," he says, unfazed. "My mom drinks hers the same way and she's eighty-six. Healthy as a horse."

"They were ripping it down," Carl says, turning back to you. "They let us go in first. We got the entire floor. Thought maybe you'd like some of it for your house. It's thick flooring. Bloody beautiful, actually."

"Well, it's not exactly my house, not officially, so I don't know about ripping up a floor."

"Oh, me and Tom would do all the work, for cheap."

"Which room did you have in mind?" You're thinking you could always re-carpet the room if it's a disaster.

"Maybe your dining room first. You don't have anything in it right now anyway. We could do the windows at the same time."

"The windows? What's wrong with the windows?"

"We'll make them bigger. Make them touch the floor. Better view that way."

It takes Carl and Tom five days to rip up the carpet, replace it with the thick hardwood flooring, sand it down, and resurface the wood. There are still remnants of gymnasium markings, fragments of red curved lines and yellow court borders, which, in your mind, make the room incredibly quirky and interesting. They also dropped the existing windows down to the floor. The brothers are extremely hard workers and they don't mind that you want to help. There's an assumed skill level in small towns that does not exist in cities.

After your house, they move through the town, and build four more rooms with their recycled flooring.

You love the flooring and the room instantly. You decide to leave it empty. It is fairly large and acts as a buffer between the kitchen area and the living room. You bring up a four-panel screen from the basement and place it at the edge of the living room to make a more distinct area.

The room becomes a cherished empty space. The simplicity of it appeals to you. The windows overlook the rising backyard, the snow and rock and pines, and then almost straight up.

The girls think you're weird. They keep encouraging you to put something in the room but you are quite in love with the hollow space. You'll sometimes take in a pillow, if you're going to sit for a while. Occasionally, you'll bring in candles. In the spring, you plan to bring in three or four fair-sized rocks and make a little Japanese rock garden, something that can be rearranged every now and then, when you feel like it. You could practise three-stone placements each morning. And each placement would suit your mood. Who needs therapy, when you've got your chopping wood and can move rocks around in your living room?

THE MORE YOU LOOK INTO the Burgess Shale, the more you realize it's about philosophy and religion, and not as much science as you'd first thought. Chaos theory, the theory of evolution and a dance with the idea of chance are woven together in the same thread of half-understanding. There's no doubt that creatures evolve but to think that humankind was destined to run things, to be the superior and dominant species is ridiculous. The only reason we're here is because of chance. We got lucky. Those five-eyed, snout-nosed creatures fossilized up there in the Shale were unlucky. It's not that they weren't entirely able to adapt and evolve. They were unlucky. Being the best and most adaptive species has nothing to do with survival. Entire species of brilliant creatures are wiped out because of dumb luck, because of chance. There is no survival of the fittest. Thousands of brilliantly adaptive species have vanished from the planet.

AFTER YOU PUT THE GIRLS TO BED, you walk around the house and turn off lights, lock doors and put the house to bed. There's a moth at the back entrance, desperate to get to the light bulb. It flutters around the light, exhausted and desperate, and you remember Elsie at Mountain Park. She called you her knight in shining armour. All the ramifications of honour and high-minded love, and chivalry. Perhaps you're an ill-made knight. Ill-made, wounded and stupid.

You pour yourself a small whisky and think about what is honourable about you. While your wife was out on the coast ramping up to a suicide, you were secretly in Paris making love to another woman. Is that the reality you've decided to go with? Of course it is — you and Claire were lovers. Nothing high-minded or honourable about that. Not that you'd planned to find Claire. But you left yourself open to adventure. Moira had been retreating for years. It wasn't just in Sooke. She'd been on a collision course with whatever was hidden in those locked-door rooms in the back of her mind.

~~~

YOU'VE ALWAYS BELIEVED MEMORY is an unreliable traveller. It has an untrustworthy half-life — a degradation of certainty that grows with each passing moment. Each lost fragment is replaced by something inaccurately designed by you.

You used to play a game with Moira. You would take an experience — one you'd been through together. Nothing extraordinary, just uncommon. Most importantly, it would have to be worthy of a story. A tale that deserved repetition. Like that time when you were stopped in Golden, on the way to Vancouver, because there were avalanches on the Trans-Canada. It was before you had daughters, when it was easy to travel on whimsical impulses. The cars and trucks were piled up in this small town all afternoon and evening. Nature and a pure white gravity said stop and you found yourselves in a bar playing Keno, trying not to drink too much in case word came that the avalanches had been cleared. The snow continued to come down, adding to the drama.

You and Moira would watch each other; listen with clever ears as you took your turn in the retelling. After, in the car on the way home from an unexpected meeting of friends at the Bistro, you would have an augmentation critique. Where did she exaggerate? What parts did you underplay so as to make some other detail stand out? How did she lie? Was the truth still there?

And now, the Golden story is so blurred by your telling and retelling, and your purposed distortions, that you've no idea what the facts are. You recall a deep feeling of disappointment and strange sadness when the RCMP reopened the highway just after midnight. You and Moira were both sad; you were moving on, putting Golden in your rearview mirror. Those strangers who taught you the rules of Keno and were thrilled when you won twenty dollars would now become the past. In the car, you realize you don't have to leave. You can stay, go to the Legion with those new friends and spend the night in Mary's Motel — a clean and reasonable suggestion from a guy named Gus who has no front teeth and is sitting at the next table. The snow is still falling as you turn the engine over. You flick the wipers on. They don't exactly clear the windows of the slushy snow with the efficiency of new blades but you've driven with worse. The Husky station has fresh coffee. Many hundreds, if not thousands, like you will drive Roger's Pass in the dark, in a snowstorm, because you all think you're going somewhere important.

CHRISTMAS COMES. Christmas always comes. You talk to the girls about how it's going to be different this year. You talk about staying until spring, about not breaking up the school year, and they are surprisingly *not* upset. They've settled in. They e-mail old friends in the city and Grandma has been to visit twice already.

Sarah wants stories about when she was young. She wants them embedded into her consciousness emphatically, so that when she is older she will not be able to tell if they are from her own memory or just remembered. Marie is removed, lurks in the shadows during these sessions, half-listening, perhaps feigning interest in something else.

You begin gently to refer to Moira in the past tense. "Your mom was a great storyteller," you say. "She used to make up amazing stories on the spot, and you'd be captivated. Then at the end you'd realize she was trying to tell you something. When you figured it out, it was like you already knew, and that you always knew." You begin to tell one of Moira's stories. This one involved a grey horse named Bert, a cat, and two little girls who were lost in the forest but weren't afraid.

It makes you happy to tell the story as you remember it because Moira appeared to be happy when she'd told it. You can see the wheels turning in Sarah's brain, recording everything — every nuance of every detail.

When you finish, snow is falling past the window as if it's in a hurry to reach the ground and gravity is more intense in front of that particular window. Christmas is only three weeks away. You want to suggest that you and the girls make each other little gifts of twigs and pinecones or homemade cards, rocks, it doesn't matter.

"It'll be hard to have Christmas without your mother," you say, "but we have each other and we'll hang on tight and weather whatever storms come. We have to press on. And Grandma is coming for a week or so. Grandma is always fun to have around."

"I don't want Christmas," Marie says. "And I don't want Grandma. I wish Christmas would just go away. I don't care. To hell with Christmas."

"Look, we don't have to do anything."

"Let's never celebrate Christmas again. Let's just get rid of it."

"That's not what your mom would have wanted. I know she would have wanted us to keep celebrating Christmas. Your mom loved Christmas. Don't you remember ..."

"She's not here. She doesn't have a say. She's gone. She left us. She chose to leave." Marie has tiny rivulets of tears across her cheeks. She turns and flees down the hallway to her bedroom. You wish you could take her out back and get her chopping wood. Her anger is identical to your own. You've now chopped all your own wood, and that of three of your neighbours. Marie will find her own way of dealing with this.

"That went well," Sarah says.

"Wit is just educated insolence, Miss Smarty-Pants."

"I've heard that before," she says.

"Your mother used to say it all the time. It's Aristotle, I think."

"Dad, I know you like to think I'm really smart but I don't know who that is."

"You are really smart and there's no reason you can't know who that is. He was one of Plato's students. He liked to walk around when he taught his own students — so he lectured and his students trundled along behind him. Plato was one of Socrates' followers. And Socrates was a philosopher, a rabble-rousing Greek philosopher." You stop talking. You forgot that Socrates wouldn't recant and was forced to drink poison. You don't have to go on. You were just playing with her anyway. Keep it light.

A memory rises up in you, of Sarah when she was two. You'd wake her up in the morning and she'd be out of bed so quickly, following you and Moira around like a miniature drunkard, her legs all wobbly with sleep. You remember loving her very much inside those mornings. You remember going to work feeling blessed to have rubbed against such a small, concentrated bundle of innocence.

Sarah looks up at you. Such horrible pain held in the furrow between her eyes that you want to cry. To hold and comfort her even before she opens her mouth. If Moira walked into the room now, you'd likely try and kill her for the pain she's caused your daughters.

"Your mother was just really sad. It was nothing you guys did; it wasn't about you, it was ... she was ... she was depressed." You've had this discussion with Sarah before. You're speaking these words as a comfort to yourself too. As a salve for your doubts. Sarah stands up and melts into your arms.

"I know," she says. "But I don't understand."

You run your idea of making little presents for each other past Sarah and she smiles. Sarah is very much like Moira in that way. Whatever she's feeling has a tendency to stay locked inside. There's a deep and brooding pool of emotion in there somewhere, which she doesn't often share.

"I miss her," Marie says. She's lying on her stomach in the middle of her bed.

"I miss her too, Mare."

"Don't call me that. She called me that. You can't call me that."

"I'm sorry, sweetie. I won't do it again."

You are both silent for a while. You can't be her mother. You have to focus on being Dad. Finally, you take a big breath. "I miss her like crazy, but sometimes I'm very angry with her for what she did. And you know it's okay to be angry. It doesn't mean you love her any less. You're just angry."

"Why did she do it, Daddy?"

You know she's not breaking your heart on purpose but it is breaking and you don't know how much more breaking it can take.

You remember Moira asleep beside you and hearing Marie start to cry. You hesitate. To leave her enough time to figure out where she is and that she's all right, on her own. But you hear her crying start to escalate, so you swing your legs over the edge of the bed and reach for your robe. When you get to the end of the hallway, Marie is in your office in the semi-darkness, looking at your computer and repeating with increasing alarm: "Where Daddy go? Where Daddy go?" You pick her up and hold her tight against your chest. "I'm right here," you say. And she pats your back with her hand like she's making sure you're real. It's very likely she wasn't even awake.

Marie was two years old. This was probably your first heartache involving your daughters.

You wish to hell you could pick her up now and bring her that same comfort. Even asleep, she must have felt safe. How does she feel safe now, when a parent has made a choice to leave, forever?

"Because she was sad."

"Was she sad because of us?"

"No. You girls were the joy of her life. You were the best part of her life. She loved you very much. It was something else."

~

SUZANNE LIVES NEXT DOOR. Her husband works for the railway and is out of town a lot. She has two kids about the same age as your girls. Suzanne wears flowered housedresses and walks in her bare feet. You cannot remember ever seeing her wearing shoes in the summer months. She's blonde and tall and blue-eyed, but plain. She has a freshly scrubbed look. Suzanne and her husband have a suite under the house that they rent out — a sort of bed and break-fast, without the breakfast. Half the places in town rent out suites similar to this one. They call theirs the Goldtrîpfchen. You assume this is a reference to the wine. It sounds alpine. It's a good name for a suite in Field.

"I notice you've got some wood to chop," you say one morning on your way to the Troubled Pig. She's in her yard shaking a rug.

"You looking for some wood to chop?"

"Just so happens."

"I'm Suzanne," she says. "Come for coffee tomorrow morning, we'll see if we can't work a deal."

"I'm ..."

"You're a Samurai without a master."

"You know what Ronin means. I'm impressed."

"It's a good name," she says smiling. "My kids know your girls."

"My dad loved *The Seven Samurai*. My name is the collateral damage from his love of that movie."

"See you tomorrow."

The next morning you work out an arrangement — Suzanne will take the girls when you need a sitter, and you'll chop wood for her.

～

Are you absolutely certain it was a suicide? All you have is circum-stantial evidence, which a major insurance company dismissed. Maybe if you knew the name of the goddamned tree, things would become crystal clear. You should fly out there and find the tree for yourself. And then? Actually finding out concerns you also. What if there is no resolution? Do you need to wallow for a while longer? Doubt, self-pity and uncertainty have become good steady and reliable companions. Are you afraid of letting go?

～

YOU ARE SURPRISED TO GET A LETTER from Maurice. He doesn't seem the writing type. His script is thin and slopes hard to the right — it's almost lying down. He wishes you and the girls a happy Christmas, and assures you he is not running around like an idiot buying things out of a sense of obligated desperation. It seems, he writes, that this is the way of Christmas for a great many.

It is late as I write this. I am taking my third glass of merlot, slightly cool, the same way you like it. I feel I must tell you where my life went off the rails. I was young, perhaps twenty years old, maybe twenty-two. I was with the Yodeler. It was a most amazing experience to sleep with her. A full-figured German woman, comfortable in her own skin. A sort of dictator lover — both demanding and yield-ing, and ultimately unrelenting.

I wanted to go into business. The Yodeler convinced me that I ought to be an artist. Business is for stiffs, she said. Nobody cares about business in the long run. Business is a grander and more stupid illusion than anything on the planet. But the arts! Art has the power to last. Music and dance, and painting, and literature ... these things give meaning to life!

So I began to study the tuba. Why the tuba? Well, when I was a child, in Grade 7, there was a girl, Bernice ... she played the tuba, and as I watched her press her lips to the mouthpiece, I truly and deeply wanted to be the tuba. I do not recall what she looked like. But her lips!!! I can still see those perfectly formed, wonderfully full lips, and the way she licked them before placing them so gently against the tuba's mouthpiece!

But the Yodeler had something quite different in mind for me. The tuba is not romantic, she said. There is no beauty in a tuba. There is nothing enduring. You should play the violin, or the cello, or you should be a painter, she said. This was not a suggestion.

I listened to the Yodeler. I started cello lessons and also began to dabble with paints. I wasted a great deal of time and money trying to play the cello and I really have no talent as a painter. Oh, I sold a few paintings. In fact, I sold enough to feed the delusion that I might be talented. And the cello is only a woman in disguise and I prefer my women to have hearts that beat and skin that is warm to the touch.

I have a keen mind for business but I did not pursue this course with all my heart. And this is where my life went off the rails. The Yodeler and I eventually broke up because we were always fighting about money.

All the best to you and those lovely girls of yours. Merry Christmas.

Sincerely
Maurice

P.S. Since I am now on my fourth glass of wine, I will share with you that I still dabble with painting but nobody sees my stuff — not even my wife — and, I have recently begun tuba lessons. My wife, the Artist, and I have a son who turns 13 this year.

P.S. again. Her name is Febe, the Artist, I mean. My wife's name is Febe.

Remember, my friend, if you can't say "no," then "yes" is completely meaningless.

꙳

A FEW MONTHS LATER, in a phone conversation with Sylvie, you will find out that Maurice owns a 49 per cent share of the Demitasse. He has a one-third share in a very popular bistro called The Bohemian and a partnership in an apartment building in Calgary. He owns several condominiums; two in Whistler, another in Edmonton, one in Vancouver, and one in Victoria. There might be a few more, she thinks. And, even though he drives a twenty-year-old wreck of a Volvo to work, Sylvie assures you that he has a Jaguar sitting in his garage at home.

Judging books by covers.

꙳

ON CHRISTMAS EVE, you and the girls gather in the town's small church with the majority of the locals. An even, ecumenical service that covers the basics is offered. Shepherds abiding in their fields, keeping a watch over their flocks, and then an angel appears and they are sore afraid. It's a good story. The church is a simple structure, like a thousand other small-town churches — white exterior, wooden floors and just a few rows of pews. There are several clusters of candles near the front.

Yesterday, at the Troubled Pig, you heard a couple of women talking about the optics of having too many candles — they didn't want it to seem too Catholic, or Anglican — but a few were all right.

There is no chance of it starting to snow just as you come out of the church, like a Hollywood movie, because it's been snowing steadily for two days — it was coming down as you walked to church and it'll still be falling when you come out. "If there are old people who need to sit down, I want you to give them your seats," you say to the girls as you come up the front step. "Oh, Dad," Marie says. "We know that." You stomp your feet in the entrance-way, and hang your coats on hooks. You let the girls sit and then stand at the back of the church with the other men, muttering Merry Christmas to everyone who catches your eye. Inside, someone has hooked up an old Hammond organ, a beautiful instrument. It makes you smile to hear "O Come All Ye Faithful" in the organ's rich, throaty Hammond tones. It's a funky sound, filled with soul, more like a jazz session than a church service, and entirely appropriate.

Inside this church is the only place you allow yourself to think about Claire. It's the irrational deal you made with yourself and with God. You need to feel healed before you'll allow thoughts of Claire outside this church. You have been inside the church three times since you arrived in Field. This is the first time you've not been alone.

You think about Paris at Christmas, with the thousands upon thousands of lights along the Champs êlysée, and the animated windows at Printemps, with the little ramps for children. You were in Paris for Christmas only once. You can see Claire standing on the balcony looking at a Paris grey sky strewn with snowflakes. Her arms are crossed in front because it's cold. Maybe she likes grey skies. Maybe she's just come out for some air. You'd like to think she's doing something unconventional, like smoking a big Cuban cigar in the bathtub. You'd like to think of Claire as your *outré* saviour. A woman who wouldn't think twice about bringing home a stranded cat, a lost dog, or a wounded man. But she might demand that you repay her at some point by being kind when it is not required. Claire is the most decent person you know. You do not let yourself drift into hope. She said she would call in a year, but you will certainly not hold her to that promise. A lot can happen with a beautiful woman in Paris over a year. You are remembering Claire fondly and wishing her happiness. You do not dwell on the lovemaking. What good would that do? You'd start to have desire and you're not ready for desire. Your last day with her is clouded anyway. There are blanks where you've no idea what you were doing. You focus on Claire's kindness. You actively push hope aside.

Sarah looks over her shoulder, an innocent happiness filling her face. She searches the men quickly, and when she finds you, there is Moira's smile. The minister — you're not really sure what he is — has just announced they're going to sing "Joy to the World," Sarah's favourite. You smile back at her and nod your head. She really likes the "and heav'n and nature sing" part for some reason. *I know*, you mouth, and then smile at her.

Of course, Claire cannot be your saviour. She can pluck you from the streets of Paris and care for you, but she cannot save you. Funny that you're thinking about saviours on Christmas Eve. Well, Jesus isn't going to do it either. You're pretty well on your own here.

"Joy to the World" was Moira's favourite. Sarah's making that connection. She's conversing with her mother inside this lovely Christmas carol. And so are you, now.

~

YOU CAN FEEL YOURSELF SCRATCHING at the icy edge of a crevasse with your fingernails, trying not to fall — perhaps a slow releasing of fingers and then falling into this morass of darkness. You're aware of it. You drink and brood at night, and in the day, you brood and drink. You chop wood. It's amazing you still have your digits, fingers and toes, hands, feet. Every morning you chop wood. It has become your routine. It is your measured way of dealing with the inner darkness. You struggle to locate just a glimmer of lightness, something hopeful hidden under all this sorrow. You're in a holding pattern, circling around and around in storm clouds, waiting to land. But your sorrow seems inexhaustible.

It's perfectly reasonable to combine grief with guilt; Moira's death and your Paris infidelity. What about Moira's infidelity? She left without saying goodbye. She left a morass of confusion and twisted speculation. She was in trouble out there on the coast. But forgiving her is easy.

Your guilt and your grief become great friends. It is not something you do on purpose but, rather, the two get tied together when you are not looking. They elope in the night and come home as a unit. You wake up one morning prepared to chop wood and there beside the axe is something new. You can barely pick the axe up.

Inanition, you find out by opening your e-mail for the first time in three weeks, is the condition or quality of being empty. Or exhaustion, as from the lack of nourishment. Or the lack of vitality or spirit. Your word of the day is *inanition*. There are a few dozen more words in your in-box but for now you ignore them and any other e-mails. It is a luxury to be able to choose not to look.

The calluses grow thick on your hands. You become very accomplished at chopping wood. You remember being at the Icefields campground with Moira. People from all over the world were staying in the camp. It was after dinner and there were a couple of guys from London, England, who were stunned when Moira picked up the axe and chopped her way through three chunks of wood with her usual expertness. She stacked them and built up the fire in the cast-iron stove. Their mouths fell open. They couldn't believe what they'd just seen. They admitted they would not know where to begin if they had to chop wood. You liked them instantly for their vulnerable honesty. You and Moira wound up drinking and talking with them in front of the fire until three in the morning.

12

CONVERGENCE

GEORGIA GETS INTO HER CAR, armed with a beautiful, magnanimous lie. She turns the key in the ignition and firms up her resolve. She's about to drive across an entire province — first by ocean, on the ferry, and then through a lot of mountains — to perform an act of kindness on the border between British Columbia and Alberta.

To Georgia, Ronin is only a voice on the phone, listening as she says she was a friend of his wife's. He remains a mysterious man whose image she pieces together from his voice and fragments of description from his wife and daughters. Ronin's mother had arrived in Sooke within hours of hearing of Moira's death, and while he was waiting to get out of Paris, Georgia was retreating. She had completely pulled away when Ronin arrived — she was working a charter boat while he was picking up the pieces of his life. But now, Georgia Engelhard Cronin has decided to come to him.

She becomes resolved to her journey when her car jerks to a stop inside the bowels of the ferry. This is her private point of no return. She stands at the rail, the ocean breeze playing in her hair, listening to a jazz band from Victoria practising on the deck. They're playing "Bye Bye Blackbird" in a loose, Miles Davis kind of way. There's a thread of recognizable melody, translated through new voices, new pains, and new joys.

Her hair flops in the wind, is scattered across her face in thick clumps, not strands. She's wearing impermeable black boots, not exactly fashionable but not ugly. Well-worn khaki trousers reach down overtop her boots. A straw-coloured wool sweater, an old friend, completes her look. She's got a down jacket and some rain gear in the trunk. She's not so stupid as to assume that it's warm in the mountains when it's warm by the ocean. She knows it's still cold up there, even though it's April.

Georgia talked to Ronin's mother a week ago. She knows he's in Field. She knows that Field is small and that she will simply ask after him when she gets there. She does not yet know how she will deliver her lie. She needs the drive, and the time, to come up with the words, time to come up with a believable delivery. It will be an awkward meeting, regardless of how much she figures out.

THE DRIVE ACROSS BRITISH COLUMBIA can be arduous, depending on what time of year it is. Spring isn't so bad. But Georgia's journey is attacked by a ferocious storm that blows in from the Pacific and stops air travel up and down the west coast. Airports are closed. Ferry services stopped. The rain falls with a hatred and wind literally blows Georgia's car eastward. It gets behind her and pushes her toward Field.

When she pulls into a gas station in Hope, Georgia has already passed the spot where her life intersected with the life-just-ending of the other driver. She had a violent twinge near that spot — an involuntary body memory. She desperately wants a cigarette and she hasn't smoked for nine years. The odd cigar doesn't count. *Life goes on*, she chants — *life goes on, life goes on, life goes on.*

When Georgia pulls out of the gas station, she has decided she won't be able to stay long in Field. She had become quite connected to the girls in the few weeks she knew them. To come back into their lives now, and then move away, would be cruelly disruptive. A visit would be all right — to let them know she cares and that she is still in their lives. Not that Georgia believes for a second that she will be welcome to stay for a longer period of time. She's just thinking about possibilities.

Hope is a nice name for a town, she thinks. Apart from the fact that she almost died here, and that her dog did, it would probably be all right to live here. She'd like to live in a place called Hope, or Love, or Peace, or Charity, or Faith for that matter.

From Hope, she drives north along the Coquihalla Highway to Merritt. Georgia turns off the main highway and heads east from Merritt. No straight lines for her. Besides, if she does it this way, she'll get to be on lake ferries from Needles to Fauquier, and from Galena Bay to Shelter Bay. She'll get a ride across Arrow Lake, twice.

Is she the type of person to stop and go to Nakusp Hot Springs by herself? Maybe she'll need a hot soak by then. If she gets there at night, when it's cool, the thought of a dip in the hot springs might be too tempting to ignore. She'll take a book with her. She's one of those women who come into the hot springs and read. They line their narrow backs up against the pool's edge and, with steam swirling and dancing all around, they read. There are too many guys out there who would take a woman alone in the hot springs as an invitation to the dance.

AS SHE CRUISES ALONG the highway, slowly rising toward the mountains, she remembers driving this highway in the heat of summer. Orchards. Vineyards. The fresh-fruit stands along the road. Georgia had felt guilty about tossing her nectarine pits out the window. She'd waited until there was nobody behind and no traffic coming before rolling down her window and throwing the pits into the ditch. In the middle of summer, in the Okanagan, this is not an easy thing.

IN THE INTERIOR, the sun is blistering as the storm continues to abuse the coast. On the Galena Bay to Shelter Bay ferry, a short, beer-bellied man, apparently travelling alone in a motor home, tries to strike up a conversation with her. Maybe it's because Georgia comes alive when she is on, or near, water that people are drawn to her. His name is Gus but Georgia is not interested in talking; she never finds out his name. He looks nice enough but he won't get any conversation out of her today.

Georgia leans over the railing, watches the ferry's wake. She has decided that she has to tell Ronin everything. Not just the lie. She's got to say the truth about sleeping with Moira and caring about her, and loving her.

GEORGIA GETS A ROOM at the only hotel in Field, which is across the street from the Troubled Pig. She's too tired to fight with Carl. She knows he's hiding Ronin, and from her brief conversation, she knows Carl is no Rhodes scholar. Eventually, she'll find Ronin and the girls. How hard can it be in a town of only a couple hundred? For now, she just wants sleep and to be still. The hotel sits on an outcrop overlooking a broad flood plain, stretching below and toward the west. The hotel's front doors face east. Tomorrow she'll find Ronin and deliver her lie. After that, she doesn't know.

She drops her clothes in a trail on her way to the bathroom, where she pours a very hot bath. With the lights out, and the door slightly ajar, she slips into the water. The Troubled Pig is also the town's liquor store. She had picked up a couple bottles of wine. The Piesporter's not exactly warm, but it's also nowhere near cold. The sweetness would be better icy cold but this will do. She drinks from the bottle and it goes down quickly.

She thinks about her journey, her mission to lie to Ronin. She begins to doubt. After her bath, she opens a window and falls into the bed without pulling the plug. She is asleep almost instantly.

"Look," she says, "I got close to your wife and I know why she drove into that tree. I know what she was struggling with. I know her demons."

The deer looks at her from across the stream with its big sad eyes and then drops its head to drink. Sunlight streams through the high branches like a light cutting into a dark church.

"It's an abortion that's haunting her." The deer stops drinking and looks up at her. "No, no, it was before you. It's what caused her pain every time she saw her kids. She stopped a child, and then she had a couple of children. She couldn't resolve that contradiction, the disaster of timing. The first aborted child haunted her. That's what drove her into that tree."

The deer stares at her, cocks its head slightly and begins to pull at the grass along the edge of the water. A shot cracks through the silence. The deer leaps up but lands in a crumpled mess of legs askew, and wrong angles, and blood, and she knows instantly the deer is dead.

GEORGIA TAKES A DEEP BREATH and sits up in bed. She scans the bedside tables for the remote. She fumbles for her glasses. She does not want to go back to that dream. Although she believes TV is a wasteland, it's better than dreaming about dead deer and ruined conversations. She wants a drink. Remembers there is more wine in the car.

A train is snaked into the valley bottom, waiting for something. The low droning hum and occasional squeaks, and bumps, and the hissing sound are a white-noise comfort. Barefoot and thirsty, Georgia tiptoes to her car in just an overcoat that barely covers her butt. She couldn't care less who sees her. She pops the trunk, finds the bottle and then looks up. A half moon is rising over Mt. Stephen, although she doesn't know it's called Mt. Stephen. The moon throws its murky light over the town. Georgia sees no one, neither coming nor going.

Back in the room, she drinks the sturdy Mâcon-Villages straight from the bottle. It's good and cold. Mountain nights are great refrigerators, she thinks. As she flips through the channels of infomercials and sports, looking desperately for a narrative of some kind, Georgia reaches over to place her bottle down on the bedside table and almost slides it off the telephone. She looks down at the phone and starts to giggle. She picks up the receiver, dials a line-out, and calls Information. They give her the number and, after Georgia works the operator over a bit, the address. There's a pen beside the phone but no paper. Georgia asks the operator to repeat the phone number and quickly writes it along the inside of her left arm.

13
MONKS

You look at your father. What's going on in there? You have come back to the city to see him. You do not think you are saying goodbye, but he appears to be barely conscious. He is sallow and still in his bed. It seems he has made the final moves in the chess match only he can understand. The product of those final moves is a quiet withdrawal from all signs of consciousness. Nothing out here seems to be registering on him.

So this is the end? This is where it stops. This is the whimper, you think. You look at his hands, flaccid by his side. Those are your hands.

Stupid to say now all the things you'd like to have said. A lost cause. But you've had a lifelong affinity for lost causes.

You step back and very gently shut the door. You pull up a chair and sit down, place your hand on top of his. Squeeze it a bit. "Look, I know you're not likely going to get this, but you never know," you say. "I know. I know ..." you whisper. You're whispering. Why? That is all that comes out. You sit there like a big dumb bastard.

You'd like to say you're sorry you didn't turn into a great hockey player — that you're sorry for embarrassing him — sorry for not being an NHL player. You want to say you know he loved you — and you're sorry you didn't understand it sooner — that you had doubts about his love but you don't anymore. Because you get it. You finally get it. Things like having a home, and clothing, and food on the table are all signs of love. Just being there in the morning is a sign. Not leaving is a sign of love. All the thousands of small sacrifices are indications of love.

You wanted your father to be someone he wasn't. You wanted the warmth, the understanding and approval. You wanted the words, and instead you got a quiet demonstration. You got weirdness too. You got the anal-retentive control freak on steroids. You got lectures instead of talking. You got harping on and on about the smallest, seemingly insignificant things. You got the yelling because to become vulnerable was unacceptable. In the end, none of that matters. Well, it does matter but it has slowly become inconsequential. He was there day after day, doing things for you. Day after day, working a job he probably didn't like all that much, so his family could have a home, food, clothing, heat, water, education and opportunity.

Today, people say they love each other all the time. There is a lot of saying and, in your mind, not enough doing.

⌒

IS IT TOO LATE TO SAY your recognition of love for your father now? Well, you could say it but the chances of it getting through are probably pretty slim. It would only mean something to you. Once again, you're drawn to the question: What's it like in there when you're lost in the fog of Alzheimer's? Maybe words and ideas get in. Maybe it's just every few words, like you in Paris, trying to decipher

French at a rate of one word understood for every three or four uttered. Maybe basic concepts, repeated often enough, get in, and everything else falls to the ground like leaves in November.

You'll often do checks on yourself to make sure you haven't turned into your father. Not the Alzheimer's. Other things, like you'll sit down and really listen to your daughters. You'll ask leading questions and then let them go, nodding and encouraging along the way. You don't harp or lecture ad nauseam about broken things. You want them to be certain you love them — and that no matter what happens, they won't forget that.

How do your kids know that you love them? You tell them, frequently. But what if you were a painfully quiet man? What if you had some inner turmoil going on and you never spoke your love? What are the signs, other than saying "I love you"?

Why are you checking up on yourself? What was so wrong with your father? You seem to have values. Morals, well, perhaps tarnished morals. A slightly bruised integrity. A sense of honour. You were fed and clothed and encouraged to get an education. You were loved, not just by your mother. You were loved by your father. In his own unique and disagreeable, and difficult way.

Irony is never a pretty thing, especially if you're at the centre of it. You start to figure it out now that your father is well into his retreat from consciousness. As he moves out of reach, you feel that hard stone of anger start to dissolve.

⁓

YOUR FATHER IS NOT AWAKE. Even when he is awake, he is barely awake. You've made the drive to Edmonton to see him, to see your mother, and to begin negotiations on the purchase of the Field house. He's fading. He seems to remember your face, but you can't be sure. You struggle to stay upbeat.

"Dad? Did you see Mom this morning?" He's propped up in bed, wearing a pajama top over a T-shirt. You notice his slippers are on the wrong feet. A TV, high up and across the room, is on but muted.

"What's that?" He's looking right at you.

"Did you see Mom this morning?"

"Well of course I saw her. She's making breakfast. We're having bacon. Bacon and eggs. She'll walk us to school."

You have a choice. You can be stupidly confrontational and insist on your version of reality or you can just go with his.

"The bacon smells terrific," you say. "I love the smell of bacon."

He pauses, inhales deeply, smiles. "She's a great cook. I need to find my math book though. I don't know where. I don't know where I left it. I'm going to get in trouble if I don't have it."

"So you like math? What do you like about math?" You're not sure if he heard you. He turns his head toward the window. Across the road, there are the sounds of children playing, small girls screaming, something squeaking. A merry-go-round?

"Dad?"

Nothing.

"Logan?"

Your mom is resigned. She no longer comes to see him every morning. She still tries to come every day but sometimes she'll miss a couple. He hasn't known her name for months, though she's certain he recognizes her face, and her voice. You can't imagine how hard this is for her — to have someone you love be there, but not there. Last month, he wandered off. He walked the whole day in his slippers, out past the city limits and halfway to Leduc. When they found him, he was dehydrated but determined to keep walking. He kept telling the policemen he had to get home for supper. He was looking for the house in which he was raised — a house that's a few thousand kilometers away in Peterborough, Ontario.

You spend the afternoon fussing around the room. You help feed him, take him to the bathroom and read to him out loud from a copy of *Huckleberry Finn* you'd left the last time you were there. Eventually, he falls asleep and part of you is relieved. You are ashamed by this feeling. It's easier for you when he is asleep. Perhaps inside his sleep, there is peace.

YOU DON'T PLAN ON TELLING the McDavids about the new hard-wood flooring, or the new windows. You'll tell them it's a pretty nice house — but that it's very expensive to heat in the winter. You'll let them know you're more than willing to give them a fair price, if they're willing to sell. You come to the meeting with a pre-approved upper limit. You plan on making an offer about $10,000 lower than this limit.

You sit at the back of the Demitasse, far away from the street. You arrive early and order coffee. Maurice tells you that Sylvie is in Montreal.

"She'll be disappointed that she missed you," he says.

He sits down, looks you in the eye and asks how you've been. You immediately start to talk about your dad. You blather, let down your guard, spill. He nods and listens, and, at the end, he simply says "I'm so sorry."

The two of you are silent for a couple minutes.

"Listen, I'm here to buy a house. I'm going to make an offer on the Field house."

"Good for you. Are they motivated to sell? Or are you motivated to buy?"

"I think they're motivated to sell. That's an interesting question, Maurice. Insightful actually."

"I used to dabble."

"Parks Canada is getting sticky about having to prove your need to live in a national park. The McDavids both work here in Edmonton."

Maurice smiles. He asks you what you think the house is worth. He asks what you're willing to spend. He asks if he might be of assistance in the negotiation.

"I'll just listen at first."

"Sure, why not," you say.

The McDavids are a mid-40s Ken and Barbie. Perfect complexions. Perfect hair. Lovely, white smiles. Their clothing seems brushed, permanently pressed, crisp. You make small talk. You introduce Maurice as an old family friend. You talk about your girls. The McDavids are about to become grandparents for the first time. Mrs. McDavid is teaching yoga. They ask about Carl at the Troubled Pig.

Finally, Mr. McDavid says it straight and simply. They are definitely interested in selling.

Maurice orders a round of cognacs. "The good stuff," he says to the waitress, who has had to take his section as well as her own.

You get up to go to the washroom, and when you get back the McDavids and Maurice are shaking hands. They shake your hand when you arrive at the table.

"Did I miss something?"

"You just bought a house," Maurice says.

"Congratulations," Mrs. McDavid says. "I know you and the girls will be happy there."

You arrange to meet at your lawyer's office the next day and then Ken and Barbie are out the door.

"Well, that was weird," you say. "I'm curious about what I paid for my new house?"

Maurice flips a drink coaster over and with his fountain pen writes a number. He slides the coaster over in front of you. You look down, start to look up but have to look at it again.

"Son of a bitch! This is $20,000 under my first offer. How did you ... What did you ...?" You pause. "This is unbelievable, Maurice."

"I believe they were very motivated. A celebratory drink is in order. It's not every day you buy a house in the mountains."

Your head is spinning. "Yes," you say, "a drink would be good."

Maurice orders a bottle of champagne. The waitress appears to be nervous opening the bottle. She fumbles with the cork — can't seem to rock it out. It could be because this bottle is expensive or because Maurice is her client. Her nervousness makes the uncorking a longer process than it should be. You pretend not to notice. When your flutes are filled, finally, you look over at Maurice. You hold up your flute and nod it towards him.

"Thank you," you say. "I don't know how you did it, but thank you. You are brilliant."

"I used to dabble," Maurice says. "It's nothing."

WHEN SARAH COMES into the house you can tell she's holding something in. She can barely contain herself. Her cheeks are flushed and she doesn't take her jacket off. You're in the gymnasium-floored dining room, sitting near the window, with a cup of coffee and a book. You do not find the bare floor to be uncomfortable. There's a special comfort in the knowledge that you helped build this floor.

"You'll never guess what," Sarah says almost out of breath.

You close your book and place it on the floor. "You're right, I can't begin to guess."

"I have something for you."

"A present? It's not my birthday."

"A sort-of present. A surprise."

"A surprise, huh."

"A big surprise."

"Hmmm."

"Well? Can you guess? It's something I found."

"I have no idea."

"Guess!" You can't remember the last time she was this excited.

"A pine cone? A rock? A fossil — you didn't find a fossil did you?"

"Nope. Better."

"Better than a fossil? Well, I give up."

"Okay, wait here," she says. Then she's out the door. You hear the bang of the door shutting and, in a minute, what sounds like several pairs of shuffling feet.

Sarah's head pokes out around the corner. "Ready?"

"Yup," you say. But you aren't. You are not ready for the five Buddhist monks in saffron robes that come into the room and all bow toward you with their hands in *namaste*.

~

YOU WOULD HAVE GIVEN ANYTHING to have been there and seen the look on Sarah's face when she saw the monks. She had been dropping rocks on jagged remnants of ice along the edge of the river, trying to break off chunks, watching them glide downstream. When she came up onto the bridge deck to come home, there they were, four of the five monks, smiling at her. They'd been watching her. Sarah's quick mind must not have taken long to connect your retold story, about the little girl and the monks carrying the statue of Buddha, to these real, grinning monks.

The monks had been travelling to Vancouver when their van broke down about three kilometres east, and they'd walked into town. They must have been quite a sight, in their saffron robes, marching along the edge of the highway, surrounded by mountains. Transplanted images of Tibet in happier times.

One of the monks speaks very good English, halting and almost poetic. He's tall and skinny, and the robes do not add any weight to his appearance. Sarah decides, that in her mind she will call him "Slim." The fifth monk, who also has a good command of English, is at Field's only garage trying to arrange for the van to be towed and fixed. They're hungry. They want to know if there is a place to eat.

It takes Sarah a while to find her footing on the slippery ground of memory, story, and reality, which have somehow melded together inside a single moment. "Well, there's the Troubled Pig," Sarah says finally. "It has good food." The first monk translates and they all giggle.

"That will be fine," the slim monk says.

Sarah starts to direct them but eventually just walks along beside them as their guide.

By the time they reach the Troubled Pig, Sarah has shared with them your story about the two monks and the statue of the Buddha. "My father used to tell me this story when I was a baby," she says. And she tells them about her mother dying last autumn. Perhaps she says something about how you're very sad and that you drink at night. That you're obsessed with chopping wood. You never find out what it was she said exactly. They do not go into the restaurant. Something convinced these monks to come and see you. One of them goes down to the garage. They sit with the soft sunlight on their faces and wait. They ask questions about the town and about the mountains. They delve no further into Sarah's personal life. When they are all there, they climb through the town to your house, Sarah leading the way.

⌐⌐

HIS NAME IS NGUCHUL LOBZANG. He is Sarah's slim monk and is the spokesperson for the group. "We are on our way to Vancouver, where we will be making a mandala," he says, "but our van is broken. Your daughter was kind enough to invite us for dinner."

You stand up and shake the monk's hand. You look at Sarah. She's beaming. You feel off balance by the arrival of the monks. You aren't certain how to proceed. But you look at your daughter and realize she has invited guests for dinner and that's good enough for you. "Well, I'm not sure what you eat but I was planning on a stir-fry of some kind. Vegetables, rice, maybe some chicken."

"It is our honour to cook for you if you will allow."

"Let me show you where everything is."

"I'll show them Dad," Sarah says. Three of the monks disappear into the kitchen and the remaining two sit with you in the gymnasium. A silence grows around you. Normally you might find this sort of prolonged silence unsettling but it is surprisingly comfortable. Finally, Nguchul clears his throat and says, "A mandala is a sacred sand drawing."

You look at him flatly. Oh, there's no doubt in your mind that a mandala is a sand drawing and that it is sacred, but you are really not interested. You were hoping for a quick meal with the monks and then everything would go back to normal. They would get into their van and trundle off to Vancouver to make their sand thing. Nguchul asks, quite unabashedly, about Moira. He asks what happened and you tell him: "She drove her car into a very large tree, at high speed." *She did it on purpose*, you want to shout. *She killed herself and tried to take a tree with her!*

Both monks close their eyes and bow to you very slightly. "I am sorry," Nguchul says. "I did not know. Your daughter said only her mother had died."

At dinner, Nguchul and Kachen talk about their sand mandalas. When Kachen speaks his eyes become very earnest and intense. He wears antiquated wire-rimmed glasses and is much shorter than Nguchul. In fact, he is the shortest of the five. "All monks at our monastery are required to learn about mandalas as part of their training. Not everyone is good at it. Those who show ability will learn perhaps two patterns in a lifetime."

"Why do you make them?"

"Those who create mandalas are purified of past negative deeds. By looking at a mandala, one can recover from physical sickness and mental problems. It generates compassion in the viewer's heart. Often, the area where a mandala is built will be blessed with prosperity, perhaps freedom from sickness, a timely rainfall, peace."

"Also, it is a demonstration of impermanence," Nguchul says. "The sun rises and the sun sets. Sand is a poor substance to build anything with."

Marie, when she arrives home after school, is hesitant. She's not sure what to make of these sudden, robed, dinner guests. She doesn't say very much and then retreats to her room.

Sarah is in awe. You watch her watching the monks. She's taking it all in — every detail.

The meal is simple but delicious. The monks, you notice, chew a lot and seem to enjoy their food a great deal. Sarah says they added their own spices to the vegetables. The conversation ranges from world peace to the Dalai Lama, Tibet, and China. You ask who Kundun is and are told this is what Tibetans call the Dalai Lama.

"There is no doubt that wars produce victors and losers," Nguchul says. "But only temporarily. Such victory or defeat cannot be long-lasting. Today, the world is small, and interdependent. Kundun says the concept of war has become anachronistic, an outmoded approach. It is past its time. We always talk about reform and changes. There were many old traditions that were ill suited to our present reality — they were counterproductive and shortsighted. These, we have consigned to the dustbin of history. War, too, should be relegated to the same dustbin."

"But we are fighting right now," you say. "We have been fighting for months. The bombs are falling now."

"Canada is not in Iraq," Nguchul says. "Canada is a great peacekeeper."

"A moot point in that we don't really have a fully active army. Our contribution would have been a drop in the ocean."

Nguchul smiles and it is such a beautiful, warm smile that you do not want to talk about war anymore. You feel lucky to be here at the table with these monks and Sarah. You are grateful to her for inviting them. There are seven people. It is a good number.

When the dishes have been washed and dried and put away, out of a purely adventurous heart, you offer to have them stay for as long as it takes to fix their van.

Between sleeping bags, couches and the futon, you find places for all the monks to sleep. You go to bed early and without drinking. Carl has dropped off another load of wood, so you've got a morning of chopping.

ー

IT'S A BIT DISCONCERTING to wake up to five monks sitting in the living room quietly staring off into space. It's not frightening but it is faintly disruptive. It's not forever, right? And right now, you welcome any distractions that happen along.

ー

WHEN YOU GET UP, the monks are meditating in the gymnasium. They're still meditating when the girls head off to school. As they move past the room, Marie rolls her eyes and Sarah's glisten with wonder. You start your chopping ritual. You go out with your coffee and cognac, and begin. You are thinking about sand mandalas this morning. The idea has seeded in your consciousness and in your imagination, and now you're playing with sand and peace and wonder. Fragments of Moira intrude like shards of broken glass. For the most part, you are able to keep her away. You still chop the wood in a fury. You're still a little frantic, but much more efficient than when you began this chopping therapy.

Your axe slices through a knotty hunk of pine you thought was going to give you grief, and a Moira memory slips through your pleasure.

She sits up in bed screaming, "No! No! No!" and you click on your bedside lamp. Breathless and confused, Moira looks around the room as if she doesn't recognize anything. Her panic threatens to explode. Her breathing is raspy, frenetic. You get in front of her, say her name, reassure. "Moira, it's me, you're all right. You're safe. It's all right. You're dreaming."

But she is not all right. Her awful dream has been gnawing at her guts.

"I know," she says. "It's just that it was too awful."

"What? What's too awful?"

She does not answer, and her persistent and private hell darkens her face. The life drains out of her eyes. They sink inwards. She has never answered your questions on the nights when her dreams turn nightmarish. In the morning she will be overly happy. And that forced happiness has started to annoy you.

The next morning, standing at the sink with your coffee, looking through the window into the backyard, you bring it up. "Let me guess," you say, "It was too horrible to talk about."

"Actually, I don't remember. I ... I wish I did. I can't remember anything except that it was horrible and it scared me."

"At some point you'll have to talk about it. It doesn't seem to be going away."

"I know, I know. But I'm not going to a shrink because I have a bad dream every now and then. I'm sorry I woke you up. I'll try not to have bad dreams anymore."

"This is more than a bad dream. Something is going on in there and I'm worried about you."

"I'm fine." She gets up from the table and moves toward the coffee on the counter. "Morning sleepyhead," she says to Sarah, who rushes into the kitchen and sits down at the table, scans the table for orange juice and reaches for it.

"Marie still sleeping?"

"Mmm."

"I'll get her," you say. You don't even look in Moira's direction as you breeze by her and down the hallway.

You've been chopping for forty minutes and the sweat is pouring off your face. Your leather gloves are soaked through and you're breathing heavily. You stop, place the axe head-down and put both hands on the handle, a move you used to see your father perform when he was shovelling snow and needed a break. You look at your work. It's a pretty big pile of wood you've created. Once you catch your breath, you begin again, more slowly now, steady and methodical. There is a small joy in this chopping. You're done with anger this morning.

NGUCHUL WALKS ONTO THE BACK PORCH, sits cross-legged and watches you swing the axe. At first you only sense someone might be there, and then he is a hazy patch in your peripheral vision. Slowly he becomes something captured inside your quick glances. The only movement he offers is the occasional lifting of an arm to sip from a mug of tea. You assume it's tea.

After you complete the chopping it's just you and Nguchul in the house. The others have gone into town to see about the van.

"I do not know much about relationships in the Western sense," he says. "I know a little about pain and suffering."

"We should get along very well then," you say.

"Kundun says that when we meet real tragedy in life, we can react in two ways. We can lose hope and fall into self-destructive habits, or we can use the challenge to find our inner strength."

If anybody else had delivered that line, you might have been insulted, or felt attacked in some way. Drinking is a self-destructive habit, and you're out drinking cognac with your coffee first thing in the morning. But Nguchul is just talking.

He leans sideways and finds a second mug — something you hadn't noticed. He holds it steaming in both hands — as if it's a small bird — and turns it once. Then in a smooth, gentle motion offers it to you with both hands. How could you refuse a presentation like that?

"Thank you," you say, and you really mean it.

"There is a story about a very famous warrior who comes to a Buddhist monk because he wants a definition of heaven and hell. He believes that monks ought to know such things. He asks this particular monk for a definition and the monk starts to laugh. 'A big, stupid brute like you,' he says. 'You're too stupid to understand anything. I'm surprised you can talk and breathe at the same time.' The warrior holds his temper and asks again. But the monk persists: 'You're too dumb. Go away. You're far too stupid and daft for such things. Not to mention ugly. Stupid and ugly.' Now the warrior's face turns red. His hair stands on end. He's shaking with rage. He draws his sword. He has the monk on the ground and is about to cut off his head, when the monk looks up and says: 'That is hell.'"

Nguchul sips his tea. Nods to himself and then continues.

"This warrior happens to be sensitive beyond his gruff exterior. A good thing for the monk. The warrior drops his sword and bursts into tears. He begins to sob uncontrollably. He feels a great humility and gratitude. Just then, the monk leans over and whispers: 'That's heaven.'"

Together, you sit and finish your tea in silence.

—

"WHAT IS THAT?" Sarah looks at Nguchul, his hands in a prayer above his heart.

"This is *namaste*," he says. "It is a Hindi word. It means many different things to different cultures. For us, it means that whatever you may look like on the outside, I see and greet the soul in you.

Or, as I am doing in this case, I am saying goodnight to you, but perhaps at a deeper level."

Sarah tries it. Hesitantly places her hands in the prayer position and looks at Nguchul. He smiles at her and bows slightly, which she mimics.

You know about *namaste* because an old girlfriend convinced you to go to a yoga class with her. You had thought yoga was all chanting and booga-booga new age navel-gazing but it turned out that this kind of yoga was all about stretching and strengthening, and you found some amazing things happened inside. It was an incredible way to refocus, and it became very important to you. At the end of a class, sudden tears, unbounded joy, grief, all rose to the surface. The instructor, a profoundly gentle woman, would *namaste* you at the end of each class. As a sign of respect and an honouring of the work you've done today, she'd say. Later, a different yoga teacher said it meant: I honour that place in you where the entire Universe exists. And when I'm in that place in me and you are in that place in you, there is only one of us.

⌇

YOU ASSUME IT'S NGUCHUL who starts writing quotations on the mirror in the bathroom. He's writing in soap, probably with the edge of a bar, or a finger. When there's no steam, the words are almost invisible, but when the mirror fogs up, the words appear clearly:

> *To straighten the crooked*
> *You must first do a harder thing*
> *Straighten yourself.*

It could be Kachen but what does it matter? It could be any one of the monks. They all know English, study English. It's just that Nguchul and Kachen are the most proficient. Besides, it's kind of nice, and you start to look forward to the sayings. Two days later, you crawl out of the shower and find this:

> *The awakened are few and hard to find.*
> *Happy is the house where a man awakes.*

⌒

A QUIET KNOCK at your door. You sit up in bed. Marie comes in. You flick on the light. She's been crying. "Come here," you say.

This is three nights in a row for Marie's bad dream. "Oh, kids get night terrors," your mother says. "It's a common thing." But you think something more must be going on here. You need to drill down and see what's at the bottom. She says it's not Moira's death, but how could that not be part of the root?

Marie snuggles in beside you and closes her eyes. They are sunken into her face. She looks ragged, her face sallow. A string of nights with disturbed sleep is wearing her out — and you too.

"Where were we?" you say. You pick up a rather tattered edition of John Irving's *Setting Free the Bears*, one of your favourites.

"At the zoo," Marie whispers.

"That's right. They're at the zoo for the first time. They're checking out the security and they've run into some rather interesting girls." You love this book because of the unexplained salt shakers and for the fact that one of the main characters gets killed halfway in.

You find your place and then begin to read. After twenty or thirty minutes, Marie falls asleep, and as you're fading into sleep yourself, you wonder why this character in the book steals so many salt shakers.

⌒

THE PHONE RINGS while you are in a sweat of chopping. You ignore it but you can hear it above the music. This morning you've picked the soundtrack to *Cinema Paradiso*. Your mother calls every day and you're in no mood for her. A few seconds later, it rings again. You drop the axe and move inside.

"This better be good."

"Yes, well, it's Carl. I'm sorry to bother you."

"That's all right, Carl. No bother. What can I do for you?" Two weeks ago, you'd enjoyed a night of entirely spontaneous scotch tasting with him. After he produced three of his favourites from a locker behind the kitchen, you ran home to gather three of your own bottles. You tested each other's sense of taste regarding the single malts. As the night wore on, the tasting part faded. You talked about Moira, about your life, shared too much probably. You're not certain if you told him about the reporter in Victoria who wanted an interview before the funeral. You were pleasant the first two times and then nasty on her third try. You have no idea what her angle was. She'd only said she wanted to talk to you about "your wife's death." What was she after? Was it a story on road safety? Suicide? You had no idea and you didn't care.

"Well, there's a lady down here looking for you and I'm wondering if it's all right to send her up. She asked if I knew where you lived. Didn't give her name."

"What does she look like?"

"Black hair," he whispers. "Tall. Looks you in the eye. She's ordered a triple espresso. She seems tired."

You never saw that reporter who wanted to talk with you, so a description is useless. "Is she carrying a notebook, or a tape recorder?"

"Hang on a second." You listen to some shuffling sounds and then Carl is back. "No, but she's got a fairly big bag — kind of a soft leather case."

You're still a little grumpy. More interested in being a hibernating bear. "She's probably harmless but I'm not too keen on company right now ..."

"I'll take care of it," Carl says. "You don't exist." He hangs up. You go back out to your wood.

―

YOU'VE WANDERED OVER to the Troubled Pig for coffee. It's not busy so Carl comes out from the kitchen and sits across from you.

"Your new guest house is in a great location," he says. "I don't mind helping. They're such hard-working buggers. They said it was all right. They said everything had been okayed by you. I can cancel the backhoe if you'd rather not ..."

"Backhoe? How big *is* this guest house?" You wonder if you're hearing things. The monks had asked if they might build a little temple. They suggested a spot near the back of your property, up the mountain, where it levels off a bit. You saw no reason to object to a little temple. But this did not sound like a little temple.

"It's three or four rooms," Carl says. "I got a shipment of wood, and rock from the quarry, coming in from the coast next week. There shouldn't be a problem pouring cement for the foundation. They seem pretty well fixed for money. They're payin' in American dollars."

"Four rooms," you say flatly. You were thinking a small *shrine* when Nguchul said temple. Definitely a problem with communication here.

"You're okay with this right? Because if you ..."

"No, no Carl. Everything's fine. But let's keep it between us, at least as long as we can."

"Oh, that won't be a problem. These guys are fanatical about the trees, the grass, even the moss. The foundation poles we're planning on puttin' in will barely disturb a thing. There's gonna be a couple of trees inside the house — right up through the roof. And the way they've designed it, you won't see it from the road."

―

Let go of anger.
Let go of pride.
When you are bound by nothing
You go beyond sorrow.

⌒

"LISTEN," YOU SAY. "I've never been big on religion. God, or what-ever it is out there more powerful and bigger than I can imagine, is fine. It's organized religion that doesn't work for me. The ideas in Christianity are fundamentally good, and the little I know about Buddhism seems to be fine, but when we start organizing and requiring and ritualizing ..."

Nguchul smiles. "Buddhism is interesting because Buddha urged people to investigate things — he didn't just command them to believe. Perhaps it is the philosophy of Buddhism you find appealing."

"But you're a monk. There's an implied commitment there. You're supposed to be big on religion."

"The Buddha also taught that the idea of firmly held notions and views are wrong. Even the Buddhist teachings. These are only guides to help us learn to look deeply, to develop our understand-ing and compassion. They are not doctrines to fight, kill or die for."

That sets you on your ass. Here's a religion that discounts itself — says don't hold too closely to these words or practices, they're just guides. Almost everything in you is vibrating with agreement. "I'd like to offer you some scotch but I don't know if monks drink. Do you?" You're holding an unopened bottle of Bowmore cask strength, one of the Islay single malts. It's a huge whisky. Bold flavours but with a subtle, smoky sweetness.

"Good Buddhists should not drink spirits."

"So I shouldn't offer?" You are slightly embarrassed by this ques-tion. You could have guessed that monks don't drink. These are holy men for Chrissake!

"I would enjoy having a drink with you," Nguchul says, smiling. He pauses. "I have been watching ... and there are things you do, like this near-empty room and your chopping meditation ... these things verge on the idea of Zen."

"Zen?"

"Not for me to explain. Not for anybody to explain. It cannot be explained. Except through living, dancing, singing, being."

"Do you guys take courses in being oblique?"

You pour an ample portion of whisky into Nguchul's glass. He appears to be in deep thought. His eyes are closed and his hands interwoven in his lap.

"I thought you said Buddhists don't drink?"

Nguchul takes one small sip, then performs that graceful smile of his, and bows slightly toward you. He makes no comment on the scotch. "I am wondering if I might ask a favour," he says.

"Ask away." You offer another dram of scotch and he lets you pour, but you know he won't be drinking it.

"I think this place would be a good one for the creation of a mandala."

"You mean in Field?"

"I think this house. Here in this room." He places his hand on the gymnasium-room floor like it's alive and sleeping, and he does not want to disturb it. "If it is all right, we will start tomorrow."

You are stunned and honoured. You're not sure what to say. Of course, you'd love to watch them do this thing, but my God! In your home?

"How long does it take to build a mandala?"

"Sometimes weeks," Nguchul says. "Perhaps more. We will pay our way while we are here."

"Oh, I'm not worried about that. Are ... are you sure you want to do it here?"

"Yes. This is the right place." He tosses back the remainder of the scotch and smiles. "In reference to your question, I said good

Buddhists should not drink. Sometimes, it is a difficult thing to be a good Buddhist."

⌒

THE MORNING THEY STARTED THE MANDALA, Uncle Bob and your mother arrived. The monks do not look up. Four of them are hunched over a pattern scratched into a hunk of plywood, and are applying tiny wisps of coloured sand with narrow metal tubes. Uncle Bob had stopped in Edmonton to pick up your mother. She is fascinated and Uncle Bob demands a drink. "Whisky if you have it," he barks.

You got Uncle Bob's letter, warning of their impending arrival, that morning. You'd just finished reading it when his car pulled up. You feel like you are running a hostel. You have no clue where you're going to put everybody.

The house became yours a month ago. You signed the papers when you last saw your dad. With a steady income from renting the city house and the insurance money, it was an easy choice, and the owners were more than willing to part with it. It had become increasingly difficult for them to prove they had a need to live in the Park, something Parks Canada was getting sticky about. The Burgess Shale folks were looking over your résumé. You hope that working up at the Burgess digs will be enough.

The monks gather into the spare room. You put your mother in your room and Uncle Bob on the futon in the living room. You hang a hammock in your office for yourself. Before you met Moira, you'd spent a month in Mexico, sleeping in a hammock very much like this one.

⌒

"I THOUGHT YOU SAID they were only staying until their van got fixed." Marie is speaking through a barely restrained anger. You're out back stacking wood and she is standing on the deck, her arms folded firmly across her chest.

"You're really having a hard time with this?"

"Dad! They're so weird! I can't have my friends over because they're either sitting in there meditating, or chanting. And now they're all, like, serious and quiet about a pile of sand!"

"Do you know what a mandala is about?"

"No and I don't care. I just want things to be normal. They're always in the bathroom!"

"You know you can use the bathroom in my room anytime you want." This may be as normal as it gets for a while, kiddo, you think. "The picture they're drawing with the sand is a healing thing. It won't be long. Just hang in there, okay?"

"But they ..."

"We have to let them finish what they started."

At breakfast the next morning, the mutiny continues.

"They're what?" Uncle Bob says. He seems outraged and insulted.

"They're building a mandala. It's a holy sand drawing."

"You mean these full-grown men sit around and play with sand?"

"It's not like that. They're not building sand castles. They're creating a beautiful picture with coloured sand. And it's supposed to be healing."

"Waste of time if you ask me," Uncle Bob says, slurping from his coffee cup.

"It's a great honour to have them do it here. Wait until you see it finished."

"But why do they have to do it here?" your mother asks. "You've got a couple of girls to think about, you know."

"The girls are fine. Hopefully they'll remember this brush up against Buddhism."

"I mean do you trust these ..."

"I know where you're going with this and it's not something I'm concerned about. I'm touched that they want to do it here." You notice the irritation, a thin, reedy edge, in your own voice.

"Have some toast," your mother says, passing you a plate with raisin toast drowning under small lakes of butter.

⌒

WHEN GEORGIA TELLS YOU ABOUT Moira's abortion, your mind begins to click backwards in time, looking for the right numbers in the combination to open the lock.

Click. Click. Click. Click. And it stops at Katya and her terminated baby — a story started with Moira and somehow continued by you.

Click. Click. Click. And it stops at Moira's steady unhappiness.

Click. Click. And there is Moira watching you and the girls play in the snow and it seems she's angry, hateful, and resentful, about something. She's outside her own family, semi-removed.

Click. But you hesitate to open the lock. Why did this messenger drive across a province to deliver this message? Why not a phone call? How close was she to Moira? Why did she wait ten months?

You're walking up Mt. Stephen Road with Georgia when she blurts it out.

She'd called from the hotel, interrupted your chopping. Your mother brought out the phone. "It's a woman," she whispered, as if Moira were going to hear. Something immoral. She put the phone down gingerly. You'll have to have a chat with your mother at some point. It has become your habit not to answer phones when you're chopping but your mother doesn't understand the concept of a ringing phone being an invitation, and not a commitment. You chopped two more hunks of pine into firewood, to underscore your own lack of commitment to telephones, then picked it up and said hello.

"She told you this?" you say.

The road is scattered with puddles, enclosed by pines and slopes gently upwards. You've stopped and turned toward Georgia.

"In her own way," she says.

"I didn't know you wore glasses?" Her frames are a subtle cat's eye shape, black plastic that contrasts sharply with her face, which is quite pale.

"I don't usually. My contacts are bugging me right now."

You walk together in silence.

"So, you think this was on purpose?"

"I don't have any doubt. She was so sad. She was sad, and I don't think it had anything to do with you, or your daughters. I believe it was this thing that was so heavy. And she just couldn't carry it any longer."

"You're staying at the hotel?"

"I got here yesterday and asked around but ..."

You smile. "Carl is very protective. Can you come for dinner this evening, about six? I'm sure the girls will be happy to see you. My mom is here. Moira's uncle Bob as well, and ..." You smile. "It'll be a rather crowded dinner party but that's my life right now."

"Thank you," Georgia says. "Can I bring anything?"

"Just yourself, and an open mind."

Your mind is reeling. Is the abortion the answer you need? It seems too simple — too perfect. But on the other hand, it makes sense.

"By the way, did you bring your dog?"

"He's staying with a friend."

You stop walking, turn slightly and look back down the road, then at Georgia.

"Can I ask you something I'm not sure I want you to answer?"

"Okay," she says with a weighty hesitation.

"I mean, well, I don't know what I mean, but I trust you. Because Moira trusted you with the safety of my kids. And because you're not exactly a stranger, though you're not close either. So, if I ask you a question, you can judge it and make a decision on whether or not to answer. I also trust you to tell the truth because you've got nothing to lose, or gain for that matter."

"I thought we could keep in touch, become friends ..."

"Well, of course. I hope that too." You pause for a few seconds. "Listen, forget it. I don't want to know."

"Must be a hell of a question."

"Something that's been bugging me but I realize how stupid ..."

"Why not ask me anyway."

"You sure?"

"Yup, I'm sure. I'll do my best to answer."

"It's really not that big a deal but I ... I don't suppose you remember the kind of tree? The one she smashed into."

"That's your question?"

"I know. I'm embarrassed. You think it's dumb."

"No, not at all." She's off-balance. "I wish I could help. I know it was very tall, and it's still there, but that's all I know."

~

NGUCHUL IS TELLING A STORY about a monk smashing a bowl of tea. This monk stands up in front of a group and announces that the tea is his soul, or spirit, and that the bowl is his body. Then he smashes the bowl onto the counter and smiles. *Is the tea still the tea?* he asks. *Is the bowl still the bowl?*

Marie gets it immediately. You watch her as the talk moves in waves around the table. You can see the light go on in her eyes, and her awareness starts to shine. She doesn't have to nod her understanding. Nor does she have to speak it. A slight parting of the lips. A minuscule smile. You watch her, fascinated, and you just know.

Georgia would have made eleven. You would never have imagined so many people eating in your home. But twelve seemed a more balanced number. So you invited Carl, who came bearing a gift of single malt — the Bowmore cask strength.

"This is a little hostess gift," he'd said, smiling like a fool as he came through the door, and then he stopped. "Shit. I'm sorry. I wasn't thinking ..."

"Carl. Relax. It's fine. I know you were just trying to be funny. This is a very generous gift."

"We are taught this from an early age," Nguchul continues. "The tea is still the tea. The bowl is no longer the bowl." One of the monks is translating everything that is said for his fellow monks, who have varying degrees of understanding, and it basically sounds as if you're at the United Nations with a translator yapping away constantly in your earpiece.

"It's one of those cons," Uncle Bob says in his biggest, booming voice. "You know — a story with a lesson hidden somewhere inside and you have to be bright as hell to get it."

"I think you mean koan, Uncle Bob." You've never been able to call him just Bob and he's given up trying to convince you to do it. "But this is a lesson, not a koan."

"How does that tie in with reincarnation?" Georgia scrunches her face, a confused look.

"I think the Bowmore might go very nicely with this rice," Carl says.

You unwrap and uncork the bottle, pour a generous portion into a glass and pass this to Carl. "Spring water," you say, passing a decanter down the table after the whisky. "Uncle Bob?" Uncle Bob squints at the bottle.

"You boys into the girly scotch?" he says.

"This is cask strength."

"Girly scotch."

"Neat then?"

"Thanks," he says.

You pour a generous portion for him.

"Richard Gere is a Buddhist, you know," your mother says. "Do you know him?"

You cringe a bit. Parents likely take lessons on how to maximize the level of embarrassment they cause for their children. Yes, Richard Gere is a Buddhist. But how many Buddhists are there in the world? You look at your daughters and wonder what you do, or say, that embarrasses them.

"Yes," Nguchul says. "The movie star."

"Jesus H. Christ!" It's Uncle Bob, who's just taken his first drink of the Bowmore. "My God, this is a hell of a drink!"

Carl smiles, shakes his head.

Your mother ignores Uncle Bob. "Richard Gere wears the beads too. The same ones I wear." She holds up her wrist and then looks at Nguchul and the other monks. Three of them are wearing their *malas*. "The same ones all of you wear!"

"I will tell you what we use them for if you like. They are a very useful tool for prayer, and for breathing exercises ..."

"You mean you boys actually practise breathing?" Uncle Bob is leaning forward. He's glowing from the whisky.

"A conscious breathing, yes, that is correct," Nguchul says.

"Stop kicking me," Sarah says, glaring at Marie.

"I didn't mean to."

"Yes you did."

Kachen interprets the conversation for the other three monks as it's moving a bit too fast for them. There is a continuous hum of background murmurs. They follow Sarah's blurting accusations and Marie's denials like they're watching a tennis match.

"Dad, Marie kicked me."

"I'm sure she didn't mean it, Sarah. Did you, Marie?"

"But what happens to the tea?" Georgia says. "Isn't that the question?"

"I'm sorry, but I don't understand how the tea gets from the floor to another bowl." Uncle Bob leans forward and twists toward

Nguchul. "That's the reincarnation isn't it?"

"Have you ever met Richard Gere?" It's your mother, again.

"It's a metaphor," you say. "It means when we die, there is a part of us, the tea, that does not stop."

"Oh, I understand that part ..."

"Maybe somebody makes the same kind of tea in a new bowl," Georgia says. "So, it's not quite the same tea, but its leaves are from the same plantation."

"I don't mean any kind of disrespect Mr. Nugchill," Uncle Bob says.

"Our ways are different." Nguchul smiles and bows slightly. This small gesture brings a relaxed and informal serenity to the table. "Yes, I have met Richard Gere, once, many years ago in India. He's a nice man. A good heart."

Your mother's face lights up with a sense of wonder and new-found respect. These monks now have her enthusiastic approval. Her eyes become those of a three year old on Christmas morning. Nguchul has met Richard Gere.

"You met Richard Gere?" She looks down the table at you. "He met Richard Gere. He was so charming in that movie *Pretty Woman*," she says. "And you know, it was Julia Roberts' best movie."

The four monks at the end of the table burst out into loud laughing and talking. In the middle of the cacophony, you hear the words *Pretty Woman* used several times.

"Goddamn chick flick," Uncle Bob says.

"That movie about the prostitute?" Sarah says.

"That's the one."

"I like Richard Gere," Marie says.

"Yes," Nguchul says, "I enjoyed this movie. Good movie about paying attention and truly seeing the consequences of actions. A movie about moral balance and seeing the right course — one based in kindness and compassion."

"Oh, Mr. Nugchill," your mother says, smiling at him and touching the sleeve of his robe. "It was a Cinderella love story."

Nguchul turns to your mother and bows. Then he turns to Georgia and speaks very softly. His voice becomes quiet and everyone at the table turns to listen.

"A long time ago in my village, the warm weather, which always comes, arrived early, and a particularly beautiful tree came into bud. Just as it seemed that these buds were going to bloom, a cold snap descended and stayed for quite a few weeks, and those buds died. When the tree again came into bud and eventually blossomed, an old man who had been watching struck up a conversation with the tree. He asked: 'Are these the same buds that died? Or are these brand new?' The tree replied: 'These are not the same buds and they are not different. Conditions were not right for those buds to blossom so they did not manifest. Conditions are right now and so the buds have blossomed.'"

He looks directly at you as he delivers the last line of his story. There's something in this story aimed at you but you're having a hard time finding it.

Nguchul smiles around the table. "The Buddha taught there is no birth, no death; there is no same, no different; there is no permanent self, there is no annihilation."

IN YOUR MIND, Moira didn't care. This morning, as you chop your wood in a rage, Moira didn't care about anything. She didn't give a flying fuck about the rain, or about her daughters, or about you, as she said goodbye to Georgia and walked from the cabin to the car. The rain is irrelevant to someone who is about to check out early. The car door is not locked and so Moira locks it by trying to unlock it. She lifts the handle and whispers *fuck* under her breath, and then truly unlocks the door. There are people who would consider this to be an omen of some kind. The door was open and they've inadvertently locked it. Turn around and go back into the cabin. Inside the car she shuffles through perhaps a dozen CDs, looking for the one. It has to be Miles Davis. *Kind of Blue.* It's the remastered version that she picks but that sort of detail doesn't interest her. Both versions were there. Some of the CDs slip onto the passenger-side floor. She leaves them there. They too are irrelevant. She backs out onto the street, and then flips the car into drive before she stops backing up. Transmissions are irrelevant too. She flicks the windshield wipers on, and she's off down the highway — headlights barely pushing through the rain. Three kilometres later, she pulls over. You'd like to think that she stops at the top of the hill, that she sits there and begins to review her life. And that she at least thinks about Sarah and Marie. You'd like to believe in Moira's hesitation, her pause, but you can't. Where does she get that last bit of resolve? Is that how it works? Is it a series of small impulses, or is it one frantic, sustained mania? Does she wait for a particular song? Does she wait for Miles to play one of his beautiful flubbed notes, one of his notes with frayed edges? Maybe she looks out the window in the general direction of the ocean. The night is dull and insipid. It's raining. There are no stars, no heavenly objects, except through faith and hope, and Moira is almost out of both. She can't see the damn tree but she knows it's there. She found it three days ago. She is operating on a very low but steady level of faith that the tree is still there. "Fuck it," she says. She slams her foot onto the accelerator and holds it there with a crazy determination, as the car veers down the highway with no hope of making the turn at the bottom. It hits the small lip at the edge of the road and is launched into the air with a sure, twisting velocity. There is the sound of breaking glass, the groaning sound of bending metal, some thing that keeps rotating, squealing, squeaking after everything else has stopped. Finally, there is only the hissing ocean overriding the sound of a muted trumpet.

14
MOUNTAIN GOATS
ARE PREVALENT HERE

"I HAVE BEEN WATCHING," Nguchul says, "noticing." He bows slightly toward you, his eyes closed, as if he is trying to find the right words but nothing will come. You are standing in the hallway that leads to the kitchen. Nguchul is leaning against the dark green wall. For some reason, the previous owner painted one side of the hallway a dark hunter-green and the other a soft lime-green. Nguchul appears more serious and focused against that rich colour. A trick of light.

Marie is sleeping in your bed. For the past hour you've been holding her while humming over and over the tune to Tom Waits's "Tom Traubert's Blues," the one with "Waltzing Matilda" in it. Tonight's bad dream was particularly unpleasant.

"It is none of my business," says Nguchul, "except that I care about you and your family. Life is suffering but we believe it does not have to be. Things can be done."

"Are you saying you can help Marie? Because I'd welcome it right now. She's my little girl ... and I ..." You have not spoken your helplessness before and something catches in your throat.

"She's in pain. I will talk with her tomorrow."

"I ... I was going to make chai," you say. "Would you like some?"

You fill the kettle as Nguchul sits at the table. You think about the monks. They came into town and decided to build a healing mandala. The work is excruciating, backbreaking. But they do it, they do it gladly, without complaint. The small temple-cum-guest-house is a gift you can't repay.

You sit at the kitchen table. You are very tired. "I found a psychiatrist in Calgary but if you think you can ..."

"Do you know the word *karuna*? It is Sanskrit. It means any action taken to diminish the suffering of others. If we are to believe that all beings are one, then to help one is to help all. It is both compassionate and logical to help others. I do not know if I have the wisdom but the effort is something. We will see."

⁓

IT SEEMS YOUR LIFE in the past little while has been made up of arrivals and departures. We arrive inside a birth, and we depart when we die. The monks would disagree. They have very different views on birth and death.

After leaving the city, and going to Paris, then leaving Paris, you arrived in Sooke. Then you left Sooke for Edmonton, for a funeral. Then you left Edmonton and arrived in Field, a small town in the mountains. Five Buddhist monks arrive and are staying with you. Your mother and Moira's uncle Bob have arrived and god only knows how long they're going to stay. Georgia arrived and she's staying too. Your father is leaving. Your grief and confusion and disappointment have arrived and it seems they are going to stay.

⁓

Spring has its hundred flowers,
Autumn its moon.
Summer has its cooling breezes,
Winter its snow.

⌒

One morning, you take a bar of soap and scrawl your own message on the bathroom mirror:

Spring is sprung,
the grass is ris',
I wonder where the birdies is?

⌒

YOU HAVE FALLEN INTO THE HABIT of meeting Nguchul each night, after the house is quiet. You begin your conversation with a discussion about how good Buddhists should not consume spirits. You both agree that they should not, then you both have a few drinks.

You are sitting on the back deck under a concentrated spectacle of stars. The day was hot, but the evening's cool, so you both wear thick sweaters, socks and boots. Nguchul has a coarse woollen hat on his head, and you, the French beret you bought in Paris ten years ago. Nguchul looks up and sighs. "These mountain stars are a worthy subject for poetry. I have no poetry in me but you ... I have seen the romantic poet side of you."

"I've never written a poem in my life. Limericks maybe, but serious poetry I leave to the experts. I appreciate poetry but writing it ... you have to be half-crazy."

Nguchul smiles. "Trust me when I say this. There is a great poet in you, I think. I could use a little more of the cognac."

You pour a liberal portion into his coffee mug. "You should write poems about these mountains," he continues. "In fact, I will start one and you finish it."

"Now?"

"Yes, now. Here is the first line." He stops and looks up at the sky. The silence is profound, disturbed only by the distant sounds of vehicles rushing by on the highway. "The mountains are stolen by falling indigo ..."

"Assumed by a splattered spectacle of stars." You have no idea where it came from. Your first inclination is to dismiss this as a stupid, childish game. Your second is to chalk it up to the cognac. You are warmed by the cognac and for a few moments the universe seems a welcoming place. You and Nguchul have created the beginnings of a mountain poem. But the brazen display of starlight soon makes you feel small and insignificant.

Nguchul inhales slowly, holds his breath for a very long time and then exhales.

"Yes, you should write poetry," he says. He sips his cognac. Lifts his eyes to the stars again. Whispers: "This is heaven."

~

IN THE MORNING, you come out to the backyard and, for the first time in a long time, you do not automatically reach for the axe. You do not look at the hazard of wood. You look up into a whirling mass of grey cloud, granite, fingers of pine, and swatches of snow. The snow is swirling and harassing the rock, looking for a safe place to rest. For months, you have been coming out here and ignoring the beauty of this place, taking it for granted, looking only inwards. Shame on you.

There are three monks in the gymnasium — you've given up referring to it as the dining room — hunched over in the final movements of the mandala. If this sand sculpture were music, it would be a Mozart symphony. They will be finished in a day or two. You've invited the entire town to see the final creation. You hesitate to call it the final *product*. A car is a product. A toaster is a product. This painstaking work of beauty is a holy work of art. There will be a ceremony in which the mandala will be wiped away and the sand dumped into the river. The ceremony will take place down the road a bit, outside the park. The warden was concerned that such a public ceremony might draw some negative reaction to the adding of foreign elements — even if it's just coloured sand — to a mostly natural environment. The Kicking Horse is a Canadian Heritage river, meaning, you imagine, that this particular river is held in higher esteem than all others.

Your mother has been cleaning like a demon, getting ready for the many visitors you expect will come. She's started baking and gathering goodies. "People will want a snack when they get here," she says.

Chakpu. Sarah told you the metal funnels they use to direct the grains of sand into the patterns is called a *chakpu.* She is always dropping odd bits of information on you. Last week she told you about Yoho National Park, which surrounds the town of Field. "Yoho is a Cree word meaning awesome," she says. "And there are twenty-eight mountain peaks here that are 3,000 metres or taller. And did you know there are more mountain goats here than any other big animal? I want to see a mountain goat."

"I think we can arrange that."

"When?"

"I'll work on it, okay?"

"Okay."

She looks off across the room. "Daddy, how will you arrange it?"

"I'll ask around and when somebody tells me where some goats are, I'll come and get you and we'll go find them."

"Oh," she says.

⌒

"OH FOR GOD'S SAKE! I can't hear a damn thing you're saying!"

The monks are chanting in the gymnasium and you're trying to have a telephone conversation in the kitchen. "I'm sorry, what did you say? A what? Look, this isn't working. I have to go outside. Hold on!" You run through the living room and upstairs, grab the cordless phone and reverse your steps. Outside, on the deck with the glass door rolled shut, the sound is slightly subdued. You never thought chanting could be so obtrusive.

"I have five monks living with me," you say. You sit down on the edge of the deck and let your legs swing like a little kid. "No, not monkeys. Monks! Buddhist monks! Who is this?"

It's a real estate agent from Edmonton. She wants to sell your house for you. "Several buyers are interested," she says. Suddenly, the monks get louder and drown her out completely. You shrug and put the phone down.

~

UNCLE BOB IS SITTING at the kitchen table reading a newspaper that's at least a week old when he puts it down and looks at you.

"I don't know," he says. "I don't know much about anything really but if you're thinking this hinges on one thing alone, you're wrong."

"What?" You wonder if it's some out-of-date newspaper story he wants to rant on about.

"No, no, not *what*; why. The question that lives up there in your head. *Why* did she do it?"

"Moira?"

"Yes. Moira."

"What about her?"

"She, the whole thing, is more complex than you know."

"Complex? What do you mean?"

"Depression. Depression is never about just one thing. Moira was always a bit depressed. Even as a kid. She was a great kid, but a dark kid, moody and turned inward. She was in therapy before you came along, kiddo."

"I know she was depressed. But I don't even know if she ..."

"Yes. Maybe we'll never know for sure, but I'm just sayin', depression is complicated. People are talking now about chemical imbalances, as part of the picture. And that's on top of all the multi-layered psychological aspects."

"How do you ..."

"How do I know so much about depression? Well, I've been there. It's kind of my constant companion, lurking there in the backwaters, waiting." He looks down at the newspaper, which is folded neatly in two. "Whenever I saw you two together, she seemed as happy as I've ever seen her. And when she was with the girls, she glowed with love. You could see it. That's what's important. All the rest is messy and more complex than we'll ever know."

You place a mug of tea in front of Uncle Bob and sit at the table.

He clears his throat. "What about you, how are you handling this ... other than chopping wood?"

"You think I'm depressed?"

"The thought crossed my mind."

"I'm fine."

"It's not your fault."

"I'm fine, really."

"Well, remember, there's nothing like standing up tall, lifting your chin and smiling to make you feel better. And that always ruins a good depression. So be careful."

～～

UNCLE BOB IS UP MOUNTAIN with the monks, along with Carl and his backhoe. The monks spend their mornings meditating and working on the mandala, and their afternoons constructing the temple.

Nguchul and Marie go for a walk. You watch them trundle off down the dusty road toward the river. A dog barks. There's a train hunkered into the valley and you can hear its low, steady throb as it waits. You only hear the beginning of their conversation.

"... but Montreal doesn't have a goalie," Marie says. "They're not going to make it past the first round without a solid goalie."

Nguchul nods. "They're a young team. Volatile. They are fully capable of playing a team defence."

"But they haven't shown anything like that all season ..."

"... the playoffs are an entirely new season ..."

"... but you don't go anywhere in the playoffs without great goaltending ..."

Now they're out of range. How in the hell did they start talking about hockey? These monks are full of surprises. When did your daughter become conversant with the subtle nuances of hockey? You're proud of her. You can't help thinking how proud your father would be.

⌇

"DID YOU KNOW that a bunch of ravens is an *unkindness*?" Sarah says. "And a group of crows is a *murder*? And did you know that the Natives say that raven is the creator, or the trickster?"

"I knew about the crows but I did not know about the ravens. An unkindness of ravens. Oh my. I rather like that. An *unkindness* of ravens. It has a ring to it, doesn't it?"

"Georgia says it's poetic."

⌇

"I SUSPECT I KNOW but why did you choose my home for this mandala?"

Nguchul and you are walking the upper road, slowly dropping toward the valley bottom and the train tracks, and home. Nguchul doesn't look like he's in shape but he's a mountain goat. You've walked the outer perimeter of the town, up the highway to the Emerald Lake turnoff and back to town. You'd like to stop for a breather, but you'll be damned if you'll let this monk out-walk you. You're not going to suggest a stop.

"You are making unhappy wood, each morning when you chop. We feel compassion for the wood."

"Was that a Buddhist joke?"

Nguchul is looking straight ahead. His face is neutral.

"That was a joke, wasn't it? It's no wonder there's never been a Buddhist comedian."

"There is much pain here. Perhaps healing will occur. As Buddhists, we believe that everything in life is impermanent, from physical possessions to plans about the future. But, as human beings, we feel certain that we are solid and permanent, and that definite events occur in our lives. We try to hang onto these moments; but, really, they are like sand running through our fingers."

Each night, instead of drinking yourself into a memory, or no memory, you and Nguchul talk into the morning. You look forward to these conversations, which twist and turn through world affairs, to peace, to sex and women. You offer up your confusion about women and Nguchul offers only his lack of experience and his insights into human nature.

~

ONE MORNING, YOU FIND MARIE hunched over the mandala, Nguchul by her side, talking softly. She holds the *chakpu* with a practised delicacy. She's putting a thin line of sand into the mandala, and is so focused she does not notice you. You glide into the kitchen silently, avoiding the creaky floorboard by taking an inelegant big step through the doorway.

~

NGUCHUL COMES ONTO THE DECK with two mugs of tea. His expression is grave. His omnipresent almost-smile is not there. You get the feeling he has something on his mind. You watch him as he sips his tea and it seems that after each sip, when a window for speech is opened, he hesitates.

"She spoke of an argument," he says finally. "The day before her mother died, Marie and her mother argued. They yelled at each other. Marie partially blames herself for your wife's death. I think she wishes she could say she was sorry for these angry words."

Why couldn't she tell you that? What the hell is it that you're doing wrong with the women in your life?

"So this is the cause of her bad dreams?"

"I do not know. I am not a psychologist. I just listened. We talked. But this argument ... she has been holding this argument inside. Her feelings and fears about it have been in a fist and now the hand has opened a little."

"I have to let her know it wasn't her fault. That there is no blame. There's got to be a way for her to release this."

"We will work a thread of remorse into the mandala. It will be Marie's contribution to healing. It is a beginning."

"You'll what? Won't that ruin your pattern? You've all worked so hard at ..." You think about what is to come. They're going to wipe it out. Destroy their work. This man, this monk, has possibly helped your daughter out of a hell. How do you speak your gratefulness? "Thank you," you say. "Thank you."

"At the bottom of this, I believe she is ashamed and embarrassed," Nguchul says. He takes a long sip of tea, several long breaths, looks up at you. "And she believes quite adamantly that the Montreal Canadians will not get past the first round in the playoffs."

~

"CARL, HOW LONG HAVE YOU LIVED HERE?"

"It's coming up on twelve years now," he says. Carl, it seems, is always wearing either an apron or coveralls. At the Troubled Pig he wears an apron and when he leaves, he is in his other uniform. This pattern was part of your understanding of Carl, but at Christmas he threw you for a loop. There he was, slipping out of an Armani overcoat and wearing a Hugo Boss suit. You did a triple-take, rubbed your eyes and looked again. Carl looked sophisticated in all the most charming connotations of that word, right down to the Italian shoes. Now, you shake that image from your head and look across the table at Carl-in-overalls.

"Have you ever seen a mountain goat in the park?"

"The curly horned ones?"

"No, those are sheep. I mean goats — they're white."

He thinks for a moment, scrunches up his face and tilts his gaze to the side. "In the park? Can't say as I have. Odd. I don't remember seeing one."

"Have you ever been up to visit the Shale dig?"

"Can't say as I have."

"You've lived here twelve years and you haven't been up to the Shale?"

"Well, you come from a city that has the world's largest shopping mall. When was the last time you were in that mall?"

You think about this for a moment. It's been possibly ten or more years. Your silence is a signal to Carl. Point to him.

⌐⌐

YOU REMEMBER WALKING through a bookstore and a book called *Hagakure* fell on the floor in front of you. You still have that book. You don't understand half of what it's getting at, but there are bits and pieces that resonate. One of those bits was about having no other purpose but being in the moment. That your life is a progression of moment after moment. So, if you can fully understand the present moment, there is nothing else to do — nothing else to want.

What if there are moments in life, small moments like the one with Maurice, the waiter back in Edmonton, and his kindness with birds, that illuminate large, complex pools of living with an astounding exactitude, a clarity so sweet it aches. If you pause for a while in the memory of one of these clear moments, you might find yourself inside a quiet bliss. One tiny act of unexpected kindness dropped in the centre of a still mountain lake. The ripples are small and inexorable. Everything in the mirror of the lake, tonnes of granite, reflected pines, a universe of ancient stars, and twelve degrees of azure-blue, are all affected.

If it's the right moment, it can, it should, change you. Maybe you exist only to crawl inside one of these blissful openings.

⌒

YOU'RE PLAYING SOFTBALL down by the river and the monks' team is winning. Kachen has a wicked curveball and he's pitching like an overdriven machine. Only Georgia can hit his pitches with any consistency. He's struck you out twice already. He slows it down a bit for the girls, and Sarah gets on base with a bunt that was meant to be a hit. Your mother is playing second base with the monks and she won't shut up. "This guy can't hit," she shrieks when Uncle Bob steps up to the plate. "He can't hit. He can't hit. Hey batta, batta, batta, batta-batta-batta-batta!" and then she launches into: "SWING! SWING!" trying to lure the batter into swinging at wild, out of the zone pitches. You don't remember ever seeing this competitive side of her.

Kachen and his three brothers, your mother, Carl and his brother Tom, line up against you, Nguchul, Georgia, Sarah, Marie, Uncle Bob, and your next-door neighbour, Suzanne.

The baseball diamond was built by the railroad, and, according to Carl, has been through various stages of decay and rebirth. Right now, it's in good condition, with a high fence backstopping home plate and a well-defined infield. You wonder about all the people who have played baseball on this diamond. What did it look like fifty years ago, eighty years ago? Probably nothing like your senior citizen loudmouth mother on second base or this saffron-robed monk standing on the sidelines wearing a Toronto Blue Jays baseball cap on his head. Nguchul was thrilled when you offered to lend it to him. Not that you followed baseball on TV. Except for the

World Series, baseball was not a game to be experienced on television. However, you loved to follow the stats in the newspapers, enjoyed seeing which teams had a shot at the playoffs, which teams are dreaming about the next year.

"The Buddha would have liked this game," Nguchul says. "In order to be good, you have to understand the entire field, you have to be present."

"What position do you think the Buddha would have played?"

"Catcher," he says without hesitation. "Because it is a position of quiet service to everyone on the field."

Kachen rips a ball past Uncle Bob, who steps back from the plate, looks hard at the demon-pitcher monk, then reassesses and steps back to the plate.

"These guys are very good," you say. "I assume baseball is something they've played before?"

"Football. Soccer as you call it, is the game we like the most, but baseball is a close second."

Uncle Bob runs his turn at bat to a full count, then hits three foul balls in a row. The second errant ball causes you and Nguchul to duck out of the way. Uncle Bob nails that ball and it's coming way too fast to get out of its way in time. But you give Nguchul a quick bump with your shoulder, you go the other way, and the ball goes in between. Must be the coffee, you think. Finally, he hits one straight down the third-base line and manages to arrive safely at first base.

When you step up to the plate, the sound of the river suddenly floods your consciousness. It's as if you step through a hazy, warm membrane and things are different on the other side. You become aware of the hushed sound of the wind through the trees at the edge of the field. There's a bee in the clover between second and third base. Time has gained weight. You swing the bat through the air and the molecules along the bat's edge seem to blur. You were trying to pay attention to everything. You have been doing your breathing exercises with Nguchul. You were thinking about

Buddha as catcher. You look at the monks out in the field. You can hear your mother's voice. Carl is on first base. Why is he wearing black dress shoes? Kachen is throwing the ball, but it's so slow! You can see a thousand ways to hit the ball — easy to hit it into the empty spot in centre field — but why is it easy? Why has everything slowed down? When is the ball going to arrive at home plate? It's taking forever. And mixed in with everything is your own steady breathing, your heartbeat, and the sound of the river.

You know exactly how hard to hit in order to knock the ball into the river. The angle, the velocity, everything is lucid. You can see the ball start to curve downward and away from the strike zone. But when the ball reaches you, you smile. You look at your mother and pop the ball into the air in a beautiful arc so that it comes down almost directly into her glove. She takes two small steps backwards and holds up her glove. Uncle Bob is stuck at first base.

You finish your run to first anyway and then walk over to Nguchul, Marie and Sarah. You look at Nguchul who is squinting into the sun.

"Something strange just happened," you say.

"Yes," he says. "You hit a pop-fly almost directly to your mother. As if you were trying to hit the ball there. And now we have two outs."

"No, something more than that. I think I had a glimpse of ... well, I don't really know. But everything slowed down ... it was pure clarity. I could see ..."

Nguchul turns and really looks at you.

"I mean everything slowed down!!! I could hear the river, the trees ... It was ... odd." You want to use words like surprising, or incredible, or amazing. Odd doesn't seem quite right but better words may come later.

Nguchul nods his head knowingly and turns back to the game. He pulls the peak of his baseball cap down to shield his eyes. "Baseball is very Buddhist," he says. "*very* Buddhist."

"IT'S A LIE," Georgia says. "I lied." She sits up, pushes her sunglasses onto her forehead, and there is misery in her eyes.

"What's a lie?" You embed the axe into your chopping block and give her sadness your full attention.

You've been chopping wood. Georgia is sprawled naked, except for sunglasses, on the deck. You're quite happy to have a naked woman on your back deck. The girls just smile when she does this. We shouldn't be ashamed of our bodies, ever, you'd told them. No matter how big, or small, or skinny, or droopy.

It's not that Georgia didn't ask if it would be all right. The day she showed up, after supper, she asked if anybody would be offended by a little nudity, as she loved the feel of air on her body. Nobody said anything. So, now, because of that silent majority, Georgia is the resident nudist.

The monks avert their eyes and shuffle by. They tolerate her, she tolerates them. Uncle Bob smiles joyfully. He does not leer. You half expected him to leer, or at least stare, but he surprises you. He's accepting and gracious with her nudity. In fact, he and Georgia have had a couple of long conversations over coffee, with her spread out on the deck in her newborn glory, and Uncle Bob in a deck chair. One morning, you catch them out there smoking a couple of cigars and pounding back the cognac, your Hennessy X.O. They stop talking and look at you like recalcitrant teenagers. You sigh and insist that they pour you one. What the hell were you saving it for anyway?

Georgia, naked and hairy in all the right places, added a new wrinkle to your morning meditation of chopping. You really had to focus. Ignore the woman and chop the wood. Just chop the wood. Don't think about the perfect puffy triangle of black hair. Chop wood. You're chopping wood and axes are sharp and can hurt you.

"I don't know why she did it," Georgia says. "She never talked about it. Only once, she told me about a bad dream with silent babies and something dark eating them, so I thought ..."

"She never talked about an abortion being at the bottom ..."

"No. We never had that conversation."

You sit down. You have that numb, hit-in-the-face feeling of all the blood suddenly draining from your face.

"I'm sorry," she says. "I thought ... well, I don't know what I thought."

Why would this woman drive across a vast province to lie to you? She's kind and wouldn't do it out of meanness. You still think of it as a suicide, you always have really, but now you've been thrown back into the land of the doubting.

It seems appropriate that Georgia is naked. There's vulnerability and truth in nakedness. Most people wouldn't want to be naked after such an admission. Or they'd cross their arms protectively in front. But here she is, propped up, with her large, round breasts, protruding nipples, and her worried face. Georgia remains open. She trusts you'll understand.

So much about Georgia's lie makes sense. It seems true to Moira's character: she's depressed about an abortion she had years before. She can't make the abortion and her two kids be part of the same reality, so she represses the abortion, shoves it so far back it has room to grow and seethe. After a dozen years, it becomes so big it has the right to demand attention. It begins to shift its weight into her consciousness. It gets aggressive. Moira cracks.

But you are looking for reasons instead of at events. Moira's dead. That's an event. The reasons do not matter. Georgia's lie is as good a reason as any other. Yeah, keep telling yourself that the reasons don't matter. Keep chopping wood like you have a vendetta against all trees — big, small, skinny or tall. The reasons do not matter. They don't matter.

Georgia was trying to ease your grief and you bought it because you wanted to. Now what do you do? You accept. Accept that Moira's gone and begin to move on. Accept that this naked woman lied to you in order to try and save you.

"It's a good lie," you say. "It was a hell of a good lie."

"I used to think a lie could become the truth simply because we wished it to be true, but that's bullshit," Georgia says.

"What the hell was it that drove her into that tree?"

"She was depressed."

"That was a given with Moira, at least in the last few years."

"Isn't that enough?"

"I don't know." You're still tilted. "All that stuff about you sleeping with Moira, and loving Moira ..."

Georgia nods her head. "She was so lost ... I, I tried to offer comfort ... and things just progressed. I'm sure I was just a release for her."

"Doesn't matter now," you say. You do not say this with any bitterness. It is a flat statement you meant for yourself. The words fall onto the hard ground and you look at them.

"It goes on." She smiles up at you.

"Yes, life goes on. I'm glad she found some comfort. I'm glad she found you."

You do not say you suspect the abortion is not something that happened before you, but rather when Moira was with you. You remember the close call and the honest conversation with Moira. At the time, your relief that it was only a close call overwhelmed your rational brain. Moira could very well have had an abortion. This could have been what haunted her.

❦

ON THE OTHER HAND, it *could* have been an accident. Abortion or no abortion, Moira loved. She loved you. She loved the girls.

15

THE REQUIEM

You have an overwhelming desire this morning to play the Górecki symphony, loud. It's usually a nocturnal visitor. But you play it regardless and the second you hear the frail beginnings of the low strings, you're swept away. The sound drives to the middle of your body like a train building and building in speed and you're there for the ride, there's no stopping it. The wheels of the train repeat themselves over and over, but the land moves by the window and changes continuously. Something is pulling your heart into, and hopefully through, sorrow. Is that what this is — sorrow? So, there you are standing in the middle of the backyard with the Górecki saturating the air. You jerk the axe out of the chopping block and the music shivers through you.

You close your eyes and release yourself into it, allow those low, minor-keyed strings to buoy you. Your back twitches in a spastic recognition.

THE OFFER COMES in early June and for two days you bubble with excitement. Your exuberance is barely contained. You have the opportunity to work on one of the pre-eminent Cambrian fossil beds in the world. You bump around the house in a state of stunned acceptance without thinking about the mechanics of time and space and how these movements might fit in with your daughters.

On day three you call the Burgess Shale Institute and say no. You say no with regret and openness. You probably explain too much, you speak your heart and your regret. When you hang up, you feel empty and a little sad. There is no way you could spend all that time at the Burgess camp with your daughters here in the town alone. It's too soon to do that to them. If Moira were here. If Moira were alive, things ... don't think that way. She's not here. You're on your own and you need to be there for your kids. The Shale's not going away. It's been working its way to this point of exposure for over 500 million years. What's your hurry to get up there? The fossils can wait; your daughters cannot.

WRITTEN IN THE MIRROR the last morning of the monks' stay is a final message:

We are what we think.
All that we are arises with our thoughts.
With our thoughts we make the world.

THE SKY THIS MORNING has a brown haze to it. Smoke from a forest fire around Golden crept into the valley in the night. The air is fresh despite the way it looks. It's uncharacteristically warm for 8:30. The monks are leaving with as little fuss as possible. At 1:30 in the morning, after consuming two drinks, Nguchul had said

"We're leaving tomorrow morning. I will miss you." They came into your life with very little fanfare and apparently they intend on departing the same way.

You pull open the side door to the van. The other monks are already inside. "I want to thank you for everything you've done." You stop.

Nguchul knows. You look at his face and you know he understands that you are grateful.

You can almost hear him saying, *There is no birth, no death. There is no hello. There is no goodbye.*

His eyes fill with something that you can only describe as compassion, or love. There is such a gentleness there. "Things manifest when the conditions are right," he says.

"I will miss you," you say. "Our talks, at night ..."

"I have known you for a very long time, my friend," he says. "It was good to see you again."

What did he say? He's known you for a long time? What the hell does he mean?"

He smiles and you know instantly it is not important. You felt an unusual connection to this monk right from the start. He's just confirming what you should have been aware of from the beginning.

You've taken an unopened bottle of your Talisker single malt whisky and wrapped it in one of your favourite sweaters. You hand Nguchul the rolled sweater. "In case you are cold in the mountains," you say. He feels the weight of it and tucks it under his arm.

"I will make good use of it, and think of you each time."

"You know, of course, that good Buddhists should not drink," you say.

Nguchul smiles. "Yes, and it is often a difficult thing to be a good Buddhist." He pauses and manages to look serious for a moment. "Remember what I said about poetry and the writing of poetry. Inside you, there is much poetry."

⟳

"I'LL BE BACK LATER in the fall, kiddo," Uncle Bob says before getting into the van. "These guys need my help. And we seem to work well together." He smiles, a boyish grin. "Truth be told, because of this diet of theirs and the steady work, I actually feel healthy for the first time in about twenty years."

"I'll look for you," you say, "whenever you come back, you're always welcome."

"You're gonna be all right, kiddo. This is a good place for you." He squints a little, as if he's trying to recall something just out of reach, or trying to find exactly the right words. "It ain't about the Shale," he says finally. "It's about loving those girls the best you can. And it's about moving on."

Nguchul turns around at the door of the van, offers his *namaste*. You notice the shiny brown prayer beads as they chatter against his forearm. He shrugs.

"Healing happens when you are ready to heal," he says. He places his hands in a prayer in front of his heart, bows slightly and enters the van. Then the monks, including Uncle Bob, are on their way to Vancouver. You watch as the van moves down the street and out of sight. You listen as it moves lower, toward the bridge road. There. They're gone. Three months late. One healing mandala late. A *small*, four-room temple late.

⟳

YOU PLAY MOZART'S REQUIEM this morning. The palpable grief, the air thick with sorrow. And the undeniable beauty. This music is mountainous, peaks and valleys and things too massive to comprehend. This morning, the first and only time in your memory, a raven watches as you chop. It sits on the tip of one of the back pines, with a stillness that is a bit unnerving.

This music brings Claire to mind. You think about Claire, wonder what she's doing. You remember her scars, the story she started to tell in Paris — going for coffee and getting caught in a bomb blast, and surviving while others did not.

In July, the heavy tourist season will be in full swing. Folks from all over the world will come to visit the Shale, or to hike, or to be in the mountains. The girls are enjoying their time away from school and they have many new friends. You wonder if Uncle Bob and the monks will make it to Vancouver. The monks are determined and focused, except you remember they originally were headed to Vancouver to make this mandala. You now own a four-room stone temple built into the side of the mountain. The hardwood flooring throughout has the markings of an old school gymnasium. The mishmash of cross-purposed basketball court boundaries — coloured lines intersecting and untangling — is as beautiful as the first room Carl did for you. Eventually, you'll run water up there. For now, there's a spring behind the new building that trickles down under the structure and then sinks back into the mountain.

As for Uncle Bob, he found that manual labour, meditation and the simple diet appealed to him, and he found the company of the worker-bee monks entirely to his liking. You were a bit taken aback when he announced over morning coffee he was going with them. Your mother is back home making her daily ritual visits to your father. Georgia stays long enough to torment the monks. She leaves visual scars in you. She leaves her body, in all its naked glory, burned into your memory. Georgia is the most overtly sexual woman you've ever met. She sunbathes in the nude. She shows up for dinner wearing see-through blouses, short skirts, and no under-wear. She likes her body and is never afraid to show it.

"I considered coming out here and making a play for you," she says, one morning when she's sunbathing out back. "You are not without your charms. And from what I can see, you're a good person."

"But I'm not your type?"

"I'm just wired for women. Tried men when I was young because I thought there was something wrong with me. Turns out there was nothing wrong with me."

"You don't look ..." You stop.

"I don't look like a dyke."

"That's not what I meant." You smile. "I don't suppose there's any way I could back-pedal my way right out of this conversation is there? I feel like I'm being insulting, and I don't mean to be. You're a decent human being, and you're attractive. The rest, I don't care about. At least that's what I see."

"I'm glad that's what you see."

You look across the yard at the pile of wood; the axe leaned against the back fence. "So, you'll go back to the coast?"

"I'll go back and pick up Jake — I'm missing my dog — and then I don't know."

"I happen to have four extra rooms, if you ever need a place to stay."

"I'll keep that in mind," she says.

⌒

YOU GO ON-LINE AND SEARCH out raven. Mystery, control and change are all ideas associated with raven. They can be harbingers of creativity. They can be tricksters too. You'd like to choose mystery, and change. There can be no ignoring the devious nature of this bird. Unkind. Ravens stir things up ... like coyote.

Georgia calls to let you know she's arrived safely home in Sooke. You tell her about the raven that watched you chop wood.

"The girls miss having you around," you say. "It's not the same around here without you flashing the monks or sunbathing."

"I would ruin you, if we slept together."

It takes you a few seconds to grasp what she's just said. "Really? What makes you so certain of that?"

"I know what I can do."

You can hear her smile even over the phone line. "You're titillating even a whole province and a bit of ocean away," you say. You hear a dog barking in the background.

"Raven is magic you know," she says. "Whether you go to him or he comes to you, it's the same thing. He sees everything cross-eyed, first one side then the other. Perhaps that's your lesson."

"That I am supposed to look at things cross-eyed?"

"Maybe the resolution of this vision is always going to make you dizzy."

Raven has been lurking at the edge of your life. You remember the raven at Pyramid Lake — the cawing scratches across the morning. You imagined ravens at the coast, on the night Moira left, silent witnesses perhaps awoken from their slumber by the sound of a car crash. These damn birds are scattered through your life.

You are still on the phone with Georgia and purposely try to cross your eyes, to direct your vision across the middle, and it makes you dizzy, almost nauseous. How do ravens live like this? It's no wonder they're sort of goofy. If you walked around constantly looking at the world with crossed eyes and feeling as if you were going to be sick any second, you'd probably be pretty goddamned grumpy.

How many ravens are there in your life?

SITTING IN THE MIDDLE of the temple's main room is a small, very worn little book of the sayings of the Buddha, the Dhammapada. There is no inscription. The giver remains a mystery. In this book, you find the messages that were written in the mirror every morning for the duration of the monks' visit, and much more.

SAINT GEORGIA WAS A VIRGIN of Auvergne who withdrew from the world and lived a life of prayer and fasting. That, and the story from Saint Gregory of Tours, who said that angels in the form of doves accompanied her coffin to the grave, is all you can find on the Internet about Saint Georgia. Is that what Georgia has in mind? Is she a virgin? So what is she the patron saint of? Doesn't she have to be the saint of some grand cause?

⌐⌐

YOU PICK UP THE PHONE and it's Rachel from the Burgess Shale Institute.

"There's been an incident with one of our guides," she says. "A small one involving several mountain goats. She's okay but she's out for the year, and is going back to school in the fall; not that you needed to know that but I thought you might like the whole picture." She takes a breath.

Jesus, you didn't know mountain goats were dangerous!

You remember Rachel from your first interview. A died-in-the-wool penny-counting bureaucrat. Trendy tortoise-shell glasses that barely concealed a hard-edged face. Your first impression of her was that she was stodgy and dull — a stiff.

She clears her throat.

"The best way to learn something is to teach it," she says. "We need another guide. It's part-time. It doesn't pay much, but perhaps it's enough. You're certainly qualified and you seemed fit. You are fit aren't you?"

So it's settled. You'll take a group of about fifteen people up to the Walcott Quarry three days a week. You'll show them around the dig and answer any questions and then you'll be back in town. Suzanne agrees to watch the girls while you're on the mountain. The elevation gain is 760 metres over a distance of ten kilometres. By the end of the summer you're definitely going to be in shape. You start your training in mid-June, or as soon as the snow pack allows. It's the 760 metres down that kills your legs and knees. Up is just cardiovascular. Down is where your body takes a pounding.

"What happened with the mountain goats?"

"Oh, nothing serious. A small incident. Nothing really. She was climbing elsewhere in the Park. Listen, thank you for agreeing to take this position. I'm sure you'll be a fine addition to the team. Goodbye."

You hang up the phone and make a decision that if you ever happen upon a herd of mountain goats, and you're not safely in your car, you'll be very, very cautious. You walk out front into the street and you are happy. You'll be making a living doing something you love. There's a train waiting at the station, murmuring low, offering a grounding note to the valley, and this throbbing diesel engine bass-note takes you back to the Legion in Golden.

YOU REMEMBER BEING AT THE LEGION in Golden, in early May. You were sitting at a table with Carl, Uncle Bob, Georgia and Nguchul. The girls were with your mother. You drove the twisted, winter-ugly road to Golden for supplies and somehow wound up at the Legion. The place was packed with an odd assortment of patrons unconcerned with fashion, drinking draft at small, circular tables. There was a gathering of the pipe bands going on so there were a lot of pipers in town. Uncle Bob is a Legion member and he signed everyone in. There were raised eyebrows about Nguchul's attire but nobody said anything. A few smiles were raised about Georgia's outfit. She was wearing a bright orange bra and a see-through blouse, a short skirt, and black leather boots. She somehow managed not to look like a hooker.

The sound of bagpipes has always been incredibly annoying to you, whining, thin and weak. You'd just as soon listen to nails scratching a chalkboard. However, when two pipers unexpectedly stood tall in the entranceway to the hall and began to fill their bags with air, and then started to make the sound that has always annoyed you, something odd happened. You did not notice the high-pitched, reedy sound; for the first time, you heard a droning note that resonates through your entire body. The bottom note grabbed your heart and resonated. A shock wave flexed up and down your spine.

Everything stops. Every head in the room turns toward the entranceway. And the melody begins, but you don't really hear it, you are fixated on the drone. At the bottom of everything is one resonating, deep note. With each refrain of melody the bottom note is punched out again. It remains steady and true. You are driven a little mad by this melodic icon. You are wondering if you might have some Scottish blood in your veins. What else could explain this hypnotic connection to bagpipes? Then, it gets better.

You hear a drum, then several snare drums in a building roll, then what sounds like a dozen pipers making their impending start-up sounds. Your initial visceral reaction is exploded. They come in a front, like the weather, through the door behind the original two. A dozen drummers and twenty pipers burst into the room on a wave of gorgeous sound. Something in you is released, and you are crying stupidly, silently, in awe. You feel very, very small. The sound is pure and innocent, and it moves in waves as these kilted men navigate the hall. Georgia reaches out and touches your knee, squeezes gently, leaves her hand there. Nguchul is in bliss. This music, you find out later, has strong similarities to Tibetan music. Carl's eyes are like a newborn's, curious and fascinated and absorbed. Uncle Bob stands up, and everyone in the room follows his lead.

~

RAVEN COMES AGAIN, of course. It's August, and you're up at Emerald Lake, floating around with the girls in a canoe, in the middle of the silky green water. The sun is blistering but the breeze is cool. The mountains this high up always remind you that winter is not far off. You're drifting around, letting the girls paddle wherever they like. You have sandwiches and juice. You've promised them you'll read one of Moira's favourite poems to them. You've gone out of your way to teach them that poetry doesn't have to be frightening or dull. The simplest poems are the best. If a poem is really hard to understand, it could mean it's been written by a bad poet. Complexity, obliqueness and intricacy — these things do not always amount to excellence. So you read them an e. e. cummings poem about the rain opening flowers. A simple love poem, one of about a half dozen Moira had memorized — that you knew of.

The two ravens swoop over your heads and you watch as they climb effortlessly inside the thermals until they eventually become two small dots above your boat.

"Dad?"

You're lying on your back looking up into the sky. It's Sarah's voice.

"Yes."

"Can two ravens become an unkindness or does it have to be more than two?"

"I think more than two. Three might be an unkindness. Four would definitely be an unkindness."

"What are you talking about? What do you mean unkind?"

"A group of ravens is called an unkindness," Sarah says.

"Oh."

Ravens mate for life. You wonder if this is a mating pair above you.

—

"LOOK, I'M NOT ONE TO PRESUPPOSE anything and I don't want to ... well, I'm just going to ask the question ... do you play hockey by any chance?"

Trust Carl to find a way into your disjointed heart.

"You don't have to be good or anything. It's not a league. We play a no checking and no raising the puck on net kind of game. We all like our teeth too much."

Your mind is reeling. And it's Carl who draws attention to your face.

"I trust that smile on your face means yes and that you'll come out and play this winter?"

You're drifting. You're warming up in the shack, the sound of the puck hitting the boards from outside. The smell of leather. The scarred wooden benches. Your hands are tingling — trying to warm up. And then you're out the door, with tightened skates and the adrenalin rising. The cold bites at your face; lets you know this is no arena. But this time you understand. You know the game and love it. You are not afraid. You fly up the wing with the puck and pass it to a streaking teammate. There is the slapping sound of the puck connecting with the stick tape-to-tape. And you know what you have to do. You move toward the net, stick blade on the ice and head up, alert and wary as a cat.

"We've got a pile of extra equipment, pads and stuff," Carl says. "You'll need a stick and skates, of course."

Your father is standing behind you with his hand on your shoulder, encouraging. He's not back in Edmonton, disappeared into the disease that forgets it's own name. *What could it hurt*, he's saying. *It's sounds like fun.*

⌒

YOU ARE WELL INTO YOUR FIRST SEASON of work at the Burgess Shale. You're quite familiar with fossils and you've acclimatized to the grunt of getting up there three days a week. The prescribed tour lecture has slowly evolved into something slightly more animated than the Shale folks expected. But you've been getting extremely positive feedback.

Sylvie's letter arrives in August. Inside the first envelope is a letter and another, smaller envelope. The smaller envelope is addressed to your Edmonton house, in Moira's handwriting. It's a letter to you, from Moira. While you were in Paris, Sylvie was picking up your mail every day religiously until you arrived back home. And this one envelope with no return address? It got mixed in with Sylvie's junk papers, she writes. A pile of papers she sorts through once a year, if that. It must have been the lack of a return address. It sort of looked like junk mail. Still, she did not throw it out.

Sylvie's letter starts by saying that you are missed, that the Demitasse is not the same without you. Maurice is well and he says to let you know that "our blue friend is back." Then she says she is sorry for her tardiness and for losing track of this letter. She hopes it is not as important as she fears it might be. She begs your forgiveness. Then she repeats all this. You call her immediately.

"Sylvie," you say. "It's all right. The important thing is that it was not lost; it was only misplaced for a while. I appreciated your diligence with the mail. I relied on you."

"I've screwed up," she says. "I'm so sorry."

"No harm done. No apology is necessary ..."

"... but ...."

"... but nothing. I appreciate your sending it. I'll see you the next time I'm in town. We'll have drinks."

This is it, you think, what you've been seeking. Moira's words. Moira's explanation. Her *why*.

You reread Sylvie's letter. You look at the envelope. Yes, it's Moira's lying-down script. The writing looks even-keeled and normal. It doesn't look like it was scratched in a fit of delirium.

All the answers are here. You read Sylvie's letter one more time and then place Moira's letter, unopened, on the bedside table. It's best to approach these sorts of things in morning light.

But you do not read it in the morning. You place it in the pages of a book on your office bookshelf and carry on with your life. You will want to remember the name of the book because chances are you'll leave the letter there unopened for quite a while. Well? Where did you put it? Was it the anthology with "Prufrock" in it? Was it e. e. cummings? The Auden? Perhaps you chose Don McKay's

Birding or Desire, another of Moira's favourites. Was it Pablo Neruda?

You know exactly where you put the letter. It's in the Miles Davis autobiography called *Miles*.

THE SEASONS DON'T FOOL AROUND in the mountains. They change with alacrity and drama. At the end of summer the nights get cold and the mornings take until noon to warm up. You have your coffee on the deck; you're drifting, thinking about what you have to do today instead of being there on the deck with the mountains and the cold edginess in the air. When the phone rings it scares you. You pick it up and say hello more gruffly than you normally would. It's Carl.

"There's some French woman here," he says. "She says she knows you. She says she's come to call. Should I send her packing?"

"A French woman? Really?"

"Yes, a beautiful French woman."

"How do you know she's French, Carl?"

"She has an accent."

"What kind of accent?"

"A French accent for fuck's sake!"

"What do you think I should do?" You think Carl's pulling a fast one. And you're not falling for it.

"I think you should kiss my friggin' ass and come down here and see her for yourself. I think you know damn well who this woman is. I think you should stop acting like you're a lord and we're the peasants who protect you."

"Carl?"

"Yes, my liege?"

"I'm sensing a lot of hostility."

"Really? I'll send her up."

"No need, Carl. I'm on my way."

SHE'S SITTING AT THE BOOTH along the wall. When you burst through the door of the Troubled Pig, she stands. You move into her arms and there is a sudden familiarity in this hug, in her spicy scent, and the feel of her body against yours. You don't think about *next*. You're just happy to hold her. You're surprised. You close your eyes and something far back releases — you feel at home.

"You live here?" she whispers. "This place, these mountains are beautiful."

"You came."

"I promised."

"Not a promise I would have held you to. I'm happy you came. I'm happy you keep your promises."

She leans in and kisses you on the lips.

"Hi," she says.

Claire has entered your life again. Just like that — on the soft breeze of a year-old promise.

You accept the awkwardness of introducing her to the girls. You accept their resistance. You and Claire are friends. She's going to stay a while. Claire's a writer. After a month, you will have the *nobody can, or ever will replace your mom* talk with the girls.

You begin to learn Claire. She tells you stories about being at boarding school, about her past loves, about growing up on a vineyard. You play it out one day at a time. Your understanding is to see how it goes. Claire begins to be part of your days. She becomes a "not guest."

"FOR THREE MONTHS we were all on a learning curve," you say. "It was amazing to watch them build the mandala."

"I would love to see the pictures someday," Claire says.

"Pictures." You repeat this word with zero intonation. You'd briefly considered, and then dismissed, the idea of taking any pictures.

"Surely you took pictures."

"It didn't seem appropriate," you say. "They were involved in something sacred and it wasn't right to try and capture it with film. It was dishonourable."

"Then you will have to make for me a description of this sand drawing."

"Of course."

"When it was finished, what did they do with the picture?"

"They wiped it out. It was all ceremonial."

"They destroyed what they made? On purpose?"

"Yes, and then they dumped the coloured sand into the river so the nagas river spirits could be happy."

"River spirits? Surely you are pulling my legs."

"It's Buddhist! I'm not making this up. The nagas spirits are in the river. Nguchul said they live in the water and that they are supposed to be very wealthy."

"Perhaps Nguchul was pulling your legs."

"Maybe, but I like to think there are spirits in the water. It makes the water seem less cold somehow."

You lean back in your chair and reach for the bottle, pour wine into Claire's glass and your own. You love the idea that the destruction of the mandala is meant to underscore the understanding of impermanence and non-attachment. But the truly beautiful thing is that, after this incredibly labour-intensive process, there is no material result at the end. No product. It's completely contrary to Western culture.

～

YOU COME DOWN OFF THE MOUNTAIN one afternoon and find Claire sitting on the back deck. She is halfway into her second bottle of wine and there are delicate rivers of mascara on each of her cheeks. Wisps of hair frame her face making the image of her seem blurred and out of focus.

"What happened?" you say. "Are you okay?"

"Non. Non, I am not okay. That is why I am drinking the life. I am having Jesus' blood. I am having the godforsaken sacrament." She attempts to pick up her wine glass but her hand can't find it and she gives it up. "Oh, it's there somewhere," she says.

"What happened? The girls okay? Has something happened?"

"Non, nothing has happened. The girls are fine. Marie is in her room. Sarah is at a friend's house, doing homework. I have read horrible things today. The newspaper is a thing of ugliness. I will never read another of these again!"

You reach down and pick up her wineglass, slide it gently into her hand, and then sit down next to her. You know about the tyranny of bad news, of death and destruction, disease and injustice that occurs in newspapers. You take a pull of wine from the bottle.

"A mother in the United States drowned her children, one by one, she called them into the bathroom and drowned them in the bathtub!" She starts to cry all over again. "What kind of monster does such a thing? And a man in Canada killed all six of his children by locking the doors of his house from the outside and then lighting it on fire! I don't understand ..."

"I know," you say. And you do know. You know about both these horrors and you wish you didn't. Ever since the girls came into your life, you have had a low tolerance for stories like this. You've slowly developed an internal firewall to keep these horrors held a safe distance away. You're still aware of them but the details don't make it through.

It appears Claire has no such firewall.

⌐⌐

"WHAT AM I DOING HERE? I do not belong. I am like a fish in the water." Claire has been crying. Her eyes are puffy and red. She is angry.

"Claire, I can't give you guarantees about tomorrow. Or next week. Or next year. All I can say is that at this moment, I love you. And I want to continue to love you."

"Well, that's something," she says. "But are you happy? You do not seem happy."

"Yes, of course, I'm happy. Why would you ask that?"

"You do not smile. I have not seen you smile for a long time."

She's right. You can't remember the last time you laughed. It's time to stop moping around like a wounded puppy and get back in the game with both feet.

"It's not you," you say. "It's life. There are things I can't let go of. They linger."

"You do not have a choice. We are in life and it is a precious thing, non?"

"Yes, but ..."

"Shall I make a listing of the good things in our life?"

"No, that won't be necessary."

"But I really think I should because you do not see it. Your daughters adore you. And they are beautiful inside and out. When did you last tell them you loved them? And look where we live — this is the most magnificent place I have ever been. Each morning I wake up and pinch myself so that I know I am not in a dream. I can walk to the river and drink out of it. Do you understand how special this is? You have enough money to live comfortably. You have a job you enjoy. Did you learn nothing about living in the moment from your Buddhist monks?" She stops to take a breath. "And you have me. I am in love with you — something I have no choice about. And I love you — and this, I choose with all my heart."

"I don't know what to ..."

"Don't say anything. Just choose to be in life with us, the girls and me, because we are waiting for you."

~

OVER THE PERIOD OF A YEAR, Claire is slowly integrated into your family. There are good moments and bad. But the good far outweighs the bad. Sarah accidentally calls Claire *Mom*, which almost rips it all apart.

"I didn't mean ..." Sarah says. "You ... I'm sorry." Sarah and Claire are eating ice-cream. Marie is sprawled on the couch in the living room, reading.

Claire looks at Sarah with a great sadness in her eyes. "It's all right. It is an honour to be called this by you. Even if it is in error."

"No, it's not all right. You're not my mom ..."

"I know, sweetie. We can just let it go ..."

"Don't call me that. My mom called me that. You can't."

"Okay."

"What are you doing here anyway? What are you doing with my dad? He doesn't need you. He's got us and we don't want you."

Claire is silent. There's no upside to pushing back. Not here. Not now.

Sarah stands up and moves to the sink, drops her bowl in the sink. Something breaks. "Why don't you go back to Paris!" And then she's down the hall and into her bedroom.

Marie closes her book and places it on the table. "She's just having a hard day. She doesn't mean any of it."

"It's all right," Claire says.

"No, it's not all right. You've done nothing wrong. I'm glad you're here. I know Sarah is too."

When it is not too cold, you and Claire come up to the small temple to talk. You call it the small temple as a tribute to the worker-bee monks and your lovely misunderstanding about its actual size. You set candles on the floor and lounge on a futon, the only furniture so far. Whenever you talk about the monks, Claire is enthralled.

"We will have a walk tomorrow," she says later. "Perhaps down along the river. It will be all right."

"Do you want me to talk to her?"

"No, we will sort it out."

And you know Claire will do just that, with humility and compassion.

─

THIS MORNING, YOU FIND A POT of coffee and a note. Claire is always leaving notes. They are a constant form of entertainment. "River. Love Claire." So you grab the French press of coffee and a mug, and head for the river. You half remember someone being sick in the night. Or was that this morning? Does one of the girls have the flu? Maybe you dreamed it.

You find Claire near the bridge, sitting on a big rock that juts out into the stream. Her feet are in the water. The sun is shining with a steady heat. Not a cloud in the sky. The small black American dippers flirt with the surface of the river — flying back and forth, back and forth. Somewhere behind you, there are chickadees. And of course, the sound of the water flowing. Flashes of reflected sunlight hop and skip across your eyes.

Claire has a mug of coffee beside her and she is smiling. Hard to believe she's here. Sometimes you shake your head and wonder why you're so damn lucky. This woman came all the way from France to be with you. She put her life there on hold, sublet her apartment, and took a leave from her work, all to be with you!

You think about cold feet. Her feet must be freezing. But she does not have cold feet about anything. She leaps with courage and gusto into life, full force. Risks her heart as if breaking it is nothing.

Claire notices you on the bridge, waves and shouts up: "It is so cold!"

"Why are you doing it then?" you shout back.

"Because I have never done it before!"

You navigate the slope of the riverbank to get to her and manage not to spill a drop of your coffee. You sit beside her and begin to remove your boots. She looks at you with a joyous smile.

"Neither have I," you say as you slide your feet into the frigid water. You smile back at her, slip your arm around her waist.

"I'm going to jump in," she says, standing up abruptly.

"What?"

But Claire is already down to her bra and panties. She drops the bra on the rock, steps out of her panties and says: "Coming?" There is a huge splash as she throws herself into the water. It takes you a little longer to get out of your clothes. The water is freezing, it never sits still long enough to warm up. Big breath! Big breath! Okay! "Oh my God!" you shout and you keep shouting it over Claire's "Yes! Yes! Yes!" And "Wow! Oh, WOW!" You flounder and laugh and splash each other — anything to keep moving in the cold water because to stop is to suffer — although splashing each other like a couple of crazed children is exhilarated suffering. Finally, you crawl out and onto the rock, which is warm and mostly dry. Claire lies on her back, with her body to the heavens. Are her breasts getting bigger? Jesus, she's beautiful!

"Have you ever been to Japan," she says.

"What? Why?" You're drying off a bit, using your shirt as a towel. You're about to join Claire and boldly bare your body to the sky, the sun and the day.

"Because I believe we are both going to Japan," she says, pointing at the gathering crowd of Japanese tourists lining the bridge, their cameras and video cameras aimed your way, while a tour bus purrs behind them.

~~

WHY DO YOU TUCK MOIRA'S LETTER into that Miles Davis book and carry on? What are you afraid of? Fear of concluding, fear of that last goodbye? Either read it or throw it out. Why do you purposely place yourself in limbo? There are people who could not have waited an hour, let alone four months, and then six, and then nine, and beyond. Is it because suicide notes are depressing? Is it that she might say some things that hurt? What are you hiding from?

There could be reminders of things in her words, and to remember these things will cause you pain. Perhaps you have chopped enough wood for one lifetime.

⌐⌐

UP AT THE TEMPLE, you're sprawled on the futon. Claire looks up from her book. "What are you writing?"

"I'm working on something."

"What?"

"I saw something today ... and ..." You had seen a dead deer beside the highway. Crows hovering and a coyote there already. You remember the grass along the highway, already turning brown but still predominately green. "... it made me want to write about it."

"You are making a journal entry?"

"A poem actually."

"I never knew this about you." Claire sounds genuinely pleased.

"Neither did I."

⌐⌐

SARAH DROPS A GLASS into the sink. It slips out of her hand and shatters.

Claire jumps, lets out a high-pitched yelp. The look of terror on her face makes you wonder what the hell is going on. For a few seconds it's as if she isn't even in the room.

"Are you all right?" Sarah notices Claire's terror.

"Yes, fine. It just surprised me."

But this is more than being surprised. Claire's face is white and she's trembling. You move to her and slip your arm around her waist.

"Hey," you say.

"I am fine. Just tired. I think I am going to take a shower before bed." She almost smiles.

Claire is wearing only a T-shirt and as she crawls into bed, you can see the scars, a couple of faint lines and several small jagged ridges.

"The broken glass was a reminder," you say, "of the thing that made these?"

"I do not remember the sound of glass breaking but there was much broken glass." Claire's voice is flat, lifeless. "I do not know why I jumped. There is no reason."

It is late but she runs into the kitchen and brings back another bottle of wine and two glasses before she begins her story. Claire takes a sip, then a gulp of wine. She closes her eyes, takes a deep breath, and begins.

She was standing in Le Viaduc Café, near the Gare de Lyon. She had a meeting with a client regarding a manual for a new piece of software. In the retelling of this story, Claire spends a great deal of time going into the details of this project. They act as a buffer in front of the events of the story, let her move into her memory at her own pace. The manual was to be in plain language. The company had come up with a stripped-down, very lean and fast Internet search engine. They'd taken the top fifty things that comparable software did, then cut that number in half according to a hierarchy derived from customer polling. They also removed any advertising.

"The speed of this engine is quite impressive," Claire says. "They're doing very well."

She's stalling her ass off, you're thinking. Why? But there is no rush. Let this unfold in its own time, you think. So you nod your head and remain silent.

Claire was standing in a café near a Metro station in Paris. It was early in the morning and her meeting was in a few minutes. She was standing at the bar, where the service was diminished but the price was half what it would have been if she were sitting at a table. It is a trick Parisians know.

"I still have an early prototype of the program," she says.

"You don't have to say any more, Claire. I only need to know you're okay."

"I need you to know. There are things — histories — that make us who we are."

"Okay. Fair enough."

Claire was in the café taking her morning coffee. She'd just gotten off the train and come out of the metro. It was a romantic Paris day with grey layered against grey in the sky. Leaves clinging to trees, sticking to sidewalks. People with raincoats and umbrellas. Collars turned up against the chill. There was the smell of wet wool, decaying leaves and roasting chestnuts.

"The sky took away the colour of the day," she says. "I was to meet with a client but I was early; there was time for coffee."

"Yes, I know days like that in Paris."

"The air was thick with water ... what is the word?"

"Humid."

"Yes, it was very humid."

Claire was standing with her back to the window, taking coffee, thinking about her meeting, planning her pitch, solidifying her bottom line as far as her billing for the project. Her laptop hung from her shoulder unobtrusively. She was thinking about her meeting when something big pushed against the middle of her back — lifted her heels off the ground — and then she heard the explosion from across the street — saw people all around her cover their faces too late. Flying glass without the sound of breaking glass — odd. Somehow she was not touched by anything except that first push of air. There was an extended, horrible moment as the café became quiet for a single fragment of time before people were screaming and yelling. Claire dropped her laptop on the floor and started to help people — mostly in shock. Offered whatever help she could — remembered a surprising amount of her first aid training. She did not feel the shards embedded in the back of her leg, just below her buttocks. Not yet. The glass had ripped right through her skirt. Only when someone asked her if she was aware her leg was bleeding did she begin to suspect there was something wrong. Sticky rivulets of blood ran down the back of her leg.

"Is it my blood?" she asked.

"It seems so."

"But how?"

"Can you feel anything," he asked.

"How can it be? My back was to the window."

"You have glass there in your leg."

"I don't feel anything."

"And yet you are bleeding." He was an older man. Grey hair, dark suit, on the floor and slumped against the bar, a towel pressed across the right side of his face. There was an intense compassion in the eye she could see but perhaps it was his voice, which was calm amidst so much chaos. But wait, he was holding his eyeglasses in his other hand. With one hand he pressed the towel against his face, and with the other he held his glasses — the arms folded over, it seemed, with careful attention. The glasses are in his hand as if it is a natural thing to take them off and hold them.

"I think I should sit down." She did not feel her injury but she did begin to feel dizzy. Cautiously, she sat on the edge of a chair, putting any pressure on her left hip. "What happened?"

"There was a bomb, I think, across the street," the man who was holding his glasses said. "You're going to be all right. You might be in shock though."

"A bomb? Why? Are you a doctor?"

He was not a doctor but he said he'd had some training. Claire started to feel her neck muscles turn to rubber and the man barked at her to stay awake, to look at him, and so she did. Claire tried to tell the man about her meeting but he kept interrupting, telling her to stay awake and not close her eyes. Then the man was telling Claire about his wife, whose name was Natalia. She's Russian, he said.

"Over here," he said to someone across the room. "She's lost a lot of blood."

"You're going to be all right, Claire."

"Nice to meet you ... Monsieur?" Claire said. But she did not get his name. And she was not all right. She was definitely not all right. There were several shards of glass, one of which was in deep and causing a great deal of bleeding. Her laptop was peppered with glass fragments. By the time they got her to a hospital, Claire was in serious trouble. She'd lost a lot of blood and was not entirely cognizant of where she was. The same shards of glass from her leg become fragments of memory.

"I was not badly hurt," she says, taking a drink of wine. "The man who told me I was injured ... he died. He was dead at the hospital. His glasses were on the table beside me. They were black-rimmed. The lenses were not so thick. One of them was cracked. I did not see that at the café. He died."

"His injuries were more than just his face?"

"I don't know." She says this as if she were standing in a huge cavern where the echo makes it impossible to speak quickly. Words overlap each other. Collide.

"I'm so sorry, Claire.

"It is, comparatively, not a big thing," she says. "People die all the time, non?"

"Not like that. Not with that sort of violence."

"I have friends in Lyon who had grandparents in Auschwitz. They lived. They survived. They recovered."

"Grieving is a personal thing. Different for everyone."

"It was ..." Claire stops.

Twelve people died in that explosion; three in the café, the rest on the street. Perhaps there is more scarring under the surface of those faint lines beneath Claire's buttocks. For now, you cannot ask more of her. Her breathing is fast and she seems to be teetering on the edge of tears.

You move in close, hug yourself up to her body. You wait a minute. Let her back away from this memory. "You're okay," you whisper. "You're okay." She nods her head, her eyes shut tight. Her tears flow now. Tears come in waves. And her tears unexpectedly cause your own tears to release.

When her body begins to relax you reach around and move your hand carefully into hers. You remember reading about the bombings in Paris but no one incident stands out in your memory. You try to imagine what it must have been like to have death so sudden and near by.

You have the opportunity to give back all the comfort and caring Claire lavished on you when you were in Paris. Compassion makes a full circle as you hold her and let her talk. When she is done, and drifting into sleep, you realize she will likely never be fully over that experience. Claire will carry her scars for the rest of her life. Yet despite this cavern of sorrow, she is happy. Most of the time, she seems happy. Is there a balm for this sort of pain? You wait until her hand is soft in yours.

"How is it that you are happy?" you whisper. "You are happy, aren't you?"

You pull the covers up over Claire's shoulders. She's always complaining about how her shoulders get cold.

"Oui. I am happy," she says. "I love ... I love ...." And then she is sleeping.

You are almost asleep yourself but you want to plant something pleasant in Claire's subconscious. "Sarah saw a robin today," you say, "down by the river. It was gathering dried grass for a nest."

16

RAVEN, AGAIN

In the morning, Claire takes the girls to Calgary for the week-end, to get ready for school, and it takes you a day of steady hesitation to work your way up to the Miles Davis autobiography. You pick *Miles* off the shelf and can see the curled edge of the letter. You tuck the book into your jacket pocket and leave for the small temple. The monks placed stones to make a pathway that was subtle and easy to climb. It switches back and forth three times before arriving at the stair to the temple. Across the valley, the mountains stretch white fingers of snow into the valleys. Some of the larches are starting to turn from green into a heady gold. In the morning, you saw your breath as you waved goodbye to Claire and the girls.

Do you really want to know what's in Moira's letter? What makes you think you're any better prepared to handle the contents of this letter today than you were a year ago? Or two years ago when you were supposed to get it?

Will the contents of the letter change your life in any way?

You've installed a little pot-bellied fireplace in a corner of the main room of the temple. You pour a few drams of the eighteen-year-old Glenmorangie into one of your favourite glasses. You light a fire to take the chill out of the room.

You are suddenly filled with fear. You remember a story you told Moira in which a man was left with nothing at the end. He was disconnected from his wife and his mistress was killed in a car crash. He'd lost his way. He had the dog and that was it. You do not want this story to be a precursor or a tragic portent. It's getting late. Claire and the girls aren't back yet. Did they say what time they were coming home? Is it supposed to freeze tonight? Are the roads okay? You don't want any tragic endings. You don't read the letter.

Where are the girls? Where's Claire? Where are they?

Do the math. How far is it to Calgary? How many hours? An hour to Banff, another forty-five minutes to Lake Louise. And then a half-hour to Field. What does that tell you? Nothing. You don't know what time the stores close or if they stopped for something to eat. Why didn't you give Claire the cell phone? Because she doesn't like cell phones and you don't blame her. Maurice used to say people used them in a feeble attempt at not feeling so alone in the world; instead, inundating themselves with banal and insipid small talk. Your father shunned them too. The guy still had a rotary phone. He had an old shiny black rotary phone, in mint condition, that you actually had to dial. You add your father to your list of people to panic about. You haven't seen him in a month. He could slip away any day. But there's nothing you can do except remember with all your heart. You start with the trip to Mountain Park and move forward from there. It's a good place to begin.

As the valley grows darker, your fear escalates. You move down to the house to be near the landline telephone. Inside your swelling panic, you start to prepare a dinner of pasta and stir-fry. You open a bottle of wine, let it sit on the counter. You set the table. And you wait. God's going to punish you. While Moira was struggling with her demons, you were in Paris making love with Claire. You are a fine example of a compassionate and considerate human being! But it was Moira who pulled away emotionally, and physically, and geographically. The connection was severed and eventually you came to believe it was permanent. Your affair with Claire was not whimsical. It was the culmination of sorrow. That's how she got in. You'd removed yourself from harm's way, had already moved away.

But your guilt still insists you're going to be punished. You know a thousand things that can go wrong on a mountain highway and this is how God will punish you. You pour a very hardy portion of wine into a mug and begin to devise a deal. You go into a panic about the meagre offerings you have to place on the table. But you have to try. *Dear God, Please don't let anything happen to them on the highway. If they get home safely, I'll stop swearing. I'll go to church more than twice a year. I'll stop drinking ... before noon ... on weekdays.* You will never let your daughters know about your doubts. For them, you will never seem uncertain about whether or not Moira's death was an accident.

God does not answer. There is no burning bush, no flood. There are no heavenly hosts, or angels. You fret and drink, drink and fret. You try to watch a movie, but nothing helps. You call your mom in Edmonton and get her machine. You look over at your neighbour Suzanne's place to see if there's a light on. There is, but you're not sure you can handle a visit right now. You pace the house noticing things that need doing but you don't write them down. You open another bottle of wine.

Just after 11 p.m., Claire and the girls pull up in front of the house and you take your first full breath in hours. You've made a good start on bottle two. Each glass was a propping up of hope and faith while everything in you wanted to be terrified. Your panic is drowning in a sea of wine, and you are quite relaxed and happy when you go out to meet them. The girls want to show you everything they've bought and you manage to "ooo" and "ahhh" in the appropriate places. You try not to slur your words.

After, when the girls are in bed, Claire asks if you're all right.

"I had a little wine," you say. "Well, more than a little! I was so worried you'd been in an accident."

"Do you think I am a bad driver?"

"No, no, no, it's not that. You're a great driver — more careful than I am — it's the other drivers, and animals, that I worry about. It was stupid of me."

She brings you in close and holds you for a long time. You sink into her welcoming softness. And then you are tucked in bed and watching as Claire undresses. You love this stripping away of layers. But tonight, there's something different about her, about her body. It seems fuller, rounder, more beautiful than you remember. Her hipbones are not as prominent.

"We should go to church tomorrow," you say as softly as something being pulled through silk. Did you say it or just think it? You must be tired, and the anxiety and whisky and wine have all worked their magic.

A small knock at the door. Whispered voices. It's Sarah and Marie. "Did you tell him yet?" someone asks. Somebody giggles. Is that Sarah? Then they're all giggling.

Are you dreaming? It's too soon to be dreaming. What's going on, what are they doing? Tell you what?

"He fell asleep," Claire says. "I think he had a hard day. We will tell him in the morning, yes? We can do it together. Come, I will tuck you in."

And then you hear a faint, "Bonne nuit, Sarah. Bonne nuit, Marie," from down the hallway.

You are suspended in the not-quite conscious state between the waking world and the sleeping world as Claire slides into bed beside you. She snuggles up to your back and kisses both your shoulder blades. She presses her body into yours. You remember the feeling of Claire's body, her breasts, belly, thighs, and long intertwined legs. Her cool skin, her smoothing touch. Or maybe you only think you feel it. But the sparkling air through the window is real. Such rarified air. You're blessed to be living here. You have Claire. Claire is coming to bed. She's tucking the girls in. You close your eyes. But wait; your eyes are already closed, you idiot. You're dreaming. How far back will this vision reach? Will you dream a woman named Katya who visits only when she wants, and who is not real? Will you be holding your daughter in your arms as she shakes off the remnants of yet another bad dream? Or will you become a small child in a dusty car headed into the mountains with your father driving, him not wanting to be on this particularly ragged road, and you just wanting to arrive.

Perhaps in this dream you will talk to your father, tell him how much you appreciate the ride, and that you love him for everything he does. You'll talk about how you know this trip is a sacrifice on his part; that you understand. You'll tell him how much you love being in the mountains. You'll draw grey-peaked and deep green word pictures. You'll describe icy clear water frothing over jumbled rocks. Water that bashes away at rock every second of every day. The sound of the wind shushing through pines. Moss-covered logs. The floors of pine forests where spongy mattresses of fallen needles make it feel as if you're walking on the moon. Clear air that is so newly born that it seems foreign when it enters your lungs. It will not be a drive focused only on arrival but a journey filled with salient moment after salient moment.

~

IN THE MORNING you are truly hungover. Claire is wearing baggy pants and a *City of Calgary Police Department* sweatshirt that your mother gave you a few years back. You have no idea where she gets this stuff — she doesn't know anyone in Calgary. Claire's hair is tied back. She places the French press on the table — the thick layer of ground coffee beans floating on top. You pick up the plunger.

"Four minutes," she says. "You'll ruin it."

"I had to take the medicine this morning," you say. "Two pills. Bad head." You can't tell if she's angry or not. She could be and with good reason. You were goofy drunk.

"The girls and I had something to tell you but you fell asleep — or should I say passed out?" She smiles at you.

Well, at least she's not angry, you think.

"We have never spoken about this," she says. "So I will tell you now and then you must promise to act excited later when the girls are up."

"Okay." What the hell's going on?

"Do you promise?"

"Yes, I promise."

Claire takes a big breath. Exhales.

—

A WEEK LATER Marie and you are sitting on the back deck in heavy sweaters watching the clouds descend into the valley. Something big is pushing the thick whiteness down the slopes and it's massing up. Claire has a meeting in Vancouver with a software company. She won't be back for a couple days.

Marie sees the tree in spite of the forest. She says it so matter-of-factly that you hardly notice it's arrived.

"Are you sure," you say.

"I love those trees," Marie says. "They're my favourite. They have droopy tops."

"What ..."

"It's the only tree with a droopy top. Hard to miss."

"You?"

"When we were in Sooke, I went there. It was on the way to the beach. I remember it."

"You went there?"

"I saw where it happened," she whispers.

You look at your daughter. Could it be possible that she's farther along the road to healing than you are? Not in a million years did you think the answer would come from her. She went there. What did she see? What horrors? But she saw the tree. She recognized the tree.

"Thank you, Marie."

"You can call me Mare, Dad. It's all right. I'm all right about that now."

"Thank you for remembering, Mare."

"Sure," she says. "G'night, Dad." She moves into your arms for a long hug.

Just like that, it's done. You know the tree.

You call Suzanne. Her kids are with their father for a couple weeks, in Golden. It was a quiet and sad separation.

"Claire's out of town for a few days," you say. "Can you watch the girls? I need to get out." When Suzanne arrives, barefooted, and her overcoat dotted with rain, she asks if you know it's raining.

"Yes, I know, and thanks for doing this."

"Are you okay?"

"I will be."

You tuck the girls in and step into the night. Your grief is so close to the surface that the air around you is poisoned. The clouds have fallen to their knees and it is raining. A steady rain, then a drizzle, and then a steady rain, fading into another drizzle. You walk through the haze resolved to keep walking until you're out of it.

Marie's information points to Moira leaving on purpose, she deliberately left you and the girls and whatever monster lurked in her subconscious. It was a hemlock, the perfect tree, given her love of philosophy, Aristotle, Socrates. But maybe it was a nearly flaw-less coincidence.

It is raining and you do not give a damn that you are soaked to the skin. One foot in front of the other. Think about walking, about breathing — one breath in front of the other. You walk the outskirts of the town and then up its middle to the main highway. Then up the highway in the twilight with all the vividness and stark delu-sions of that special light hidden inside the rain. Soon you are at the Takkakaw Falls road, and still you do not care about the rain. Nobody gets pneumonia or a cold from getting wet; you simply get wet and cold.

You are wrestling with the certainty that Moira left deliberately. You are walking in the rain as if it does not matter, like that friend of Claire's in Paris when you first saw them. What the hell was her name? It's all tragic and romantic not to care about the rain, or the cold, or the snow. The rain stops and the cold humidity begins to work you over, becomes not so romantic. You vaguely remember a quote in the *Hagakure* about trying to learn something from a rain-storm — about trying to avoid getting wet but becoming drenched anyway. The writer of this book suggests that if you accept the fact that you are going to get soaked in the beginning, you will avoid being perplexed — but will still get just as wet. You're just bloody cold. Romance and stupidity are kissing cousins.

The road climbs a little and you soon find yourself on the side of a mountain, serpentining upward at angles, risking the slippery stones and slick foliage in the swirl of misty-white ground fog. You're climbing higher, not thinking of getting back to town, or the darkness, or how you'll navigate your way down off this slope. You become single-minded. After a half-hour of grunting and slipping, you look up and see that the clouds have broken above you. A few more minutes and you're looking at the first haphazard array of stars against the beginnings of indigo.

You half expect to find Katya up here, hunkered down under an outcrop, all decked out in exceptionally wrong clothing. Tennis gear or a bikini, or dressed like some 17th Avenue hooker in Calgary. She'd confront you about the stupid symbolism of what you're doing — trying to walk your way to some clarity. She'd likely scold you, say none of this matters, that climbing up the side of a slippery mountain in the rain is stupid — it solves nothing. But there are no phantoms on this tricky slope. Just a cold movement of air across the valley bottom.

You begin to shiver. There's no time to sit and contemplate. Time only to stop, take a good look, maybe a few conscious breaths, then stumble home. You would never have thought about conscious breathing a few months ago. Nguchul, the great non-teacher, waited for you to come with questions. Then he'd answer them with epigrams that had subtext piled on top of subtext. You'd ask what he was doing. *I am breathing,* he'd say. Well, of course, you're breathing; we're all breathing. *But I am only breathing.* You're not sitting? *No, I am only breathing.* You're not thinking about the mountains or the birds, and that pine smell? What about the bear that just walked into the yard? He looks kind of hungry. Nguchul would stop talking and you'd watch him for a few minutes. It was as if he'd packed up all his consciousness into a suitcase and taken it inside his breathing. A few days later you'd ask for a lesson in breathing. *Is there some trick to this breathing you do?* It had become your daily ritual to sit and only breathe. Even a few minutes of this exercise gives a renewed focus and energy. It is only the beginnings of meditation. You know this. But you are amazed at how rested you feel afterwards.

You close your eyes. Take a deep breath. Stop. Exhale. Take a deep breath.

It can be very dark on a beach with no moon and a few faint stars. Starlight is nothing compared to the ocean's darkness. Tonight, the ocean is an ill-tempered lion. Out there, it roars at the steady certainty of moving inland and then being drawn back out.

At the edge of the beach, shadow pines rip darkness into the sky. They are frozen witnesses, indifferent and mute. It's a bit frightening to hear that sound building and building, then pounding the shore some unknown distance in front of you.

Listen. The beach stones are suspended in frothy water. This suspension is only for a few moments. As the water is pulled away, the stones fall together — a symphony of clicking. Exhale.

You're not sure about the moon. Maybe there was a frail curve of moon. The stars could have been brilliant and crystalline that night. You were not there to play witness to Moira's passing, which took place on the edge of the Pacific while you were across the other ocean, walking the streets of Paris, drowning in a culture you barely understood but loved because it remained a wistful abstraction.

Had you been standing on that beach around midnight on the last day of August you might have heard the bang. There are no skid marks. But even if this exit was planned, wouldn't you brake at the last second? Wouldn't some life force in you shout: No! and cause your foot to slam on the brakes? Why no skid marks? Did her brakes fail? These questions form a beautiful labyrinth. They draw you in and you wander aimlessly looking for a way out.

At such a speed the vehicle virtually folds over itself.

There are things you do know. The colour of the rental car, its make, model and year were included in the report. The estimated time was 'round midnight. Miles Davis. The flubbed note denied. Miles was in the CD player. She knew. Miles Davis is a love of yours. A final love note? It was still playing when they arrived, they said.

You wish you'd asked what kind of tree it was. Small things like this can be comically important. The details of moments become everything. If you'd asked back then you might have found your way out of the swirling labyrinth. Because the tree has a genus, a species, a common and a scientific name. It gives it meaning.

Take a deep breath. Exhale. She didn't need the Miles Davis. You see, the ruined sound of ocean meeting land is a fitting end for anyone.

You open your eyes and there it is. The raven is flying above the valley, toward you, barely moving its wings, using the current, gliding closer and closer. You are transfixed on this black dot as it moves in a steady, smooth line. You thought at first it was an eagle, or a hawk. You're not certain it's a raven until it gets above your head, looks you over. Then it makes the muffled fa-wumph, fa-wumph sound with its wings as it grabs the air and moves where it wants to go. You'll never know for sure that this bird is a *she*, but you thought of it as *she* immediately. She takes a couple strokes with her wings and is gone up mountain, out of your vision. You imagine she might have been sleeping in a high pine when the weather blew in, and when the clouds broke she decided to move, saw you across the valley and decided to come over and take a look.

It's going to be dark soon and you're not in the city. The moon will be nearly useless even if it manages to climb above these high horizons. You pack up the image of this twilight raven in your memory and start down toward the road, and home.

ACKNOWLEDGEMENTS

I would like to thank Paulette Dubé, who did not hesitate to give her permission, when I asked about using her beautiful poem, and for her words about raven. Thanks also to agent and *mom extra-ordinaire*, Hilary McMahon, who said she could not shake these characters out of her head for weeks, and to Amy and Alison at *Westwood Creative* for their steady support and work. Thanks also to Gail Sobat, Kerry Mulholland, the boys of the Raving Poets — Mike, Gordon, Eds, Mark. Harding — you're in here and I appreciate your stories more than you know (I hope you realize that your life is not off-track — you're right where you're supposed to be). Anna and John at Miette Hot Springs Resort, for the Greek coffee, medium sweet, and for tolerating me through days of re-writing and re-structuring in #35. I am very grateful to Donya Peroff, for her penetrating questions, brilliant edits, Dominic Farrell, copy editor for his sharp eye, and Marc Côté for calling this novel a book of mercy.

Balts, Zen master, poet, gardener, lover of radishes, for insisting that I ought to write more about the mountains.

Acknowledgements

References to the *Hagakure* used with grateful permission:
Hagakure: The Book of the Samurai by Yamamoto Tsunetomo
Translated by William Scott Wilson.
English translation copyright 1979, 2002 by William Scott
Wilson and Kodansha International. All rights reserved.